The Best Revenge

Andrew Grey

Dreamspinner Press

Published by
Dreamspinner Press
4760 Preston Road
Suite 244-149
Frisco, TX 75034
http://www.dreamspinnerpress.com/

The Best Revenge

Cover Art by Dan Skinner/Cerberus Inc.   cerberusinc@hotmail.com
Cover Design by Mara McKennen

ISBN: 978-1-935192-68-8

Printed in the United States of America
First Edition
March, 2009

eBook edition available
eBook ISBN: 978-1-935192-69-5

Dedication: To Dominic, my love, companion, and dearest friend, and to a small, beautiful little girl with four legs.

Chapter 1

TYLER'S ANTIQUES was his life's work. He'd built the business from nothing and in five short years, his was the premier antique shop in town, located in the heart of the city's antique district. The owner and lifeblood of Tyler's Antiques was Tyler O'Connor. This was no dingy antique store filled with things everyone's grandmother had thrown away. The items in this shop were high-end, quality antiques from the nineteenth century. There were no fakes, reproductions, or refinished pieces either; only quality antiques in their original condition. The shop was organized into display rooms, with partial walls and half-walls creating the room spaces. Some of these rooms were set up as living rooms, bedrooms, parlors, libraries, and offices. Each display room contained furniture, rugs, lamps, artwork, sculpture, clocks, chandeliers, and display pieces. All were displayed perfectly and all were for sale.

This particular Monday morning, Tyler was walking the floor of the shop as he did every morning, making his to-do list for the day. The shop required constant dusting and cleaning. No piece on display was ever allowed to get dusty. Included on his list were minor repairs that needed to be made as well as errands that he needed to run after the store closed or pieces in the back that needed work completed. Once his morning rounds were done, he opened the store for business promptly at nine each day.

During the week, Gladys would normally come in to work at about one in the afternoon and work until closing. Gladys was approaching sixty and worked for Tyler in order to get away from her retiree husband for a few hours in the afternoon. Having Gladys in the store gave Tyler time to make minor repairs, to work on pieces that needed to be prepared before being put on display, and for client appointments or to see items that people wished to sell. However, Gladys had recently fallen and broken her leg. Tyler missed seeing Gladys every day. She had worked for him for the past three years and was one of a small group of people that Tyler considered as close friends. She had told him she would be back to work in a few weeks, so until then, Tyler was on his own.

With the store open, Tyler knew that it would be slow for the first couple of hours and he decided that he would try to complete as many of the items on his list as he could before noon.

As he walked to the back of the store, he caught a glimpse of himself in one of the many mirrors. "I still look pretty good," he said out loud to himself. In truth, Tyler was almost stunningly handsome. He was tall and slim, with a nice gym-built body, sandy hair, and deep blue eyes. He went to the gym five mornings a week before the store opened. Gym time was his time. He hadn't dated in years and had no real interest in dating. He just wanted to keep himself looking good, and good-looking he was, not that it did him any good at all. Many of his customers were gay and they all thought he would make a great catch. A few had tried to be caught, but Tyler wasn't interested. No one had managed to catch his eye, or his heart. He'd just never felt that certain connection with anyone, at least not for a number of years.

By noon most of the items on his list were completed and a few customers had wandered into the store. He spoke with each of them. Some he had seen before. One couple was new in town and just wanted to look around. Since no one else was in the store, Tyler gave them a brief tour and answered their questions. They ended up buying a light fixture for their new home, which meant that Tyler would probably be seeing them again.

As he was eating his lunch, the telephone rang. "Good afternoon, Tyler's Antiques." Tyler's phone voice was always upbeat and happy, regardless of how he actually felt.

"Well, good afternoon. My name is Alice Burke and I'm interested in selling a number of antique pieces. I'd like to make an appointment to have you come and look at them." She sounded formal and stiff even over the phone.

"What type of pieces are they, Mrs. Burke?"

"My mother was a collector of antiques and these are some of her pieces. I don't know what you would call some of them, but they are very nice."

"I'm sure they are." Tyler got calls like this all the time. Usually the people had items he wasn't interested in because they weren't up to his quality standards. "Can you describe one of the pieces?"

"Sure. There's a two-person sofa, you could call it, in medium-colored wood decorated with carved ladies heads."

That description made Tyler take notice. "Are there other pieces like that?" Tyler realized that she may have some quality pieces after all.

"My, yes. There are eight pieces that match." This actually had potential.

"All right, Mrs. Burke. I will be happy to set up an appointment with you. When would you like me to come over?" His calendar was out on the desk and he was already checking available dates.

"Can you come this evening at seven?"

Tyler checked his calendar and found that he was available. "Yes, Mrs. Burke. I had a cancellation for this evening and I'm available. Could you please give me your address and telephone number?"

She provided Tyler with the information he'd requested. He thanked her for calling, and told her he would see her at seven that evening.

What Mrs. Burke had described sounded quite promising, but Tyler had learned not to get his hopes up. He spent the rest of the day meeting customers and completing his list of items. At five o'clock, he closed the store and went upstairs to his apartment. Entering the apartment from the antique store was like entering a different world. Where the antique shop was full of items and always changing, Tyler's apartment was largely furnished with simple, modern furniture. The only exceptions were a large carved Victorian table in the living room and a large walnut Victorian bed. Both of these pieces had been left to him by his grandmother and he treasured them. The apartment consisted of a large living room, kitchen, bathroom, and two bedrooms. One of the bedrooms was his and one was set up as a guest room. In the three years he had lived in the apartment it had been used all of four times.

Tyler prepared himself a frozen dinner, cleaned up the dishes, and got ready to meet Mrs. Burke.

At about six-thirty he grabbed his jacket and headed down the back stairs to where his truck was parked. Tyler had two vehicles. One was a relatively new car, and the other was a truck with a trailer that he used to pick up and deliver furniture as well as transport items to antique shows. He got in the truck and headed to the address Mrs. Burke had given him. The address was in Shorewood, an affluent suburb north of the city on Lake Michigan. The house was quite small and he was worried that he'd wasted the trip.

Parking the truck in front of the house, he went up the front walk and rang the doorbell. The door was answered by a small woman in her late sixties. She had severe facial features and looked like she'd spent her life lecturing children. She invited him inside, and he saw that he hadn't wasted the trip; the house was full of wonderful antiques.

Tyler introduced himself. "Mrs. Burke, I'm Tyler O'Connor."

"Pleased to meet you, Mr. O'Connor. I'm Alice Burke." They shook hands.

"Please call me Tyler." She smiled. "So Mrs. Burke, which items would you like to sell?"

"Well, Tyler, I'm moving to a condo and I'll have much less room. Why don't we start in the living room and I will tell you which items I would like to sell. We can then move to the next room."

"That'll be fine. I'll write down a description of each item and what I'm willing to pay you for it. If you have a price that you would like to get for an item, please tell me. I believe in being fair and honest. I don't haggle, and when we're through you can tell me which items you would like to sell based upon the price I quote you."

"Tyler," she beamed, "that sounds completely fair." She seemed pleased that the process would be easy for her.

As they walked through the house, Tyler was surprised at the number of items that she wanted to sell. Among them was an eight-piece walnut living room set with carved ladies heads, two side tables with marble tops, a small, intricately carved writing desk, four lamps, a glass-fronted bookcase, and a three-piece bedroom set. In all his years in business, Tyler had only had one other parlor set with so many matching pieces. Tyler completed his list of the items along with the price he was willing to pay. Mrs. Burke suggested that they sit down at the kitchen table and discuss the remaining details. When they got into the kitchen Tyler noticed that the walls were covered with religious plaques and pictures and he couldn't help but feel a little uncomfortable. They sat down at the table and went over the list of items and the prices, and she seemed surprised at the prices he was willing to pay.

"To be honest, Tyler, this is more than I thought the items were worth." As she was speaking, a young man entered the kitchen and sat down at the table. She introduced the young man as her son. "Tyler O'Connor, this is my son, Mark." Reaching across the table, Tyler and Mark shook hands. When Tyler took Mark's hand it was like a spark shot through him. "Mark, I'm selling some of the items in the house to Tyler."

Looking at the list on the table, Mark commented quietly, "That's quite a list. Mom, did you show him the big old table that's upstairs in storage?"

"No, I didn't. Would you take him up and show it to him? I just can't go up the stairs again."

"Sure, Mom." Mark indicated that Tyler should follow him, but Tyler was having difficulty concentrating. He was absolutely captivated by the gorgeous man across the table. It had been some time since anyone had captured his interest like that. Finally, he was able to get up from the table.

Mark led Tyler up the stairs and into a small storage area off one of the bedrooms. When Mark opened the door to the room, Tyler found himself staring into Mark's incredible green eyes and he completely lost his train of thought. "Tyler, that's the table."

Tyler pulled his eyes away from Mark and looked at the piece of furniture. He almost whistled when he saw it. Of all the items he had seen in the house, this table was the best by far. Mark turned on the light so Tyler could see the table better. Tyler looked over the table carefully and was trying to decide on a price for it. He was alternately looking at the table and Mark. In the light Tyler could see that Mark was not beautiful, but was definitely handsome. He was slightly taller than Tyler, with dark wavy hair, a handsome face, a young lean body, and those incredible green eyes.

"Well, Mark, I've seen what I need to see. Let's head back downstairs."

Mark led him back down the stairs and Tyler found himself looking at Mark's tight bubble butt. When he reached the bottom of the stairs, he shook his head slightly to clear his mind and joined Mrs. Burke in the kitchen.

"Mrs. Burke, how much do you want for the table?" Tyler was trying to keep his excitement under control.

"Tyler, it's just taking up space. How about fifteen hundred dollars?" She just wanted to start clearing out the house.

Tyler knew that price was low. "Mrs. Burke, it's a really nice table. I'll pay you three thousand, which seems much more reasonable to me." Tyler could tell that Mrs. Burke was pleased.

Tyler totaled up the amount for the items he was buying and wrote Mrs. Burke a check. He also wrote up a bill of sale for the items he was purchasing, indicating each of the items Mrs. Burke was selling and the amount she was being paid for each item, and had her sign it. Then Tyler got to work. He packed each item, and loaded them carefully into the trailer.

"Mark, would you be willing to help me load some of the larger items? I'll gladly pay you for your time."

Before Mark could say a word, Mrs. Burke chimed in, "Mark will be glad to help you. It's the Christian thing to do."

He saw Mark roll his eyes. "Of course I'll help, Mom."

Mark helped Tyler load the large items into the truck. Tyler was happy to get to spend a few extra minutes with Mark even if it was just loading the truck. When everything was in the truck, including the table from upstairs, Tyler said good night to Mrs. Burke and thanked Mark for his help. Mark followed Tyler out to the truck and for a second Tyler thought Mark was going to ask him a question, but then he changed his mind.

"Look, Mark, I really should pay you for your time."

Mark shook his head. "Could I ask you where your shop is? I'd like to see Mom's stuff when you have it on display." Tyler handed Mark one of his business cards and told him to stop by the store any time. Closing and locking the trailer, he wished Mark a good night and drove back toward the store.

It was almost nine when Tyler got back to the store. Backing the truck up to the back door, he carefully unloaded the small items into the store room, leaving on the truck only the large pieces of furniture that he couldn't move by himself. Locking the truck and making sure the store was secure, he headed up to his apartment.

He got cleaned up, had a small snack, and got ready for bed. He couldn't stop thinking about Mark. He kept seeing those green eyes. Tyler chastised himself. "Look, you'll probably never see him again, so stop wishing and go to bed." He cleaned up the dishes from his snack and got into bed. He did allow himself the small luxury of wishing for a second that the bed wasn't so big and that someday he wouldn't sleep alone. Then he turned out the light and went to sleep.

Chapter 2

THE following Friday was one of those dreary days that happens in May when the wind is off Lake Michigan, keeping the city shrouded in clouds. The morning had been slow and Tyler had managed to get all of his to-do list items completed. He was sitting at the computer completing paperwork when the bell on the front door sounded, indicating that someone had entered the store.

Looking from the computer screen, Tyler was surprised to see Mark Burke standing in the doorway. Mark was looking around the store and Tyler found himself watching Mark and enjoying the view. Tyler didn't know what it was, but Mark just seemed to distract him.

"Mark. Came to see the store?" Tyler approached Mark and they shook hands. Tyler again felt the same spark that he had the last time he'd touched Mark.

"Yeah, I was curious about the store." Stammering slightly, he continued. "And I wanted to see Mom's things on display." Mark was looking around, peering at some of the furniture arrangements.

"Would you like me to give you the tour?"

He smiled brightly. "Sure… that'd be great." Mark seemed a little nervous or excited. Tyler couldn't quite tell which. With a smile to hide his own excitement, Tyler showed Mark through the store, explaining how the items were displayed and answering Mark's questions about some of the pieces. At the end of the tour, Mark asked, "Where are the rest of the items you got from Mom?"

"Well, the parlor set is being reupholstered, and the other pieces are in the back. I need to work on them before they're put in the shop." Taking Mark to the back room, Tyler showed him the pieces and explained what needed to be done to make each one saleable.

"Can I ask where the large table is? That was always one of my favorite pieces, but it was too big for the house, or so my brother always said." When he talked about his brother, a shadow passed across Mark's face. Tyler noticed it but said nothing.

"I'm particularly fond of that piece myself, so right now, I have it in my living room. I'm still deciding if I want to keep it or sell it. That's the one advantage of being an antique dealer. Besides, it needs some work and I wanted to be able to take my time. It got pretty banged up." Tyler led Mark back to the front of the store and offered him a chair. "I was able to put the smaller items and lamps in the store right away."

Mark looked around the store. "Yeah, I did notice a few of the items."

"Well, let's see: three of the four lamps have already been sold. Lighting is hard to find and good lighting is getting pretty rare, so it doesn't stay in the store for very long." Tyler was looking at Mark and he suddenly felt the urge to smile. Sitting and talking with Mark just seemed so natural. "Can I offer you something to drink?"

"That'd be great. Do you have a diet soda?"

"Diet Coke okay?" Tyler took two sodas out of the small refrigerator behind the counter and handed Mark one. Mark opened the can and sipped the soda. He kept looking at the store and back at Tyler.

Tyler got the feeling that Mark wanted to ask something, but was either afraid or too shy. Tyler decided to let Mark off the hook. "I keep getting the feeling that there's a question you want to ask, but aren't sure how to ask it?"

Mark looked at the floor. "Well, kinda."

"Go ahead and ask. I won't bite." Tyler figured paving the way would ease Mark's hesitation.

"Well, I've been thinking about some things a lot lately and… well… um…." Mark stopped talking. He seemed to be trying to make up his mind about something. Tyler was looking at Mark and he saw his expression change and a determined look seemed to replace his doubts. "Tyler, I want to ask you something. I don't know if I'm doing this right, so I'm just going to ask. Would you have dinner with me… you know… like, as in a… date?"

Tyler was surprised, pleased, flattered, and a little confused all at once. He quickly composed himself and thought for a minute. "I think I'd like that." The smile Tyler got lit the entire room and he couldn't help smiling back. It had been a long time since he'd been on a date.

The answer seemed to open the floodgates for Mark. "I'm so relieved. I wanted to ask you when you were at the house but I chickened out. Maybe you weren't gay, maybe I was imagining the spark I felt when you shook my hand." Mark took a breath. "Maybe you weren't checking me out when we came down the stairs."

Tyler couldn't help but laugh. "Well, Mark, I am gay, I felt the same spark you did, and I was checking you out as we came down the stairs. Was I that obvious?"

Now it was Mark's turn to laugh. "Well, kinda." Mark was still laughing and Tyler joined him. They had just settled down when a young couple came into the store. Tyler greeted them and they said they just wanted to look around. After offering to answer any questions they might have, he went back and sat near Mark.

"So, when would you like to have dinner?" Looking into Mark's deep green eyes, Tyler saw Mark's lips move, but he didn't hear anything. Shaking his head to clear his thoughts, Tyler said, "Sorry. I was kind of… lost for a second."

Mark smiled. "I was wondering if you were free for dinner tomorrow night?"

Tyler smiled back. "Yes. Where would you like to go?"

"How about Italian? We could go to Magellan's. It's private and, from what I hear, quite nice."

Tyler couldn't help smiling again and he felt little happy butterflies in his stomach. "That sounds wonderful. I close the store at five, so is seven o'clock okay for dinner? I'll make a reservation."

"Sounds good. I could meet you here at about six-thirty and we could go together. Parking is so difficult near the restaurant." Tyler smiled and indicated that would be fine. Between customers, Mark and Tyler talked for the next few hours. At about three, Mark got up to leave. He said goodbye to Tyler and headed for the door. When he reached the door, he turned around, walked back to Tyler, and gently kissed him on the lips. "I'll see you tomorrow at six-thirty." Tyler watched as Mark left the store and walked down the sidewalk.

Tyler was excited and had so much nervous energy he couldn't sit still. He forced himself to finish the paperwork he had been working on when Mark came in. At five o'clock, he closed the store and turned off the shop lights. Instead of going up to his apartment, he decided to prepare some of the pieces that needed work to be put on sale. He spent the next couple of hours working in the back room, and he managed to get three pieces done and ready for sale. Heading up to the apartment at about seven-thirty, he made dinner and spent the evening watching television until it was time to go to bed.

ON Saturday, Tyler spent the day doing his usual work. The store was busy and for that he was extremely grateful. When the store was slow, the days plodded by, and he desperately wanted time to move quickly. He had put the three pieces he'd worked on the night before in the store and one of them had already sold. He made a note that on Wednesday, the day the store was closed, he would need to rework some of the store displays. At five he closed the store and bounded up the stairs to get ready for dinner.

When Mark arrived at six-thirty as promised, Tyler met him at the entrance to the store. He was wearing a pair of dress pants and a blue button-down shirt. Mark looked sharp in a pair of light khakis and a deep burgundy shirt. Tyler opened the door to the shop and let Mark into the store. Mark just stood there like he didn't know what to do.

Tyler chuckled to himself and took the lead. Leaning forward, he gently kissed him on the lips. Tyler felt Mark open his mouth slightly and Tyler probed his lips gently with his tongue. Mark's full lips felt warm and inviting, and heat spread through Tyler's body.

Slowly breaking the kiss, Tyler whispered, "Shall we go to dinner?"

Mark smiled. "Yes, if you promise to do that again later."

"I think I can promise that."

Tyler led Mark to his car and they chatted on the ride to the restaurant. When they arrived, the hostess seated them at a table and took their drink orders.

"So, what do you do?"

"Well, I've been working in an art gallery for the last few years. I majored in art in college and I really love it. I also paint and sculpt. I've basically turned my room at home into a studio. My dream is to be a working artist and to be able to make a living at it."

"You're still living at home?"

"Yeah. When I finished college, Mom hurt herself and I moved back in with her to take care of her. My brother and sister are both married and have kids, so I agreed to take care of her."

"Your mom told me she was looking to move."

"She keeps talking about moving into a condo, but I think she's just talking. The truth is that she would need to move into assisted living because she can't fully take care of herself."

"Does she know you're gay?"

The look on Mark's face was almost painful. "No, and I don't know how she'd react. She's very religious. You saw all the stuff she's got up around the house, and she keeps buying more." Mark took a deep breath. "I probably should have told her a long time ago. I had a boyfriend in college for about six months, but we broke up and I can't help thinking it was because I wasn't out to my family. He was, and his family was, very supportive, so he figured everyone's family would be and couldn't figure out why I just didn't come out. I am out in other aspects of my life, but I just can't seem to get the courage to tell my family. After the breakup I tried to change, to make myself 'normal,' but… all that did was hurt me more."

"I understand…. It can be hard. You have to do what's right for you and what you feel comfortable with, although the secrets and covering up can be a burden."

"Yeah, I know." The waitress came over to take their orders. As Mark was placing his order, Tyler looked around the restaurant and saw some friends sitting a few tables away. When the waitress left, Tyler waved.

"Who are they?" Mark asked skeptically.

"They're customers and good friends, Tom and Bill. I'd like to say hello. Would you mind?"

"No. I'll come with you if that's okay." Tyler nodded and they made their way to the other table.

As they approached, Tom and Bill stood to greet them. Tyler made introductions. "Tom Carter and Bill Jenssens, this is Mark Burke." The men hugged Tyler and shook hands with Mark, exchanging pleasantries. Bill almost invited them to join their table, but Tom gave him a quick look and the invitation died on his lips.

"Tom, before I forget, I have an item at the store that I set aside for you to look at. Stop by in the next few days. I put it aside just in case…." Tyler didn't want to intrude. "We'll let you enjoy your dinner. Have a good evening." Tyler put his arm around Mark's waist and led him back to their table.

"They seem nice, and they're both so handsome," commented Mark.

"They really are. They are a wonderful couple. It's hard to believe that they're in their forties, isn't it?" Mark did look a little surprised. Looking across the restaurant, Tyler caught a glimpse of Bill and Tom as they leaned across their table and kissed gently.

Mark saw it, too, and looked at Tyler quizzically. "I guess I'm not used to public displays of affection."

Tyler smiled. "Tom told me once that he and Bill refused to censor their behavior in public. If straight people can do it, so can we." Tyler shook his head; he'd always wished for what those two had in each other. He then gently reached across the table and lightly stroked Mark's hand.

Mark smiled. "Tyler, please tell me about you. I know about the store and what you do but I don't know much else."

"Let's see. I'm twenty-nine, going to be thirty next month. When I graduated from college with a degree in business I started working for a large company. I absolutely hated it. I had always loved antiques and since I had put some money aside, I decided to try to be an antique dealer. I started selling out of an antique mall, and slowly built the business into what I have today." There was a certain pride in his voice.

"As far as dating, I haven't dated much in the last few years. I did have a few boyfriends in college. The longest relationship lasted almost a year, but after college he eventually got a job on the west coast. For the last few years, my life has largely been the store."

Tyler was still holding Mark's hand when the server brought their dinners. After dinner and before dessert, Tyler asked Mark about his art.

Mark seemed to sparkle as he told Tyler about the pieces he was working on. "'Right now I'm doing mostly portraiture. I like being able to paint a picture of someone and have the portrait show some hidden characteristic of the person. It's the same thing with my sculpture."

"What medium are you using?"

"For sculpture I'm working in clay, I'm experimenting with cast bronze, and I like to paint using oils. It gives me time to work and blend. But, for some pieces I use acrylics." Tyler could tell by his enthusiasm and the twinkle in his eye that this was Mark's passion.

After dinner, Tyler drove them back to the store. "Would you like to come up for a while?"

Mark smiled. "That would be nice."

Tyler led Mark up to the apartment over the store. He showed him around the apartment and offered him a seat. "Would you like a drink? I have soda, wine, or water."

"A glass of wine, if you're having one." Tyler poured two glasses of white wine and handed one to Mark. The two of them sat together on the sofa talking, laughing, and getting to know each other for the rest of the evening.

At close to midnight, Mark got up to leave. "Tyler, I had a wonderful time."

"I did too. I'd really like to see you again." He was hoping that Mark felt the same way and he was rewarded with a bright smile.

"I'd like to see you again as well, but…." Tyler wasn't sure what the "but" meant, but he knew it wasn't good. "I don't want to wait until next Saturday." Now it was Tyler's turn to smile.

"The store is closed on Wednesdays and I usually use the day to make store changes and repairs. I should be done by three or four in the afternoon."

"What a coincidence. Wednesday is my day off from the gallery. I could come by at about four and we could decide what we want to do." Mark kept flashing those smiles and Tyler couldn't help smiling in return.

"Sounds great!" Tyler led Mark out through the store rather than the back apartment entrance. Before opening the door he kept his promise, wrapping his arms around Mark, and giving him another gentle, deep kiss. He then unlocked the door, and Mark almost skipped down the sidewalk. Tyler relocked the door and smiled to himself all the way back upstairs.

Chapter 3

IT was a beautiful day, at least in Tyler's mind. It had been raining all day, but tonight Tyler had another date with Mark and he didn't care what it was doing outside. Tyler had been working all day to rearrange the store displays and get new merchandise ready for sale. He was working near the front of the store when he heard someone rapping on the door. When he looked, he saw Tom standing in the doorway, trying to stay out of the rain. Unlocking the door, he let him into the store.

"Sorry, Tyler, I know you're closed, but I was in the area and saw you in the store."

Smiling, Tyler said, "No sweat. I could use a break. You want to see the lamp I set aside for you?"

"That would be great." Tyler took him into the back room and showed Tom the lamp. Tyler was right—it was exactly what they'd been looking for. They settled on a price and Tom bought the lamp, writing Tyler a check.

"Hey, Tyler." Tom leaned close, conspiratorially. "You and Mark looked awfully chummy. Are you dating?"

Tyler got a sheepish grin and nodded. "That was our first date." Smiling, he added, "I'm seeing him again tonight." Tom could tell that Tyler was really excited. "Say, can I ask you a question? I'd like your opinion on something. It's about Mark."

"Sure." Tyler had never asked Tom for relationship advice before, so Tom was really intrigued.

"Well, I'm a little worried. Mark's not out to his family and he's not had much more relationship experience than me. I'm just wondering if I could be setting myself up for a fall."

Tom couldn't help but laugh and Tyler looked disgusted. "Tyler, with any relationship or potential relationship there is the opportunity to get hurt. But—and this is a big but—there is also the potential for great happiness and fulfillment." Tyler was watching him closely. "You want my advice, here it is: don't worry about it. We were all inexperienced at some point. As for his family, that will come in time. Look, he's not too big a closet case. I saw you two holding hands at the restaurant." Tom smiled. "Give him time and support. The potential for love is always worth a little patience and understanding." Tom patted Tyler on the shoulder. "I can tell you like him. Take it slow if you like, but follow your heart."

"Thanks, Tom."

"We all get the jitters when we meet someone new. It's normal. Just enjoy yourself and enjoy the feeling. There's nothing like it." Tom checked his watch. "Oh, god, I've got to get back to work. I'll talk to you soon." Tyler let Tom out and went back to work. Late in the afternoon, he wrapped up the last of his changes to the store and went upstairs to get cleaned up. As he was taking a shower, the phone rang. Tyler stepped out of the shower and answered the phone.

"Hello."

"Tyler, it's Mark. I'm down at the front door of the store. Could you let me in, please?" From Mark's tone, he could tell that there was something wrong. Tyler turned off the shower, put on a robe, and went down to the front door of the store. Mark was standing in front of the store in the rain, looking like a drowned rat. He opened the door and let him in.

Mark just stood in the front of the store and dripped all over the floor. He didn't move and he didn't say anything. "Mark, what's wrong?" Mark didn't answer; he just shook his head. Tyler could tell he was trying to keep himself composed, but wasn't having much luck. "Come on, Mark, let's get you upstairs." As Tyler ushered Mark upstairs, he could see that he was walking stiffly. Tyler got Mark some towels from the bathroom and laid out dry clothes. When he came into the kitchen, he could see that Mark was completely soaked and dripping all over the floor. If he wasn't so miserable, it would have been cute.

"Mark, go in the bathroom. I put some towels out for you and a pair of sweatpants and a T-shirt. Get yourself dried off and you can tell me what's wrong." Without saying anything, Mark shuffled off to the bathroom. As he moved, Tyler could see that Mark was definitely walking stiffly, like he was hurt. Tyler quickly went into the bedroom to get dressed as well. A few minutes later, Mark came out wearing the clothes Tyler had put out for him.

Mark sat on the sofa. He didn't move and he didn't say anything. Tyler just waited, and finally he started to talk.

"About two hours ago, I was up in my room at home painting, when I heard my brother Roger come into the house. He was really mad about something. I couldn't hear what he was saying, but he was talking loudly to Mom. Then I heard a few words. 'Fucking faggot.' Roger raced up the stairs, burst into my room, and started hitting me. Grabbing me by the neck, he dragged me downstairs and into the kitchen." Mark was sniffling and Tyler gave him some Kleenex. "Mom was in the kitchen. She told me that a friend of Roger's had seen us at the restaurant the other night holding hands. She then asked me if I was gay. When I answered yes, she told me to get out of the house, that I was no son of hers, and that I would burn in hell." He sniffled into a Kleenex.

Hearing this, Tyler's insides started to turn. The pain that he'd felt years earlier and thought he'd buried started to come to the surface.

"They wouldn't even let me get any clothes or my art stuff. I just grabbed my keys and came here." Mark was starting to sob pretty heavily. "I didn't know where else to go."

"I'm glad you came here." Tyler wrapped his arms around Mark, pulled him into a tight hug, and let him cry. Mark just sobbed. Tyler held him until his tears subsided. "Will you show me where Roger hit you? I noticed you were walking like you were in pain." Lifting the T-shirt, Mark showed Tyler a large red mark, which was already starting to turn purple, on his left side.

"It's more sore now than anything. I don't think he broke anything." Shaking his head, he huffed, "Even when we were kids, Roger was always a bully."

"Have you had anything to eat?"

"Yeah, I had lunch before Roger got to the house. I could use something to drink, though." Tyler brought himself and Mark each a Diet Coke. They sat on the couch and Tyler just held Mark. Suddenly, he jerked. "Oh shit, we were supposed to go out tonight. I ruined everything!"

"Shhh." Tyler wiped the tears from Mark's cheek with his fingers. "We were going to decide what we were going to do. I vote we order a pizza, watch TV, and talk. I'll get the guest room made up and you can stay here."

"I couldn't put you out. I'll just go h—" Mark was about to say home and then it hit him that he didn't have one and he started to cry again. "I don't have any place to go," he sobbed. Tyler just held him to let him know that he wasn't alone. "You do have a place to go. It's the room right over there." Tyler knew he had to get Mark to do something. "Come on. Help me make up the bed."

Tyler got fresh sheets, pillowcases, and blankets, and made up the room for Mark. He also laid out some clothes for him to sleep in. Stepping into the bathroom, Tyler put Mark's wet clothes in the washing machine. When he was done he rejoined Mark on the sofa. "Look, tomorrow you can call your mom. Tell her you want to get your things. If she gives you a hard time, tell her that you'll bring the police if you have to."

"The police? How will they help?"

Smiling devilishly, Tyler quipped, "I know a particular police officer who will be more than happy to accompany you to your mother's to pick up your things."

"But…."

"Oh, ye of little faith, this particular police officer, Officer Davis, is gay, cute, and doesn't take crap from anybody. Now that we have that settled, let's order dinner, and after dinner I have a story to tell you."

The pizza Tyler ordered arrived and they sat on the couch watching TV while they ate. After dinner, Tyler turned off the TV, opened a bottle of wine, and poured them each a large glass.

"What's this for?"

"It's medicinal. I promised you I'd tell you a story. After I do, I'll need it."

"That bad, huh?"

All Tyler could do was shake his head. "Mark, I have only told this story to one other person and that's Tom, one of the people you met the other night." Taking a drink of wine, Tyler told his story.

"When I was in college I met Blake. He was a dream: smart, funny, good-looking, popular, everything in one package. We dated for about two months and Blake said that he wanted us to be exclusive. I was on cloud nine. He took me home to meet his family and he asked to meet my family. I explained to Blake that I hadn't told my parents I was gay and at first he didn't say any more about it. After a few months, he started asking when I was going to come out to my parents. Once we'd been dating for six months, I realized that I wasn't being fair to Blake, my parents, or myself, so I decided that I would go home and tell my parents. The next weekend, I traveled home to visit my parents. On Saturday, I asked my mom and dad to come into the living room. I had something I wanted to talk to them about. I sat them down in the living room, told them I was gay, explained about Blake, told them that I loved them, and tried to explain that they didn't do anything wrong. Being gay was just part of who I was."

Tyler took another drink of wine, got up from the sofa, and started to walk around the room. "They didn't say much when I told them. They just looked at each other and told me that we'd talk about it some more later. The next day when I left to go back to school they hugged me goodbye like they always did and I told them that I'd like to bring Blake to meet them the next weekend."

Tyler was still pacing through the room. "The next weekend we arrived at the house on Friday evening. The house was dark and my parents weren't home. When I went up to the door there was a note taped to the window. The note said, "Your things are in the garage. Take them and go." Tyler felt the hurt and pain start all over again. "I looked at Blake and showed him the note. I was devastated, just like you feel right now. Opening the garage door, I saw a pile of six or seven boxes with a sign that read 'Take these.' That was it. They didn't even write my name on the boxes, or use my name on any of the notes. Blake helped me get the boxes in the car and he drove me back to school. I cried the entire drive back. At one point, Blake had to pull off the road, because he was crying with me."

"When we finally got back to school, Blake loaded the boxes into my room, took me to his room, put me to bed, and held me in his arms the entire night. The next morning, I started to look through the boxes. Most of them were things from my room. Two of the boxes were things from the house. Pictures of me that hung on the living room walls, things I had made Mom in school, gifts I had given them, even the church family portrait of the three of us. It was as though they were wiping me completely out of their existence. When I realized what those boxes meant, I completely lost it. Thank god Blake was there to help me through the turmoil. On Sunday, Blake convinced me to call my grandmother and tell her what had happened. Grandma had always been cool, and to this day I still can't figure out how she raised my dad. Anyway, when I told her what happened, my grandmother rescued me from complete despair. She told me that she'd known I was gay for years and that she didn't give a crap what my parents thought, she still loved me. Then she called my father every name in the book and asked me to come visit her the following weekend and to bring Blake. She wanted to meet him."

"I did visit Grandma the next weekend and she held me and loved me and told me that it was going to be all right." This was the point in the story that Tyler's eyes filled with tears and Mark stopped Tyler from pacing, sat him on the sofa, and gave him a hug. "We spent the weekend together and when I left Grandma handed me a check. She said that she wanted to make sure that I had enough money to finish school. When the weekend was over I went back to school. I made sure that I called Grandma at least twice a week just to see how she was doing. About two weeks later when I called no one answered the phone. The next day I got a call from a lawyer telling me that she had passed away three days earlier. He also told me that the funeral had been the day before, and that he was calling because he needed to set up an appointment with me to discuss Grandma's will."

"Since I didn't have a car, he agreed to come to campus to meet with me. We met in the student union and he explained that Grandma had changed her will recently and that she had left everything to me with the exception of ten thousand dollars to pay for her funeral and tombstone. It turned out that Grandma had more than any of us knew. There was real estate, stocks, the house, and all the antique furnishings. Most of the items were liquidated for me by the lawyer. By the time the estate was settled, I had graduated college. I was working for a large corporation, but wasn't happy. I had been selling antiques in an antique mall and decided to open an antique store. At that time, Grandma's house was being sold, and needed to be emptied. I used the antiques as the initial inventory for the store, keeping the few pieces that meant something to me. The rest of the money from Grandma is invested. I have yet to touch any of it."

"To this day I have never heard a word from either of my parents or any of my other relatives. It is as though I don't exist to them. They live twenty miles from here, but it might as well be on another planet."

Tyler was drained, but finally telling another person what had happened had lifted a burden he didn't know he carried. "Look, Mark, what I have I accomplished on my own without help from anyone except Grandma, and I'm grateful to her every day. The reason I told you that story is to let you know that you're not alone and I do understand how you feel. I also want you to know that it will get better and tomorrow we'll see about finding members of your family that aren't as closed-minded as Roger and your mom."

Tyler hugged Mark to him, gently rocked him, and kept telling him things would be okay.

Together they drained the bottle of wine and spent the evening consoling each other and just being there. When it was time to go to bed, Tyler made sure Mark had everything he needed to get ready for bed, said good night, got cleaned up himself, and got into bed. He had turned out the light and was just getting comfortable when he heard a soft knock on the door. The door opened a little and he heard Mark.

"Tyler." The voice was very tentative.

Echoing the soft tone, Tyler murmured, "Yes, Mark."

"Um, can I sleep with you? I don't want to sleep alone." As a response, Tyler lifted the covers to allow Mark to get into bed. It was then that he realized he was naked. He had always slept that way and didn't give it a second thought. Mark saw he was naked, but instead of shying away, he slipped off his T-shirt and sweatpants and got into the bed.

Tyler just wrapped his arms around Mark and pulled him into his body, making sure he felt warm and safe. Kissing him gently on the lips, he wished Mark a good night. Mark snuggled next to Tyler like it was the most natural thing in the world, and soon they were both asleep.

Chapter 4

TYLER woke feeling very contented and a little confused. Then his mind cleared, and he remembered what had happened and why there was someone else in bed with him. Tyler was lying on his side and Mark was spooned into him with his arms wrapped tightly around his chest, something big, hard, and insistent pressing into Tyler's butt. Tyler smiled and slowly rolled over to face Mark, who was still asleep. Kissing him gently on the forehead, Tyler slowly got out of bed, put on his robe, and padded into the kitchen to make coffee and start breakfast.

After starting the coffee, Tyler took Mark's clean clothes from the laundry and quietly put them at the foot of the bed. Mark was still asleep and he decided to let him sleep as long as possible; the rest would do him good. Padding to the bathroom, Tyler performed his morning routine and stepped into the shower. As he stood in the shower washing himself, he could still almost feel the warmth of Mark's body. Images and the feeling of Mark's naked body next to his flooded into his mind and his body responded immediately. Allowing himself to go with those feelings, he stroked himself slowly at first, allowing his foreskin to slide over the crown of his cock. Enjoying the feeling, he slowly picked up speed. Feeling his balls start to contract, he whispered, "Oh, Mark" as he came.

Stepping out of the shower, he dried himself off, put on his robe, and headed into the kitchen for a cup of coffee. Finishing his coffee, he headed into the bedroom to wake Mark and get dressed. Stepping into the bedroom, Tyler got a surprise and an eyeful. Mark had shifted in the bed and pushed down the covers. He was lying on his back with the covers pushed down around his hips, giving Tyler an unobstructed view. Mark was incredible. His body was lean, toned, and slightly tanned. Fine, thick, dark hair covered his chest and stomach. Tyler loved a man with a thick mat of chest hair. His erection reached almost to his navel; his balls were large and hanging low. Tyler's breath hitched and he couldn't take his eyes off the exquisite man lying in his bed. Shaking his head slowly, Tyler moved to the side of the bed, slowly pulled up the blanket to cover Mark, leaned down, and kissed him gently on the forehead while he lightly rubbed his shoulder.

Mark opened his eyes slowly, not quite realizing where he was. At first, he smiled when he saw Tyler, but then he remembered what had happened the day before, the pain flooded over him in waves, and he started to tear up. Tyler gently sat on the edge of the bed, took Mark into his arms, and hugged him tightly while gently rocking him. When the pain subsided, Tyler released him.

"There's coffee in the kitchen. Get cleaned up. I'll make breakfast, and we'll talk." Looking down at Mark's side, he asked, "Does the bruise still hurt?"

"A little, but it feels better this morning." Mark headed to the bathroom and Tyler couldn't help peeking at Mark's butt. He was pleasantly surprised to see that it was perfect, dimpled, and completely smooth. Tyler felt his own body ache, but he pushed it away, silently chastising himself. Mark was hurting and all he could think about was how badly he wanted him. When Mark had left the room, Tyler quickly dressed and headed to the kitchen to make breakfast.

Mark soon joined him in the kitchen, and they had a breakfast of bagels, orange juice, and coffee. "I need to leave soon or I'll be late for work." Mark worked at the Peter Barrett Art Gallery two blocks away from Tyler's Antiques.

"Why don't you come back to the store for lunch? We can eat together and call your mom to arrange to get your things. She may be more reasonable when your brother isn't there." The look on Mark's face was pure agony. "I know this'll be hard, but I'll be there with you. I promise."

"Okay. I'd feel better if you were there when I called her. Thank you." Mark finished his breakfast and they headed downstairs. At the front door, Tyler kissed Mark tenderly, hugged him tightly, and told him he'd see him at lunch. Tyler knew from his own experience years before that Mark would crave comfort and he was determined to be there, just like Blake had been there for him.

The morning passed quickly. The store was unusually busy, but thoughts of Mark were always in the back of his mind. Did they have a real connection? Was he just latching on to Tyler because he needed him? Was Tyler projecting his own pain and need onto Mark? Was he just being silly and over-analyzing? He figured he might be overanalyzing and decided to put the other questions out of his mind for now and concentrate on Mark. At about noon, Mark came through the front door of the store, and he actually seemed to be smiling.

"Looks like you had a good morning." Tyler was pleased.

"Yeah, I did. I told Peter what happened. He was so supportive. He asked if I had a place to stay. When I told him I was staying with you he just winked at me and said 'Good.'" Mark had a questioning look on his face.

Tyler was smiling now. "I've known Peter for a long time. We often help each other. I sometimes find paintings and need his advice and he sometimes gets decorative art objects and he asks my opinion. He's a great guy. I'm glad you told him." Tyler figured if Mark could tell Peter what happened he had at least started to process and deal with it. "I ordered lunch from the deli down the street."

The words were barely out of his mouth when Steve, the deli delivery man, brought in their lunches. "Mark, this is Steve." The two men shook hands. Tyler paid for the food and Steve asked if Tyler needed him this week. "Could you stop by this afternoon for a few minutes? I have some large pieces of furniture that need to be moved." Steve nodded and left.

"Can I ask what that was about?"

Smiling at Mark, Tyler explained, "Steve helps me move furniture and with deliveries. His dad owns the deli." Leaning in, he bumped Mark's shoulder playfully, as if to share a secret. "He works for beer."

The look on Mark's face was priceless. "Beer?"

"Yeah. His dad won't allow him to have beer in the deli. He won't buy beer, and he doesn't want it in the house. So when Steve helps me I pay him in beer. I have cases of it in the back; he stops by whenever he needs some." Laughing now, he added, "To this day, his dad can't figure out where he's getting it." Mark was laughing with him now and they sat down behind the counter to eat lunch.

"Isn't Steve old enough to buy beer for himself?" There was a worried look on Mark's face like he thought maybe Tyler was corrupting a minor.

"Steve's about twenty-three, but he's a little slow and his father worries about him so he keeps him on a tight allowance and makes him account for all of the money he gives him."

"Doesn't his dad pay him for his work?"

"Oh yeah. Most of that money is put into savings for Steve. His dad is trying to make sure that Steve is taken care of. He really means well and he loves Steve to death. He just wants him to be able to take care of himself and be responsible when he's no longer around. It's actually pretty wonderful."

They finished their lunches and Tyler handed Mark the phone. He started to tense up and get very nervous. "Look, Mark, before you call your mom, I want to tell you something…. Look at me." He turned his head and looked Mark square in those deep green eyes. "Mark, you did nothing wrong. I'll say it again. You… did… nothing… wrong." Mark seemed to find his courage and dialed the phone.

"Mom, it's Mark. Don't hang up…. I need to get my things. I will come with the police if I have to. All right. Fine…. I'll be there then…." As the conversation continued Tyler saw Mark's expression change from confusion and hurt to anger. "All right, but I'm not coming alone, and if Roger is there we'll kick his ass into next week. Goodbye." When he hung up the phone Mark was breathing hard and the anger was still flashing in his eyes.

Tyler waited until Mark was ready to tell him about the conversation. "Mom says that I can pick up my stuff Saturday at five-thirty. She won't be home and she specifically said she didn't want to see me. She also told me to be sure to leave my key on the table when I left. She told me that Roger would be there to make sure I didn't steal anything and I told her I wasn't coming alone and if he was there we'd kick his ass."

I smiled broadly. "I heard that part. Mark, you did great."

"But until Saturday, I only have these clothes."

"After the store closes tonight, we'll indulge in the great American gay pastime… shopping."

"I can't afford new clothes." He was starting to get stressed again.

"I'll make a deal with you. I'll buy the clothes if you're willing to help me in the store for a few hours."

Mark smiled broadly. "Okay. Deal." They finished their lunches and both of them returned to work.

That evening, just before dinner, the phone rang. Tyler answered. "Hello."

"Tyler, it's Peter Barrett."

"Oh, hey, Peter, how are you?"

"Great. I was calling to speak with Mark. Is he there?"

"Sure, I'll put him on." Tyler handed the phone to Mark and went into the kitchen to fix dinner. After talking with Peter, Mark hung up the phone, bounded into the kitchen, and threw his arms around Tyler. "I can't believe it. Peter called to tell me that one of the pieces that he let me put in the gallery sold. He said he got full price for it and he said that he isn't taking a commission. He'll have a check for me tomorrow. It was a small piece and it only sold for about three hundred dollars, but it's the first piece I've ever sold." Tyler hugged him back and congratulated him. He was glad that some good things were happening for Mark.

That evening after dinner, Tyler took Mark to the mall and they bought him enough clothes to last until Saturday. Mark seemed to enjoy the shopping and Tyler was happy to see him smile. When they got back to the apartment Mark put his purchases in the guest room and joined Tyler on the couch.

Looking around the apartment, Mark commented, "Tyler, I guess I'm surprised that your apartment isn't full of antiques."

"To tell you the truth, I never really gave much thought to the furniture in the apartment. In the past I've used part of the apartment as storage when I have more inventory than I can handle." Pausing a minute and thinking, he said, "The table in the corner and my bed are two items from my grandmother's that I kept. The bed was hers, and I remember crawling into it with her when I was scared. I always felt safe and secure when I was in that bed." Tyler looked over at a large carved table. "We used to sit in her living room and play cards for hours. We always used that table as our card table. Grandma was a crack gin rummy player. She and her friends would play every week, for money no less." He smiled and laughed lightly. "Grandma was a regular card shark. She used to fleece the other little old ladies." The memories were making him smile.

Tyler stopped talking and seemed to be deep in thought. "I seem to remember that there were a few boxes of other things that I kept. I'll have to see if I can find them." He was quiet for a while, just remembering and thinking.

Mark leaned against him and rested his head on his shoulder. "Did your grandmother live in town?"

"She had one of those Victorian houses just off Newberry Street on the east side. I drive by the house sometimes, just to see the place."

Tyler hugged Mark to him, found the remote control for the stereo, and turned it on. Soft soothing music floated through the apartment, and after a few minutes, Tyler could feel Mark start to sway slightly with the music. Eventually Tyler got up from the couch and held out his hand to Mark. Without either of them saying a word, Tyler took Mark's hand and wrapped his arms around him. They danced around the living room for the next hour, holding each other tightly and occasionally kissing softly.

At bedtime, they were sitting together on the sofa. It was starting to get late and Tyler had something that he wanted to talk to Mark about. Tyler wasn't sure how to bring up the subject. He finally decided to use the direct approach. "Mark, last night, when you slept with me…." Tyler stopped because the look on Mark's face was pure agony.

Mark started to sob. "You don't want me either."

Tyler reached to hug Mark, but he squirmed away and stood up. Tyler stood up, went to Mark, and held him tightly. "That's not it at all." Gently placing his hand on Mark's chin, he moved his head so he was looking at him. "When you came to my room last night I was surprised and a little confused. But, sleeping with you felt like the most natural thing in the world." Tyler stopped, trying to find the right words. "Mark, I really enjoyed sleeping with you. I just didn't want you to feel obligated. The guest room is yours for as long as you need it."

Tyler could feel Mark relax and the tension started to leave his body. "Last night in your bed, I felt so safe and warm and I want to feel that way again. If it's truly okay with you, I do want to sleep with you, but I'm not ready for anything more."

Tyler kissed Mark tenderly. "Nothing will happen until you're ready, if you're ever ready. Take your time; a lot has happened in the last week, and you don't need to rush." Tyler wasn't sure if the last comment was for Mark's benefit or his. He hoped Mark was interested in going further, but that had to be Mark's decision… period.

Mark was in the bathroom while Tyler shut off the lights and got the coffeemaker ready for the next morning. When Mark was done, Tyler went into the bathroom to clean up and get ready for bed. Mark was already in bed, but when Tyler walked into the bedroom, Mark turned on the bed sidelight, got out of bed, and stood in front of him.

"We slept together last night and we're going to sleep together tonight. I wanted to see you. After all, I've undressed you with my eyes for the last two days." After looking for a minute, Mark whispered, "You're beautiful." Well, that answered the question of whether Mark was interested. Tyler felt a wave of relief and desire course through him.

He whispered softly in return, "So are you, Mark. Let's get into bed before we get cold." The truth was, if he stood staring at Mark for much longer, he was going to get hard, and he was trying to avoid that if possible.

Tyler got into bed and held the covers up for Mark, who immediately snuggled up next to him just like he had done the night before. Turning off the light, Tyler said quietly, "Good night, Mark."

"Good night, Tyler." The kiss from Mark was so gentle and soft he almost thought he imagined it.

Chapter 5

MARK woke up early on Saturday morning feeling pretty good. Yes, he knew today was going to be hard, going to get his stuff from his mom's, but he was also thankful. Lying next to him in the bed was Tyler—warm, strong, and supportive. Not to mention hot. Tyler had kept his word and they'd just slept together for the past three nights. Peter gave Mark the day off, so he didn't have to go to work. He was just enjoying the feeling of being in bed with Tyler, feeling warm and safe, and not having to get up to go to work. It had been a warm night so they were sleeping with only a sheet over them. Tyler was still asleep on his back, the sheet conforming to his body, and Mark could see the distinct outline of Tyler's erection through the sheet. Prying his eyes away, he snuggled next to Tyler, wrapping his arms around his chest.

"Morning, Mark," Tyler murmured sleepily.

"Morning, Tyler." Mark softly kissed him on the lips. Wrapping his arms around Mark, Tyler drew the artist to him and kissed him deeply, almost passionately. Tyler felt Mark's erection rub against his and it took all of his restraint to break the kiss and slowly pull away. He was keeping his promise, but it wasn't easy. Kissing Mark again, Tyler got out of bed and headed sleepily into the bathroom. Mark put on Tyler's robe and went into the kitchen for coffee. As he was finishing his first cup, Tyler came into the kitchen. He was already dressed to go down to the store.

"Tyler, we're supposed to get my stuff today. I was wondering if there is a place I can set up as sort of a studio. I've got some ideas that I'd like to try out, but I need a place to work."

Tyler thought for a minute. "There's a storage room in the back of the store. That might work for you. Come to think of it, it might be perfect. I'm just using it for parts storage. If I remember, it has large windows that face south. If you uncover them you should get lots of light during the day."

"What do you mean, parts storage?"

"Well, sometimes I buy items really cheaply because they're in poor condition. Lamps, dressers, desks, whatever. I strip them down for parts. You know… lamp bases, switches, drawer pulls, and things like that. I use the parts to repair other pieces."

"Oh. I don't want to cause you any trouble."

Giving Mark a hug, Tyler said, "I'll give you the keys to the truck and you can go to Home Depot and get some shelving. I'll show you where to put the shelves and if you'll clean out the store room and organize the stuff on the new shelves, you can have that room for a studio."

Mark gave Tyler a hug and a long kiss. "Thanks, Tyler. I'll get dressed and go to Home Depot right away." Mark bounded into the bedroom to get dressed. About ten minutes later they were heading down to the store. Tyler showed Mark where the new shelving needed to be placed.

"I need to get the store opened. Here are the keys to the truck. Get the shelving and I'll show you the storeroom when you get back." Tyler threw Mark the keys and gave him some money. Mark then got in the truck and headed to Home Depot.

When Mark got back, Tyler was still busy with customers. When he had a break, Tyler found Mark. "Did you get everything?"

Mark was still really excited. "Yeah, I think I got everything I'll need." He seemed pleased.

Tyler was smiling as well. "Steve will be over in a few minutes to help you with the shelving and cleaning out the storeroom." Tyler leaned over and gave Mark a gentle kiss. Mark looked around the store to see if people were watching, but Tyler shrugged and smiled. "Let them get their own man."

Steve arrived a few minutes later. He and Mark went to the stockroom to put the shelves together and start cleaning out the storage room. Mark was surprised by how quickly Steve was able to put together the shelves. Tyler came back for a few minutes when there were no customers in the store to show Mark the storage room. By eleven o'clock the shelves were put together and Mark had started cleaning out the room. Steve had to go back to the deli to change clothes and help his dad with the noon rush. "I'll bring your lunches at about one if that's okay. The lunch rush will be over and I can stay to help for a few hours."

Mark smiled. "Thanks, Steve. That'll be great. You were a big help." Steve walked out of the store with a big smile on his face.

Tyler walked up to Mark. "Looks like you made a friend."

"Yeah, he's really nice and really handy. He had those shelves together in no time." Kissing Tyler again, Mark said, "I'm going to go back to work. Call me when lunch arrives." Mark headed back to the storage room and started to unload all the boxes from the room. There were boxes lining the floor and one set of shelves against the back wall. Moving the items to the shelves, he organized the items as he cleared the floor. When the floor had been cleared, Mark could see that it was a good-sized room and would be perfect for him to work. He started opening the boxes on the shelves and noticed that these boxes didn't contain parts.

The first box contained lots of framed pictures, and when Mark took out the first picture he gasped. Staring back at him was Tyler as a teenager, with what he assumed were his parents on either side of him. Mark was stunned. He looked through the rest of the items in the box and he knew that this was one of the boxes that Tyler's parents had packed when they removed him from their lives. The second box contained items that looked like they were made by a child. Mark knew immediately that this was the other box that Tyler's parent's had packed. He wasn't sure what to do with these boxes, so he put them at the far top of the new shelves.

There were still four boxes left and Mark hoped that they weren't more of the same. When he took the third box from the shelf, it was quite heavy, and he carefully set the box on the floor. Opening the box, he was surprised to see that it was full of tissue paper. He carefully took out the first piece and unwrapped what looked like part of a clock. Taking out the second item in the box and removing the packing, it looked like a statue of a scantily clad warrior with a sword and an upraised arm. Then Mark remembered he had seen a modern reproduction of one of these at a friend's house. They were called swinging mystery clocks. The statue was the base, and the other piece was the clock and pendulum combined. The clock was designed so that the entire clock piece would swing back and forth on the arm of the statue, thereby serving as its own pendulum. Mark figured that this had to be one of the pieces from Tyler's grandmother. Thinking he'd surprise Tyler, Mark took the clock upstairs to the apartment, set the statue on the table, and balanced the clock movement on the arm of the statue. The clock looked very impressive.

Heading back to the storeroom, Mark opened the next box and found a pair of silver candelabra. They had been carefully broken down and packed away in silver cloth. They seemed very light. Mark turned them over and he realized they were so light because they were made of thin hand-hammered pieces of silver. Carrying this box upstairs, he carefully assembled the candelabra and put them on the table next to the clock.

The next two boxes contained paintings. Each had been packed carefully. Four small paintings looked like they belonged together as a series, and the other two paintings were larger. All of them were in gold-leaf frames. They were all dirty and needed to be cleaned, but Mark could tell that they were all high-quality works. He carefully repacked each of the paintings and put them back on the shelf in the storage room. He was just finishing up when Steve came back to tell him that he'd brought lunch.

"Thank you, Steve. Are you joining us for lunch?"

"No, thank you, I already ate. What do you want me to do in here?"

"Would you take down the blinds from the windows and sweep down the ceilings, walls, and floor?" Steve nodded yes and smiled. "But first could you come with me to the front of the store?" Steve followed Mark.

Tyler was sitting at the counter waiting for Mark to join him. The store was quiet for now. "Tyler, I have something to show you. Would it be okay for Steve to watch the store for a few minutes?"

Tyler was puzzled, but he saw Mark's excitement and agreed. "Steve, we'll only be gone a few minutes."

Tyler headed to the back room, but Mark directed him upstairs. "Go into the living room." Tyler headed into the living room and Mark heard a gasp.

"Mark, where did you find these?"

"In the storage room. I also found two boxes of paintings. They look to be of good quality in nice frames, but they need to be cleaned. I left them on the shelves in there until I can look at them better. I hope that's all right?"

Tyler hugged Mark tightly and kissed him strongly. "I haven't seen these in years. Thank you for finding them and bringing them up here." Then Tyler's mood changed and he became very tentative. "Did you find anything else?"

"Yes, I found two other boxes. When I looked inside, I knew what was in them and just put them on one of the top shelves." Mark didn't really want to tell him about those boxes at all.

Tyler turned his eyes back to the table and the happiness returned. "Thank you again. I remember those from Grandma's house." Turning back to Mark and kissing him again, he murmured softly, "We should get back downstairs."

Tyler and Mark went back to the store and ate their lunches. After lunch, Mark spent most of the afternoon with Steve getting the storage room walls wiped down and the floor mopped. They also cleaned the windows inside and out. When they were done, the afternoon sun shone brightly through the windows and Mark knew this would be a good place to work.

Late in the afternoon, Mark went upstairs to get cleaned up and to prepare himself to pick up his things at his mom's. He heard Tyler coming up the stairs. When Tyler entered the apartment, Mark was ready to go.

"Let's get this over with as soon as possible. The quicker this is done, the quicker I can move on."

Tyler knew this would be hard and he wanted to make the most of Mark's resolve. "How much is there? Do we need to bring the truck?"

"No, your car should be big enough to hold everything." Getting in Tyler's car, they headed to Mark's mother's house.

Pulling up in front of the house, they noticed that there appeared to be someone home. Mark was concerned that Roger was there, but as they got out of the car, a woman came out of the house. "Marky, how are you?" She ran up to Mark and threw her arms around him. Mark could feel his eyes filling with tears. After a minute, she broke the hug and looked at Tyler. "Who is your friend?"

"Amy, this is Tyler. Tyler O'Connor, this is my sister, Amy." Tyler shook Amy's hand and she led them into the house, talking to Mark the entire time.

"Mom told me yesterday what happened. She and Roger were almost proud of it. I was mad as hell and told them so." She barely stopped to breathe. "Anyway, when mom told me you were coming to pick up your things I wanted to make sure I saw you to let you know that I love you and I don't care who you love." She finally took a deep breath. "Marky, I'm proud of you for standing up and telling them the truth." She scooped Mark into another hug.

"Thanks, Amy. Your support means a lot. At least I haven't lost my entire family." Mark sniffled a little. After entering the house, they headed right upstairs to Mark's room. He looked in, afraid of what he might find, but everything looked the same as when he left it. Mark marched directly to the closet and took out two suitcases. "Amy, start emptying the drawers into these. Tyler, please take all of the hanging clothes down to the car and lay them on the backseat." Everyone got to work. Amy packed like a fiend and Tyler hauled things to the car when they were packed. Once all the clothes and other items were set, Mark started packing his art supplies. Soon the art supplies were in boxes and the room was pretty bare. Mark then went into the closet and hauled out a large box painted the same color as the walls. "Tyler, please load this in the car last. These are some finished paintings. I always hid them from Roger, figuring he'd damage them to be spiteful." Grabbing the last of the stuff from the room, they headed outside and loaded everything in the car. As they were heading back to the car, Mark remembered that he still had his key.

"Tyler and Amy, I'll be right back. I need to leave the key." Mark marched into the house. He came out a few minutes later with a smile on his face. Tyler noticed it, but Amy didn't.

Mark hugged his sister again and gave her the phone number at Tyler's. "Don't give it to Mom or Roger and don't tell them where I'm staying. I'll call you in a few days." Hugging his sister again, he added, "I love you, Amy!"

"I love you too, Marky. Keep in touch." She headed back up the walk and into the house.

Mark and Tyler got into the car and headed back to the apartment. "Selfish bitch!"

"Where did that come from?" Tyler looked at Mark in surprise.

"Tyler, she didn't even offer me a place to stay. Granted, I would have said no thank you—she and her bratty kids drive me crazy—but she at least could have offered." He then shifted his hand to Tyler's leg.

Tyler was enjoying Mark's touch. "Don't blame your sister. At least she's being supportive." They were quiet for a few minutes as they drove. "Mark, when you came out of the house you were smiling. What did you do?"

"Who says I did anything?" The look on Mark's face spoke volumes. "Mom said to leave my key on the table and I did. I made sure that it would be on the table when she got home." Mark was laughing so hard he could barely get the words out. "I superglued the damn key to the top of the kitchen table. I know it sounds petty, but I couldn't help myself."

Tyler was now laughing as well. "Serves her right." When they had calmed down, he said, "Mark, let's get your stuff unloaded and go get some dinner."

When they got back to the store, Mark put all of the art supplies in his new studio, and Tyler moved all of Mark's clothes to the guest room closet and dresser. The remaining items they put in the second guest room closet. The box of finished paintings Tyler put in the living room. When everything was unloaded and reasonably put away, they left to eat.

Dinner was at a small café near the apartment. Mark thought the food excellent and the company even better. During dinner, Mark reached across the table and took Tyler's hand. "Tyler, I just want to thank you for everything. I appreciate everything you've done to help me." Mark looked into Tyler's eyes—those big, beautiful blue eyes. After dinner, when the waitress asked them about dessert, Mark declined, telling the waitress that they had dessert waiting for them at home, and asked her to please bring the check.

When they got back to the apartment, Tyler brought out the box of paintings. "Mark, I'd like to see your work. Would you show them to me?"

Mark opened the box very carefully and removed four unframed canvasses, lining them up against one of the walls. Tyler just looked at the paintings. He was speechless. Three of the paintings were landscapes and they were absolutely beautiful. The fourth painting was a portrait of Mark's sister Amy as she might have looked ten years ago. It was a stunning portrait. Her eyes danced and her personality jumped off the canvas. Finally Tyler found his voice. "Mark, they're stunning. Hell, stunning doesn't begin to describe them. They're magnificent, beautiful, moving, and enthralling." Tyler stopped. "They're you." Tyler just couldn't stop looking at the paintings. "I love them, Mark. They're incredible."

Without saying a word, Mark slowly turned and walked into Tyler's bedroom, got undressed, and climbed into the bed. Tyler locked up, turned off the lights, and walked into the bedroom, still thinking about the paintings. When he walked into the bedroom, a sight more beautiful than the paintings greeted him. Mark had pulled down the covers on the bed, lying on his back, naked as the day he was born, his green eyes flashing at Tyler. Tyler got undressed and got into bed next to Mark.

"Tyler, I tested negative last year and you know I haven't been with anyone since college. I also know you were tested last year because I found the results slip on your desk and I know it's been a long time for you as well." Tyler nodded. "Tyler, what I'm saying is that I'm ready."

"Mark, are you sure? I don't want you to feel pressured."

"I'm sure." Mark gently turned toward Tyler, kissing him with heat and want. Tyler returned the kiss, adding his own passion. Slowly breaking the kiss, Tyler gently lifted himself off the bed, kissed Mark again, and whispered that he'd be right back. Tyler quickly found the stereo remote control, turned on some very soft music, went to the kitchen, found a candle in a drawer, lit it, and carried it to the bedroom. He then rejoined Mark on the bed, turned off the bedroom light, wrapped his arms around Mark, and gave him a kiss hot enough to melt the polar icecaps.

Mark returned the kiss with all of his pent-up passion and desire, thrusting his tongue deep into Tyler's mouth, tasting him. Tyler's kisses seemed to reach deep into him; it was as though he could feel them deep in his heart. Tyler broke away to look at him. In the light of the candle, Tyler could see the flames reflected in Mark's eyes. After a few seconds, Mark pulled his lips back to him.

"Ty, don't stop. Your kisses are magic." They were, too. Each kiss seemed to help heal some of his pain, made him feel wanted, special, cared for.

Tyler's only response was to gently bite and pull on Mark's lip.

Tyler's weight on top of him felt reassuring and solid. Tyler's cock rubbing against his set him on fire with each movement, the flame of desire inside of him building and burning to a white-hot intensity. Mark felt Tyler's lips on his neck and throat, kissing, licking, and nibbling, sending pulses of pleasure through his body, his back involuntary arching, his legs stiffening against the mattress.

Mark was making these wonderful sounds as Tyler explored his shoulders and neck. "Ty, love that. Ummm… yeah, right there. Don't stop." Mark gave himself over to the pleasure, allowing himself to feel what Tyler had to give.

Tyler renewed his ministrations. "Don't intend to!"

Mark kept hearing moans and whimpers of pleasure and he realized they were coming from him. Tyler's hands were all over his body, gently caressing his chest, sides, hips, legs, and arms. The feel of Tyler's hands on his body made him burn. His skin got hotter everywhere Tyler touched, making him need and want Tyler more and more.

Tyler wanted to feel every inch of Mark's body all at once. He needed to make sure he was really there and this was really real. Running his fingers through the hair on Mark's chest had him moaning with delight.

"Mmmmm, Mark. Love this, love the way you feel." Tyler was nibbling Mark's ear as his hands wandered over his body.

"Tyler, your touch is thrilling." Mark was almost gasping for breath he was reacting so strongly to Tyler's touch. It was almost overwhelming.

Tyler worked his hand to Mark's cock, taking him in his grasp. Mark gasped loudly at his first touch. Tyler ran his hand over the shaft and used his thumb to caress the already leaking head.

Slowly and gently, Mark felt Tyler's weight lift off of him. He opened his eyes and saw that Tyler was kneeling next to him.

"Mark, you're magnificent…." Tyler licked his right nipple. "Beautiful." His left nipple. "Moving." His stomach. "Enthralling." He nuzzled Mark's cock with his nose and lips. "Captivating." As he heard the last word spoken, Mark felt Tyler's lips encircle the head of his cock. The words stopped as Tyler continued to take more and more of Mark into his mouth.

Mark gasped as he felt the warm wetness of Tyler's mouth engulf his cock, tongue tickling the head, making him squirm and writhe on the bed. Tyler heard Mark making the most wonderful sounds of pleasure and happiness— encouraging, thrilling sounds. As Tyler took more of Mark into his mouth, those sounds filled the entire room.

"Mark, I'm going to drive you out of your mind." Mark's cock slid over Tyler's tongue and the taste of Mark filled his entire mouth, spurring him on. As he ran his tongue along the sensitive ridge, Mark started to almost purr, the sounds of pleasure coming from deep within his chest.

The feel of Tyler's mouth on his cock kept sending Mark into exquisite agony. He started to buck almost involuntarily as Tyler's mouth and tongue continued to send waves of pleasure through him. Mark whimpered between breaths, "Tyler, you're driving me to the edge. Gonna come soon...." Rather than pull away as Mark expected, Tyler took Mark's cock deep into his mouth. Mark bucked hard against Tyler's mouth. All control left him, and hot streams exploded from his cock, shooting into Tyler.

Tyler swallowed deeply, savoring the tingly, salty sweetness of Mark on his tongue. "You taste like heaven," he moaned between gasping breaths.

Mark opened his mouth to speak, but found a pair of lips and tongue already there, probing and kissing. Mark tasted himself on Tyler's tongue and lips, felt Tyler's weight on his body, and felt Tyler's cock gently rubbing against his own. He moaned into Tyler's mouth as they kissed. "You taste sooo good." Tyler's caressing hands never stopped stroking his back, kneading his butt, and his lips never stopped kissing. Mark felt Tyler tense, his back arch, and his hands grab onto his butt as Tyler's cock throbbed against him as he came on Mark's stomach, panting and moaning into his mouth and pulling on his lips.

"Mark, I'm still seeing stars. It's never been like that." A feeling of warmth and happiness washed over Mark as he heard those words. Pulling Tyler's lips to his, Mark devoured his mouth, savoring the feel and taste of Tyler as he floated on waves of happiness, joy, and utter acceptance like he'd never felt from another person in his life.

Tyler's lips kept kissing and his hands kept caressing long after they had both climaxed. Slowly the pace and urgency of the kissing and caressing slowed, but didn't stop. Whispered words reached his ears. "Mark, we should get cleaned up. Come to the bathroom in a minute." Slowly, Mark felt the weight lift from his body, and the kisses stopped. Soon, Mark heard the sound of water running. In a sex-induced daze, he got up from the bed and headed into the bathroom, where arms wrapped around him and drew him into the shower. Those arms and hands, Tyler's arms and hands, washed his body, caressing and kneading his skin, adding feelings of inner warmth to the steamy wetness of the shower. When Tyler had washed him, Mark washed Tyler's body with the same gentleness, care, and tenderness, communicating through his hands and body the same feelings and assurances he'd received from Tyler. Wrapping his arms around Tyler, he held his body close, pressing them together until the water cooled.

After using large, fluffy, soft towels to dry and massage each other's skin, they fell into bed, holding, kissing, and caressing.

Wrapping his arms around Mark, Tyler spooned into Mark's back, allowing his entire body to press against hot skin while he kissed him on the shoulders and neck. "Mmmm, Mark, I love the way you taste." Continuing to kiss and explore Mark's body, his hands stroked the hair on Mark's chest and stomach. Tyler rolled Mark over so he was facing him, kissing Mark deeply. Using his weight, Tyler shifted them in bed so he was lying on his back with Mark on top of him. "Mark, I love the way your hairy chest feels against my skin." The words were mumbled between breaths, and he wiggled his chest against Mark's, luxuriating in the soft feel of Mark's chest hair against his smooth skin. Running his fingers through Mark's curly hair, he pressed his lips to Mark's.

Soon Tyler felt Mark's lips and tongue against his neck, licking, sucking, and gently biting. Those lips moved to Tyler's nipples where they teased, nibbled, and played. The lips kissed across Tyler's stomach where they swirled and sucked on his navel. Moving to the head of his cock, kissing… licking… teasing. Tyler gasped as Mark's warm mouth surrounded his cock, taking in more and more of him. Using his hands, Tyler guided Mark as he shifted his body to straddle him. "Want to taste you, Mark. Can't get enough." Tyler then guided Mark's cock deep into his mouth, his hands on Mark's butt, kneading and caressing.

Both Mark and Tyler were moaning loudly, encouraging each other to continue. Spreading Mark's cheeks, Tyler slowly inserted a wet finger into Mark's perfect puckered entrance. Tyler found the magic spot, curling his finger slightly as he slowly moved his finger back and forth.

"Tyler, you're… ohhhhh…." Mark's breathing became heavier and faster. Tyler carefully added a second finger as he ran his tongue around Mark's crown. The sensation sent Mark over the edge. "Ooohhh, aaahhhhh." He bucked hard, and Tyler felt Mark's orgasm shoot down his throat.

Mark swallowed Tyler to the hilt, working Tyler's cock deep down his throat. The taste of Mark still on Tyler's tongue combined with the magic of Mark's lips was too much, and he came, bucking into Mark's mouth. Mark collapsed on top of Tyler and slowly shifted his body. Wrapping his arms around him, Mark pulled him into his chest, kissing him deeply. "I've never experienced anything like that before. You're incredible."

Speaking between breaths, Tyler gasped, "You're pretty amazing as well, you know." As their breathing returned to normal, Tyler pulled the covers over both of them and snuggled next to Mark. They both quickly fell into a deep, contented, happy sleep.

Chapter 6

SUNDAY mornings were always special for Tyler. The store didn't open until noon, and he had all morning to read the paper and relax around the apartment. However, this morning Tyler was especially grateful because Mark was snuggled up next to him sound asleep, and they didn't have to get out of bed. He slowly and gently shifted position so he was facing Mark; and as he wrapped his arms around him, he could feel Mark entwine his body with Tyler's. Within minutes, Tyler had dozed off again, to be awakened a few minutes later by the feel of Mark's hot, rock-hard cock pressing insistently against his stomach. Tyler breathed heavily as his own body responded. Mark was still asleep, and Tyler didn't want to wake him; they had both had a rough couple of days.

Tyler continued to hold Mark, until he rolled over in his sleep. Tyler gingerly got out of bed and quietly headed for the bathroom, closing the door silently. Tyler got cleaned up, started the shower, and got under the spray. Letting the water course over him, he felt the bathroom door open, and soon he felt a hard, warm body pressing against his back.

"Mmmm. Morning, Mark," Tyler cooed, as Mark reached around to stroke his smooth chest and stomach.

"Morning, Ty," Mark whispered, kissing his shoulder and nibbling gently on his ear.

"Oh, that feels so good… you feel so good." Mark wiggled his hairy chest against Tyler's back, causing jolts of pleasure to shoot through him. Mark actually felt Tyler shudder. Slowly, Tyler turned around, brought his lips to Mark's, kissing him deeply, exploring his mouth with his tongue, gently pressing him against the tile wall of the shower. With Mark pressed against the wall, he was at Tyler's mercy. Taking one nipple and then the other into his mouth, Tyler sucked and nibbled on each one slowly and deliberately. Mark started making happy pleasure sounds that echoed off the tile of the shower.

"You like that, Mark?"

"Yeah, that's, oh… right there." Tyler sucked again, receiving the same response. Sucking a little harder made Mark's voice almost disappear. Tyler loved that sound, loved that he could get Mark to make that incredibly happy sound. Tyler moved from nipple to nipple until Mark actually started to get hoarse.

After the nipples, he moved to the navel, darting his tongue in and out, tickling him slightly, but teasing him as well. Mark was starting to thrust his hips slightly, his heavy cock bouncing against Tyler's cheek. "Ty, touch me please!" The begging was almost too much. Mark begging for him, wanting him. It was the sexiest sound ever.

Kneeling in front of Mark, Tyler gently nuzzled his balls before taking them into his mouth. They were pulled so tight to Mark's body that he was able to get both into his mouth at once. Now that was heaven. Those orbs were so soft and hot, rolling around in his mouth, his tongue lapping and shifting them.

"Ty, that's, oh god. Don't stop, please." Mark's knees were starting to shake as Tyler stroked his cock. "Love that. Oh goodness." Mark looked down; the sight of his cock in Tyler's hands was unbelievable.

Tyler looked up and saw tears in Mark's eyes. The expression on his face was pure ecstasy.

"You're gonna love this." Tyler opened his mouth and swallowed Mark's cock to the root. It had taken him three attempts in order to determine the best way for him to take all of Mark down his throat, but he got it this time. When he looked into Mark's face, there were still tears in his eyes.

His breath came in gasps. "Ohhhh, no one has ever…." Mark was groaning and writhing in pleasure. Each time Tyler took Mark to the root, Mark would slap the tile wall with his hands as the tears continued to roll down his cheeks.

"Ty, that feels so good." Mark stroked Tyler's hair as he continued to take all of Mark. "So magical." Mark rubbed his eyes, wiping away the tears.

Gently turning his new lover around, he tapped the inside of his thigh, indicating that Mark should spread his legs, while Tyler massaged and kneaded his butt. Kissing the small of his back, Tyler spread Mark's cheeks, exposing his opening.

Tyler teased the rim of his entrance with his tongue, and with each touch, Mark moaned and whimpered in delight.

"No one has ever...." Mark couldn't believe the sensations surging through his body. His muscles seemed to be contracting on their own as he felt Tyler's tongue teasing and probing his butt.

"Never?" Tyler grinned from ear to ear. It was thrilling to know he was the first to give Mark this type of pleasure.

Mark could only shake his head as Tyler impaled him with his tongue, taking his breath away. Mark threw his head back in a silent gasp, his knees nearly buckling under him.

The water from the shower traveled down Mark's back and flowed over the perfect pucker as Tyler probed it with his tongue. Waves of pleasure flowed through Mark as Tyler continued tonguing his opening, and his moans and whimpers built to a crescendo of pleasure. Using his fingers to tease the edges, Tyler darted his tongue in and out.

Mark's breathing was quick and shallow, and he whimpered, "Oh god, Ty, that feels so good. Don't stop!" Tyler kept fucking Mark with his tongue, probing and darting around his entrance, savoring the musky smell and taste as he steadily stroked his own hard cock. "That... feels... so... in... cred... ible...."

Soon Mark was bucking his butt against Tyler's tongue, groaning deeply as he came on the wall of the shower. His orgasm was so strong that his knees buckled and he nearly collapsed on the floor. Steadying him and turning Mark around, Tyler kissed him deeply. Mark reached Tyler's cock, stroking the silky skin as he returned the kisses. Tyler bucked against Mark's hand, his need for release so great it hurt. Moaning deeply, he came in great heaves on Mark's hand and stomach.

Turning off the water, they stepped out of the shower and took turns drying each other. They were getting dressed when Tyler turned to Mark with an inquisitive look on his face.

"Mark, why the tears? Was something wrong?" Tyler was more curious than concerned. He had seen the way Mark reacted, but the tears were a puzzle.

Mark's eyes filled again. "No one has ever done that for me before."

"Done what?" Tyler was a little confused.

"Taken me all the way. When I saw you do that, the pleasure was just too much." Mark wiped his eyes again and started to feel a little embarrassed.

Kissing Mark gently, Tyler said, "I've never had that effect on anyone before. It's so sexy and hot. Making you that happy is the hottest thing I can think of."

"Yeah?" Mark looked Tyler deep in the eyes to see if he was kidding. He wasn't.

Tyler nodded his head forcefully. "Oh, yeah!"

TYLER opened the store at noon with a big grin on his face. Mark was back in what was now his studio, getting himself set up. It was a beautifully sunny day and Tyler was hoping that Mark would be inspired and start painting. Since there were no customers, Tyler spent the next hour or so dusting all of the furniture in the store before poking his head into the studio to see what Mark was doing. Mark had already set up his easel, had a canvas on it, and looked to be working. Rather than disturb him, he quietly went back to the front of the store.

At about one o'clock, Tom and Bill entered the store. They had turned into regular customers who stopped in at least once a week, in addition to close friends. Tyler met them in the front and shook hands with both of them.

While Bill was wandering around the store, Tom and Tyler chatted. "So, Tyler, are you still seeing that cutie from the restaurant?"

Tyler nodded his head yes. "As a matter of fact, he's staying with me." Tyler could see that Tom was surprised. He gave Tom a brief synopsis of what had happened with Mark's family. Tom knew Tyler's story and he easily understood the bond that had formed between the two men.

"Tyler, Bill and I wanted to ask if you and Mark would like to go dancing with us this evening. We're going to Snuggles. They have a smoke-free room off the bar where there's a dance floor, they only play slow romantic songs, and you can hold each other and dance all night long if you want."

"That sounds nice." The thought of dancing with Mark made Tyler smile to himself.

"It is. Bill and I went there on one of our early dates. In fact, it's where Bill and I first confessed our feelings for one another. It has a special place in our hearts." Tom had a nostalgic look on his face.

"I'll ask Mark and give you a call before the store closes. When I last checked, he had a canvas on his easel and looked to be working. I really don't want to disturb him."

"Is his work any good?" Tom wasn't being critical, just curious. "I've been thinking that I want to have a portrait of Bill done."

"Down at Peter Barrett's there are a few pieces of Mark's work on display. He actually sold his first work a few days ago. He was so excited."

"I really would like to see his work, but I don't want Bill to know. I want the portrait to be a surprise for his birthday or Christmas."

Bill joined them when they were done talking. "Bill, I have something I need to show Tom. Would you mind watching the store for a few minutes?"

"Sure, no problem." Tom and Tyler headed upstairs to the apartment. The four paintings were still leaning against the wall. When Tom looked at them, he stopped moving and just stared. "You're right, Tyler. These are incredible. The portrait is breathtaking and I love the landscape of Lake Park. The detail of the bridge is so lifelike. Bill and I love to walk through the park, and that bridge is one of our favorite spots." Tom just kept looking at the paintings. "Tyler, here's a card with my work number on it. Please have Mark give me a call at work. I would be honored to have him do portraits of both of us. Also ask him how much he wants for the Lake Park painting. I would love to buy it for the family room." They headed back downstairs to the store.

At the front of the store, Bill was casually talking to a customer who had just come into the store and wanted to look around. Tom said that he wanted to poke around the store, leaving Bill and Tyler alone at the front.

"Bill, I have a sensitive question to ask you, but before I do, you must promise not to tell a single soul. Not even Tom." Bill was surprised that Tyler was so serious.

"Okay, I promise. As long as it's not illegal."

"No, nothing like that. It's just that… well… Mark is a little… big, if you get what I'm saying." Bill still looked confused. He smiled and nodded his head. He seemed to understand, but Tyler needed to stress the magnitude of his problem. Whispering, Tyler continued, "Bill, he's about nine inches long and as big as your wrist." The surprised look on Bill's face told Tyler that he fully understood.

Bill's eyes were still wide. "Tyler, are you telling me that Mark is hung like a horse and you don't know how you'll be able to take it?" He started to smile. "You are one lucky man."

"Yeah, I know. I mean, it's been a long time for me and I want to be able to give myself to him, but I'll need some help." The look on Tyler's face was dead serious.

Bill nodded his head. "I know exactly what you need to do. Go to the leather store at The Room. They have a number of butt plugs in various sizes. Get one each in medium and large. Use the medium one first and leave it in for twenty to thirty minutes. When that's comfortable, move up to the larger size." Tyler nodded, taking all this in. "The plugs will help stretch the muscles without pain and you can wear them under clothes. I recommend that you get one made of glass." The look of shock on Tyler's face was priceless. "Think of them as butt-plug-shaped paper weights. They are very smooth and easy to clean. When you're there, ask for Chuck, and you can use Tom's or my name. He knows both of us and he's very helpful."

Tyler felt a sense of relief knowing there was something he could do. "Thank you. I knew you'd be able to help."

Tom rejoined them and they said goodbye. Tyler promised he'd call them to let them know about that night. There were no customers in the store, so Tyler peeked in on Mark. He was sitting at the easel looking off into space. He smiled when he saw Tyler, and came out of the studio.

Tyler kissed him sweetly. Reaching into his pocket, he handed Mark Tom's card. "This is Tom's work number. He wants you to call him this week at work. I showed him the paintings upstairs and he wants to commission you to do portraits of both of them. He also wants to buy the Lake Park landscape, if you want to sell it."

Mark hugged the stuffing out of Tyler, pushed him against the wall, and kissed him with passion and need. "Oh, Ty. Thank you!" He was so excited he was nearly bouncing off the walls.

"The portraits are a surprise, so don't say anything about it when Bill's around. They also asked if we'd like to go to Snuggles dancing tonight. I told them I'd ask you. I'd like to go, but I didn't know if you would."

"Dancing sounds great. I'd love to go." Kissing Tyler again, he said, "By the way, when the store closes, I need you to come upstairs right away. I'll have something for you." He winked as he turned and went back into the studio.

Tyler approached the front of the store as a customer entered. As he got closer, he realized that the man looked a lot like Mark. Tyler was immediately on his guard.

"I'm Roger Burke. You bought some items from my mother about a week ago." The look on his face and his demeanor were definitely that of a bully.

"Yes, I did. What of it?" Tyler was immediately defensive.

"Look, I've got your check right here. I want the items you bought back." The look on his face was confrontational. He was looking for a fight.

Tyler crossed his arms over his chest. "No."

"What do you mean no?" He was starting to raise his voice.

"First thing, the sale was completed properly…."

Roger just started talking over him. "Look, we haven't cashed the check, so that transaction hasn't been completed."

Tyler was starting to get angry, but realized he needed to keep himself under control. Losing his temper was not going to help. "Your cashing the check has nothing to do with it. Your mother signed a bill of sale stating that a check was acceptable payment and that ownership of the items listed immediately transferred to me."

"If I don't get those items back, I'll…." Roger was waving his hands at Tyler, gestures that were designed to intimidate. They failed.

Mockingly, Tyler said, "You'll what? Throw a hissy fit, cry back to Mommy?" Tyler got very serious. "I don't care what you think you'll do. Those items are mine. You can't have them back, you won't get them back, and in fact, some of them have already been sold. Now you—" Tyler was about to throw Roger out of the store when he saw Mark coming toward them.

Roger pointed at Mark. "What is that… that… faggot brother of mine doing here?" The hatred and venom were almost frightening. Mark stopped moving, but Tyler motioned him to come forward.

Slipping his arm around Mark's waist, he spat, "He's here because you and your mom threw him out of the house. He's here because he's my boyfriend." Tyler just stared Roger in the eyes and he could see him backing down.

"Look, I know you cheated my mother on those things you bought." His voice had none of the authority or bravado it had a few minutes earlier.

Tyler just laughed at him. "I most certainly did not. I paid her a fair price for each item. Furthermore, I paid her more than she asked for on some of the items. Now, you have thirty seconds to leave this store. You are not welcome here! If you come back here I'll have you arrested for trespassing. Mark, you're my witness that he's been warned."

"You'll be sorry!" Roger was sputtering.

"No, Roger, you will! If you try to cause trouble for either Mark or me, I will call friends. Big, strong friends. They know how to handle bullies like you. Roger, like most bullies, you're a coward, a chicken shit coward! Now GET OUT before I call the police!" Roger turned and walked out of the store. He was still mad, but he wasn't used to someone standing up to him and he didn't know how to react.

Mark stood silently next to Tyler. "I didn't know he was here until he saw me. I heard raised voices and came out to see if you needed help." Tyler hugged Mark to him.

"Mark, he's not going to hurt you ever again if you don't let him. He's a bully, and you stand up to bullies. Besides, he nearly wet his pants when I told him I'd call some big, strong friends." Tyler started to laugh and Mark did as well.

"This is the first time I've ever seen him flustered. Why did he stop by, anyway?"

"He wanted to return my check and get the items back that I bought from your mom. Why he would do that I have no idea. I think he's nuts." Turning to Mark and lightening his tone, he asked, "Don't let him bother you. Okay?"

Mark nodded. "Yeah."

Tyler decided to change the subject. "Are you done working?"

Mark's face brightened when he thought about his work. "No, not yet." Looking at his watch, he said, "It's three-thirty; I'll work for another hour. Then I'll meet you upstairs."

"Okay, cutie. See you upstairs." Tyler squeezed Mark's butt as he headed back to the studio. Mark had taken about two steps when Tyler rushed up to him, slipping his arms around his waist. "Don't you even think about Roger. He's not worth the concern." Tyler kissed Mark on the neck and released him. Mark turned to look at Tyler again, flashing those incredible green eyes, before heading back to the studio.

Tyler spent the rest of the afternoon helping customers. He was particularly pleased because he sold a large bookcase that had been in the store for more than a year. He was also drained from his confrontation with Roger and he hoped Mark could put him out of his mind.

Just before closing, Tyler called Tom and told him that he and Mark would love to go dancing with them that evening. At five, Tyler locked the door to the store, put the day's receipts in the safe, and headed upstairs to the apartment. As he entered, Mark came out of the bedroom wearing only a small pair of shorts that left little to the imagination. The outline of Mark's semi-hard cock was clearly visible. Tyler's body responded immediately, creating a visible tightness in his pants.

Hugging Mark and rubbing the crotch of the shorts, he asked, "Are these my surprise?" Tyler let his hand slip past the waistband, lightly brushing Mark's cock and cupping his balls. Mark's cock was now fully erect and pressing hard against the fabric. A moan escaped from deep in Mark's chest.

Mark shook his head, gently pulling Tyler's hand out of the shorts. "I'm glad you like them, but no. These are just to give you something to think about. Your surprise is in the bedroom." Mark took Tyler's hand and led him into the bedroom. The bed had been stripped except for the white sheets. "Tyler, I want to paint you... nude." Mark was a little unsure how Tyler would react.

Tyler just smiled and started to undress. "What do you want me to do?" Tyler finished undressing.

Tyler standing in front of him naked and hard was almost too much. Mark had to quash the urge to rip off his shorts and throw Tyler onto the bed. He closed his eyes before speaking. "I need to do some sketches first." Cautioning Tyler, he said, "Now, I am not going to show you the sketches or the painting until it's finished. Okay?"

Tyler nodded. "All right, Mark. I trust you."

"Lay on your stomach with your head facing the foot of the bed." Tyler complied. "Prop your chest up slightly using your arms. Basically, I want you to look like you're lying on the bed, watching for me to come into the room so you can seduce me."

Tyler smiled. That was exactly what he wanted to do right now. The sight of Mark's cock in those tight shorts had him grinding his hips into the bed. He had to forcefully stop himself from moving.

Mark spent a few minutes positioning Tyler. When he was done, he got himself into position. He was looking at Tyler at a slight angle, so Tyler's face and shoulders were in the foreground, with Tyler's butt and legs visible by looking over his shoulders. Once Tyler was positioned, he rumpled and draped the top sheet. Stepping back, he felt he had gotten the look he wanted. Sitting in the chair he'd positioned, he started to sketch. As he sketched, he cautioned Tyler, "Please try not to move or change your expression. I know it's difficult, but please try."

Tyler didn't move, but his cock was hard as steel, pulsing and leaking all over the bed.

Mark sketched and drew for the next hour. The only sound in the room was the pencil scraping over the paper and the sound of Mark's and Tyler's breathing. Mark stretched his hands for a minute and then went back to sketching. "I still need a few more sketches. Please be patient. I'll make it up to you." He continued to draw at an almost furious pace. When he finally got up from the chair, he walked over to Tyler and kissed him.

"Mark, there's a digital camera at the desk in the store. Do you want to get a picture before I move?" Mark raced down to the store, grabbed the camera, and raced back to the bedroom. He then took a number of pictures from slightly different angles. Putting down the camera, Mark crawled on the bed, wrapped Tyler in his arms, and kissed him. "Thank you for being patient. I think I got what I needed."

Tyler rolled over and pulled Mark on top of him and started to remove the shorts, but Mark stopped him gently. "We need to get dinner and meet Bill and Tom in an hour. We really don't have time right now." It didn't matter to Tyler. He shifted positions and tugged off Mark's shorts. Drawing him to his body, he cupped Mark's head in his hands and kissed him with passion, heat, and need. Mark returned the kiss, adding his own passion and want.

"Mark, I wanted you here with me now because I need to tell you something. I wanted to feel you next to me with no separation when I told you. This afternoon when I was arguing with Roger and he threatened you, I realized something important, something I haven't felt in a very long time. Mark, I wanted you to know that I'm falling in love with you and I'm falling hard."

Tyler could see tears in Mark's eyes. "Ty, you're not alone, because I'm falling in love with you as well."

Tyler was hard as a rock and he could feel Mark's erection pressing against his skin. His breath was coming in deep gasps as he pulled Mark's lips to his, kissing him deeply, letting all his emotions flow through the kiss.

"Tyler, we need…." His words were cut off as Tyler thrust his tongue deep into Mark's mouth, pulling on his lips.

Mark could feel Tyler bucking against him, grinding his cock against Mark's.

The feel of Mark's cock against his was driving Tyler wild with desire. Mark was enjoying it as well. Those sexy pleasure noises had started and just kept building with each movement. Tyler slipped his hands beneath Mark, cupping and squeezing his butt.

Their cocks slid easily past each other. They were both leaking so plentifully, they provided their own lube. Mark's kisses were becoming more insistent, his teeth scraping and pulling on Tyler's lips. His moans were becoming more insistent and breathier. Mark opened his mouth and no sound came out.

Tyler was finding it difficult to form words as well. His cock sliding past Mark's was sending shocks up and down his spine, throwing his body into absolute overdrive. Finally, he managed to form a word. He squeaked out, "Mark," as he shot hard between their bodies, his body convulsing for what seemed like hours.

The feel of Tyler's come against his skin sent Mark flying and his own cock throbbed. He threw his head back against the bed as he shuddered and thrashed to a climax.

Slowly, Tyler lifted his weight off Mark as he kissed and petted him. Tyler padded to the bathroom for a washcloth and towel. Returning to the bedroom, he cleaned up Mark before washing himself.

Mark sat on the edge of the bed and stood up. "Ty, we need to get dressed quickly."

"Uh-huh. I'm moving as fast as I can. You wore me out."

Mark laughed. "I wore you out?"

Tyler smiled at Mark. "Yeah, those shorts did me in." Tyler reached over and pulled Mark to him. "You looked so sexy and hot in those shorts, but you look even better naked." The look on Tyler's face was pure lust.

Mark smiled back. "We need to get ready or we'll be late." Mark started getting dressed.

"Tom said it was very casual and he suggested we wear loose-fitting shirts. He said it makes it easier to caress while dancing." Oh yeah, dancing and feeling Tyler's skin at the same time; now that was gonna be heaven.

They both got dressed. Mark wore a pair of jeans and a red button-down shirt. Tyler wore jeans and a loose fitting T-shirt. After grabbing a quick bite to eat, they headed out to the bar to meet Bill and Tom.

Snuggles was a small, quiet bar that catered to an older crowd. The bar had two rooms; the first had tables and a bar, while the second had the dance floor, a few tables, and was nonsmoking. When Tyler and Mark arrived, Bill and Tom were already there and had grabbed a table around the dance floor. Tom was wearing a pair of leather pants and a white T-shirt. Bill was wearing leather pants and a leather vest with no shirt underneath. Tyler got drinks and brought them to the table. The four men sat and talked for a while before getting up to dance.

Tom leaned across the table and winked at the two of them. "I know why you were late."

Mark and Tyler looked a little sheepish. "I was posing for Mark." Tyler's eyes met Mark's as he smiled at him.

Mark excused himself and went to the bathroom. Bill leaned over to Tyler. "You were doing more than posing for Mark. Your lips are all scraped and swelled." Tyler couldn't help but smile. He was just so happy.

Tom patted him on the back on his way to the bar. "It's good to see you so happy, Tyler. It really is."

Tyler thought for a minute and realized that he was happy, truly happy for the first time in a very long time. Mark was quickly becoming a very important part of his life. The thought scared him a little, but delighted him even more.

Mark returned to the table as Tom returned with drinks. They spent a few minutes laughing, talking, and enjoying their drinks before getting up to dance.

The music was slow and mellow, and Bill and Tom moved to the dance floor first. Tom wrapped his arms around Bill, slipping his hands under the vest and drawing him to his body. Tyler and Mark got up to dance as well. Wrapping his arms around Mark, Tyler rested his head against Mark's shoulder. The two men swayed and moved to the music.

Mark whispered to Tyler, "I didn't realize Bill and Tom were into leather."

Tyler smiled and tightened his hold on Mark. "Oh yeah, they are both really into leather. Remind me to tell you about it sometime." Tyler nibbled gently on Mark's ear. "You smell so good, and you taste even better." Mark gently kissed Tyler as he slipped his hands beneath Tyler's T-shirt, caressing his back. "Oh, that's really nice." They kept dancing and kissing for the next few hours. The music, the closeness, and the kisses relaxed them both, allowing them to just feel each other. At about eleven, the four of them sat down for a rest and a drink. Finishing their drinks, they danced for another hour.

At midnight, the four men said good night and headed home. Tyler and Mark got back to the apartment and got ready for bed. Tyler climbed into the bed where he had posed for Mark a few hours before. The memory was enough to get Tyler hard and anxious for his lover to come to bed. When Mark came into the bedroom, Tyler lifted the covers so he could get into bed, pulled Mark close, and kissed him hungrily. "I've waited all evening to get you naked with me here in bed."

"Are you going to turn off the light?"

"No, I want to see you. Your body is so sexy and I want to be able to see what I'm doing." Tyler kissed Mark with deep passion. Pressing Tyler into the mattress, Mark added his own desire. "Love the way you kiss."

Tyler explored Mark's mouth with his tongue.

"Oh, Ty, that feels so good." Mark pulled and tugged on Tyler's lips as they kissed. Tyler moaned into Mark's mouth as Mark wrapped his hand around him, stroking slowly and gently.

"I can't get enough of you." Tyler cupped Mark's butt in his hands, kneading and massaging.

After slinking down Tyler's body, Mark took the head of Tyler's cock into his mouth, slowly sliding his tongue around it as he extended his lips down the shaft, until he felt Tyler's pubic hair tickle his nose. Tyler was whimpering with delight as Mark fondled his balls. "Oh,

Mark," were the only words Tyler could form. The sensation of Mark's mouth on him took his breath away.

Tyler watched as Mark worked his cock into his mouth, taking him deeply. Tyler ran his hands through Mark's dark hair, caressing his head and cheek as Mark sucked him. God, Mark was good at that. Really good. The room filled with pleasure noises, moans, whimpers, and soft groans, and he realized they were coming from him.

Gently lifting Tyler's legs toward his chest, Mark tickled his scrotum with his tongue. The gasping and whimpering got louder and more insistent. Mark licked and sucked a path to Tyler's entrance, probing and sucking on the opening. Tyler moaned loudly as Mark used his hands to spread his cheeks and his tongue to probe his butt.

"Mark, don't stop. Feels so good!" Using his hands, Tyler guided Mark into a new position. "I want to taste you, Mark." Straddling Tyler, Mark lowered his cock into Tyler's waiting mouth as he lifted Tyler's legs, impaling him with his tongue, deeply probing and licking Tyler's entrance.

Mark felt Tyler take all of him again and again as he fondled his balls with one hand and fingered his ass with the other. "Oh god Tyler, I'm so close." The sounds of passion filled the bedroom. Whimpers, moans, gasps. "Ty, I can't take much more." Tyler swallowed Mark as he inserted a slicked finger into his opening. "Oh Ty, gonna, oh!" Mark arched his back and exploded deep into Tyler.

Without lowering Tyler's legs to the bed, Mark took Tyler's cock to the root in one movement, using his lips to pump Tyler's cock as he gently inserted a slicked finger into Tyler's butt, pressing against his prostate. "Mark, I'm so close!" Mark added a second finger as he probed and stretched. "Oh god, Mark," were all the words he could manage as he erupted in Mark's mouth. Mark swallowed deeply, savoring the tingling sensation on his tongue.

Mark brought his mouth to Tyler's, kissing him deeply as he wrapped him in his arms. "Never going to let you go."

"Good. Don't want you to." The kissing and petting continued as Tyler pulled up the covers. "Love the feeling of being in your arms."

"Good. Love having you in my arms." Tyler turned out the light.

Tyler was holding him close, gently rubbing his chest. "Ty, what's with Bill and Tom and the leather? You said you'd tell me about it."

"Mark, do you know what The Room is?"

"Isn't that the leather bar near Snuggles?" Tyler nodded. "Don't they have a big monthly event?"

"Yeah, they call it the revels." Tyler gently kissed Mark on the forehead. "Tom got dragged to the revels by a friend about two years ago. To make a long story short, he ended up accidentally overthrowing the Master of the Revels. Consequently, he became the Master."

"You're kidding?"

Tyler chuckled lightly. "No. The night he became Master, he also met Bill, and from what he tells me, it was instant attraction."

"Is he still the Master?"

"No, he stepped down about a year ago. He still does one revel a year, usually in June. The one he did last year was their wedding." Tyler was quiet for a minute. "I don't know if he's doing one this year. I could ask him, if you'd like to go." That really wasn't Tyler's thing, but if Mark wanted to go, he'd take him.

Mark actually thought about it for a minute. "I don't think so." He snuggled closer to Tyler. "Good night, Ty."

Tyler could hear Mark's breathing even out as he fell asleep and he smiled to himself as he drifted to sleep too.

Chapter 7

THE following Saturday, Mark was watching the store. Tyler had said that he needed to run an errand. He wasn't willing to explain. He just kissed him, winked, and told him he wouldn't be gone long. It had been a good week. Mark had called Tom on Monday and they had worked out the details for the portraits of him and Bill. Tom was going to sit for his portrait, but the portrait of Bill would need to be done strictly from pictures. Tom wanted the portraits as a Christmas gift for Bill, so Mark had plenty of time. To add to his good fortune, Tom had purchased the Lake Park painting and didn't even blink when Mark had quoted his price. He didn't charge what Peter would have in the gallery, but he had asked a fair price. To top it all off he was making excellent progress on the painting of Tyler, and even Mark had to admit that the painting was good. So good that a few times he was staring at it and got hard. He wanted to have it done in two weeks, in time for Tyler's birthday.

Tyler had been gone for about fifteen minutes when a striking man came into the store. Mark couldn't help but notice that this man was sex on wheels: tall, handsome, broad- shouldered, muscular, tanned, not a hair out of place. Perfect in every way. He also exuded an air of self-assurance. He was even dressed perfectly. After allowing him to look around the store for a few minutes, Mark approached the man and asked if he could help him.

"I'm looking for Tyler O'Connor."

"Tyler is out of the store for a few minutes. I expect him back shortly."

"Oh. I'm an old friend of his in town for the weekend," he said and offered his hand. "Blake Stevenson."

Shaking the offered hand, Mark replied, "I'm Mark Burke. Can I offer you something to drink? He really should be back at any time."

"Water would be great."

Mark got a bottled water out of the refrigerator under the counter and handed it to Blake. "Can I ask you how long you've known Tyler?" Mark was a little curious, but mostly just making polite conversation until Tyler got back.

"We went to college together." It dawned on Mark. This was Tyler's college boyfriend. At that moment, Tyler walked through the front door of the store carrying a medium-sized brown bag. Blake took one look at Tyler, walked over to him, and hugged him tightly. Tyler was a little surprised and didn't react until Blake stepped back and Tyler was able to see him clearly.

"My god, Blake, what a surprise. It's been what, eight years? How are you?"

"I've been great. I'm in town for the weekend and thought I would try to see you." Leaning in close, he offered suggestively, "Thought maybe we could get together, you know, for old time's sake." Tyler didn't know how to react to that. He said nothing and stared. Mark, on the other hand, heard every word. He just waited to see how Tyler would react.

Choosing to ignore the offer as absurd, Tyler continued, "What are you doing these days? I had heard you were a stockbroker in California."

"Yeah. I started my own small brokerage office a few years ago. It's been a bigger success than I ever expected. I sold it a year ago and made a bundle. Now I'm scouting other business opportunities." There was a smug, self-satisfied look on his face.

"That's great. I'm glad things are going well for you." Turning to Mark, Tyler asked, "Have you met Mark?"

"Yes, he was very helpful when I arrived." Tyler looked at Mark and smiled. Mark, on the other hand, was confused and a little angry. Why hadn't Tyler turned down Blake's offer?

"Excuse me, please. I have some work to do." Mark then headed briskly back to the studio.

Tyler watched Mark go. From his walk, he figured something was wrong, but he really couldn't figure out what. He then realized he was ignoring Blake.

"So when do you fly home?" He was trying to concentrate on what Blake was saying while at the same time wondering what was wrong with Mark.

"My plane leaves in the morning. Ty, would you like to get together later for a drink? I'd really like to catch up, you know, see how much has changed, how much hasn't." The look on Blake's face was pure sex.

Tyler smiled blandly. "Blake, it's good to see you, but I'm seeing someone." Thoughts of Mark turned the smile from bland to radiant.

"So am I. Robert and I have been together for four years, but that doesn't stop me from having some fun when I'm out of town." Tyler found that repulsive. Was this the same person he had been in love with in college, the same person who had held him and comforted him that traumatic night when his parents disowned him? Tyler realized it wasn't.

"No, thank you, Blake, but it was good to see you." He was trying very hard to keep a look of revulsion off his face.

Blake plowed on, completely oblivious to anything but what he wanted. "Call me if you change your mind." He put a hotel card on the counter with a room number written on it. Tyler didn't touch the card. After scooping Tyler into another hug, Blake left the store and walked to his rental car.

Tyler was shocked and confused. He was trying to reconcile the person from his memory and the person who had just left his store, but he couldn't. Tyler picked up the hotel card and threw it in the trash. He had no intention of calling Blake. Mark was more of a man and a much better person than the Blake that just left the store. There were no customers in the store, so Tyler went back to see what Mark was doing.

He found Mark in his studio behind his easel just staring out the window. He wasn't moving, just staring.

"Mark, do you want to get some lunch?"

"No! I'm not hungry." The tone was severe and he sounded hurt.

"Is something wrong?"

"No.... Yes.... God, I don't know. Why don't you tell me?"

"Just tell me what's on your mind." Tyler was a little confused and a little worried about Mark's reaction.

Mark finally started to move and began packing up his paints. "Maybe I should just go." His voice was high and soft, and Tyler could tell something was hurting him.

Tyler walked up to Mark, placing his hands on his shoulders. "Mark, what is wrong?" Tyler was starting to get worried.

Mark squirmed away. "Well, I heard Blake proposition you and since you didn't tell him no, or even tell him you were seeing me, I figured you were interested." Mark's voice was almost squeaking and Tyler could tell he was close to tears.

"Mark, first thing, I didn't react to his offer because it was ridiculous and pathetic." That got Mark's attention. "Secondly, you had already been talking to him, so I thought you had introduced yourself as my boyfriend. The person I saw today isn't the Blake I remember or care about. The person I loved in college was sensitive, caring, thoughtful, and loving, just like the person I love today."

"What? Who?" Mark's head jerked up and he just stared at Tyler, his face hard.

"Mark, the person I love is you." Suddenly, the room got very quiet, the only sound the pinging of the paint brushes that slipped out of Mark's fingers and hit the floor. "Mark, you have no reason to be jealous or threatened by anyone where I'm concerned." Mark was out from behind the easel like a shot, launching himself at Tyler, pinning him against the wall as he kissed him hard, pulling on his lips, thrusting his tongue into his mouth, making needy, almost wanton noises as his eyes became blurry.

Tyler was instantly hard and it took all his self-control to keep from tearing off Mark's clothes and taking him right there. Mark kept kissing until the front doorbell rang, indicating that there were customers in the store. Reluctantly, Tyler and Mark broke the kiss and Tyler went to the front of the store to greet the customers, straightening his clothes as he walked. Mark went back to his studio and spent the rest of the morning tying to get something accomplished.

Mark had to work at the art gallery in the afternoon and evening, so Tyler didn't see Mark again until dinnertime. He spent the afternoon in the store. After the store closed, he had some pieces to deliver and an appointment to look at some items for sale. Steve met him at closing time and the two of them completed the deliveries and headed over to see a longtime client who was moving to a smaller home and needed to sell some of the pieces she'd collected.

Heading back to the store at about seven, Tyler noticed a car parked behind the store near the back door. Getting out of the truck, Tyler was greeted by Officer Sam Davis.

"Hi, Sam. Haven't seen you in a while. How are you?"

"Hi, Tyler. Hey, Steve." Steve waved and started to unload the items from the truck into the back room of the store as Tyler and Sam talked.

"Tyler, we got an interesting call at the station today from a Roger Burke. He says that you purchased some items from his mom and took advantage of her." Sam was almost laughing.

Tyler just shook his head. Roger would stop at nothing to get what he wanted, no matter how unreasonable. "Well, Sam, I did buy some items from Alice Burke about two weeks ago. We had a good visit, she showed me the items she wanted to sell, I told her the price I was willing to pay, and she agreed. I do have a signed bill of sale from Mrs. Burke."

"So what's his problem?"

"Roger Burke is a bully. When I was at the house I met his brother Mark. Mark and I went out for dinner a few days later. Some friends of Roger's saw us, and told him. He told his mother and she kicked Mark out of the house. He's been staying with me ever since. Roger tried to cancel the sale last week, but it's not possible because some of the items are already sold, and besides, I am not going to give in to a bully."

"We all thought that this guy was a bit crazy, but I had to check it out and I wanted to let you know what was happening."

"Sam, I have proof and a signed receipt. He's just bullying. Besides, the items weren't his but his mother's. He has no business being involved. I'm starting to wonder if there isn't something else we just don't know…." Tyler thought for a minute. "One other thing: For at least one of the items she quoted me a price and I paid her more than she quoted because it was worth more. Mark was there for that conversation."

"Well, I just wanted you to know. Say, could I get a copy of that bill of sale? I'll add it to the file."

Tyler started heading through the store to the counter. "Sure, no problem. Thanks, Sam. Hey, stop by for a drink sometime. I'd really like you to meet Mark."

"I'll do that. By the way, what does he do?" Sam was just making conversation.

"Right now he's working for Peter Barrett. He's a gifted artist. He's sold a few pieces and he just got a commission." Tyler made a copy of the bill of sale for Sam.

"This looks great. I have to call him back. I'm going to tell him that there's nothing we can do. The sale is well documented. I'm also going to try to pressure him a little and tell him that this sounds like a family dispute. While I'm at it, I'll also mention that making false, unsubstantiated claims is a crime. That should shut him up!" Sam and Tyler headed back through the store to the rear exit.

"Thanks, Sam. Let me know if you find out anything more. This guy is a real nutcase and he's violent. Mark had bruises from him after they kicked him out of the house." Sam waved goodbye and got into his car.

Tyler helped Steve unload the rest of the items into the shop. It had been a good evening. His client had wanted to sell a number of pieces, including some rare, hard-to-find items. After completing the unloading, Tyler gave Steve a case of beer and he went home happy. Tyler went upstairs and started to fix dinner. Mark would be home soon and he was looking forward to picking up where they had left off that afternoon. As dinner was cooking, Tyler went to the bedroom to prepare for Mark's arrival.

When Mark returned from work, Tyler had dinner nearly ready. The table was set for the two of them with candles, Chopin was playing softly on the stereo, and the lights had been dimmed in the apartment. Tyler heard Mark on the stairs and met him at the door with a kiss and a glass of wine.

"Mark, sit down and rest a while. Dinner should be ready in ten minutes." Mark sat on the couch and relaxed. "How did it go at the gallery?"

Mark sipped his wine. "It was quite busy. Saturdays usually are, particularly Saturday evenings. People like to wander through the area and look around." Taking another sip of wine, he added, "A woman was interested in one of my paintings. She spent a long time looking at it. I'm hoping she'll come back and buy it. Maybe if I sell another painting soon after selling the first, Peter will let me hang more of my work."

That got Tyler thinking. "I have to go see Peter this week. He wanted me to stop by and look at something he found. Have you told him about the other commissions you've received?"

"No, I haven't mentioned it. Why?"

"Never you mind. Just trust me." Bringing the food to the table, Tyler teased, "Come and join me for dinner, I've got dessert planned as well." Mark saw the look in Tyler's eyes and knew dessert would be special.

The dinner was wonderful. Mark and Tyler talked, laughed, and kissed their way through the meal. After dinner, Tyler put the dishes in the kitchen and joined Mark in the living room. Sitting together on the sofa, they were soon kissing passionately. Mark pressed Tyler into the sofa cushions and started to open the buttons on his shirt. "Mark, why don't we move this into the bedroom?" Lifting himself off the sofa, Tyler bent down to kiss Mark. "Give me a minute and then join me." Tyler slowly walked into the bedroom, clicking the stereo remote to change the music.

A few minutes later, Mark turned off the living room lights and followed Tyler into the bedroom. The lights were off and the bedroom glowed with candlelight. The bed had been turned down, extra pillows had been added, and in the background, deep romantic symphonic music created a mood of pure romance and love. The bathroom door opened and Tyler stepped naked into the bedroom. Slowly, he approached Mark, took him into his arms and kissed him gently and tenderly as he slowly started to undress him. Pressing his body to Mark's back, Tyler reached around Mark as he slowly undid the buttons of his shirt, slipped it off his shoulders, and let it drop to the floor. Mark toed out of his shoes as his pants were opened and they fell to the floor. Mark stepped out of them, leaving him wearing only his briefs.

Tyler nibbled Mark's ear as he whispered, "I want you to move in with me." His hands rubbed Mark's stomach.

"Tyler, I've been living here for weeks." The voice was very soft and raspy. Tyler's hands were roaming over his body.

"I know, but I wanted to make it official. I want you to know that you're wanted and loved, so would you please make your home with me?" Tyler nibbled on Mark's neck and shoulders.

Breathlessly Mark replied, "Oh, yes, Tyler." Tyler's hands and mouth were working magic on his body.

Tyler ran his hands through the hair on Mark's chest, gently teasing his sensitive nipples. Slowly, Tyler worked his hands into the band of Mark's briefs, lowering them past his butt, allowing his cock to bounce free.

"Mark, lie on your back on the bed. I have something special for you." Tyler watched Mark's butt wiggle slightly as he complied with his request. "You are going to love this."

Reaching for the light mint massage oil he had placed on the nightstand, Tyler slowly worked the muscles of Mark's shoulders and upper chest, being sure to apply just enough pressure to relax the muscles. As Tyler continued massaging Mark's arms, chest, and legs, using long, firm, slow hand movements, Mark continued to relax and just let himself float on the sensations provided by Tyler's hands. Those hands touching, massaging, kneading every part of his body, love and affection communicated with every touch, every movement. The long strokes allowing Tyler's love to flow deep into Mark, communicating in a way that mere words just couldn't. Gently rolling Mark onto his stomach, Tyler straddled Mark as he massaged his arms, shoulders, and back, working his hands across and into the knotted and tense muscles. Moving down his body, Tyler stroked and massaged the legs.

As Tyler worked his skin and muscles, Mark could feel the heat within him rising. Tyler's touch was like a branding iron on his skin, each caress, each touch building Mark's desire for more.

Using a small dab of oil, Tyler massaged and kneaded Mark's butt, working in the oil and relaxing the muscles. Gently reaching between Mark's legs, he cupped his balls in one hand as he massaged his crack with the side of his other hand. Tyler continued to massage and stroke with the next pass. Over and over Tyler rubbed and stroked Mark's entrance. With each caress, it flexed and contracted. Tyler gently slipped an oiled finger into Mark while he continued to stroke Mark's balls. As Tyler inserted the finger, Mark raised his butt and pushed upward, moaning as the finger pressed deeper. "Man, Mark, the noises you make… so sexy."

Slowly he withdrew and reinserted the finger. This time, Mark's moan was reasonably coherent. "More, Tyler, more!' Tyler added a second finger and still Mark moaned for more, "Tyler, I want you! Need you!"

"Are you sure?" His voice was low and deep with need; he was so hard it was almost painful. Tyler added a third finger, making sure Mark was ready for him.

"Oh god, yes. Please, Tyler, I need you! I love you!" Gently, Tyler rolled Mark onto his back and got a pillow. Mark lifted his legs to expose himself completely to Tyler. The sight was one of the most incredible things Tyler had ever seen. The love and trust conveyed in that simple act was almost overwhelming.

Placing a pillow beneath Mark, Tyler positioned his lubed cock at Mark's entrance and gently pushed forward. "Relax, Mark," he whispered softly. Tyler slowly pressed into Mark, whispering sweet words of love, and massaging his lower back and butt. He was soon buried inside Mark, not moving at all. "Mark, you feel so tight, so warm, so incredible."

"Ty, I can feel your heart beat, you fill me so completely." Mark let his head fall back on the pillow, the sensations overwhelming his senses.

He felt Mark start to press to him and he very slowly started to move inside Mark, using long, very deliberate strokes. Tyler kept a very steady pace as he heard Mark moan each time he entered him and whimper when he withdrew. "Oh, Ty…. Oh, Ty…. Oh, Ty…."

Bending forward for a kiss, Tyler was surprised and delighted as Mark thrust his tongue into Tyler's mouth and sucked on his lips. Locking his legs around Tyler's back, Mark pressed Tyler's head to his lips, moaning into Tyler's mouth as they kissed. "Ty, you feel so good… love having you inside me."

"Love the way you feel around me." The warmth and tightness of Mark's body was like nothing he had ever felt before. "Mark, you look so hot." Tyler completely withdrew his cock.

"Yeah? You make me feel hot." Mark threw his head back on the pillow as Tyler drove his cock deep into him again. Tyler withdrew again, reentering with a single long thrust, nearly taking Mark's breath away.

Tyler was flying, the noises Mark was making driving him wild with desire. Steadily he picked up the pace. As he did, he felt the urgency of Mark's kisses increase and the moaning start to turn nearly breathless, almost pleading. Tyler caressed Mark's legs and thighs as he continued to drive himself deep into Mark.

"I just can't get enough of you, Mark!"

Those words sent Mark soaring on wings of pleasure. Mark cried, "I love you, Tyler!" as his orgasm sprayed over his stomach and chest. Tyler lasted just a few more strokes as he cried out his own declarations of love, his cock pulsing deeply into Mark.

"Mark, that was wonderful. You were wonderful." His kisses were warm and loving.

"Ty, that was amazing. Promise it will always be special like that." Mark just glowed from their lovemaking.

Placing his mouth close to Mark's ear, Tyler whispered, "Making love is always special."

Slowly Tyler withdrew from Mark, lying next to him on the bed. When their breathing returned to normal, Tyler kissed Mark and headed to the bathroom. Tyler turned on the shower to warm, returned to the bedroom, and ushered Mark into the bathroom. Candles had already been lit, casting the bathroom in the same warm glow as the bedroom. Tyler gently pulled Mark into the shower, wrapping his arms around him, kissing him deeply as he massaged his back. Tyler then carefully washed Mark, starting with his hair and working down his body to his legs, using his soapy hands to massage and caress every inch of his skin. Mark then washed Tyler, caressing his body and kissing his lips. When the water started to cool, Tyler turned off the shower, wrapped Mark in a large towel, dried his body, and whispered for him to get into bed. Tyler then dried himself and went into the kitchen to get their nightcap.

Tyler returned to the bedroom with two glasses of champagne and a bowl of strawberries. Handing Mark a glass, Tyler set the bowl of strawberries on the nightstand, placed a large berry between his lips, and pressed the berry to Mark's lips. After sharing the berry, Tyler whispered, "Mark, I love you," while reaching for another berry and gently placing it into Mark's open mouth.

"I love you too, Tyler. More than I ever dreamed." After feeding each other the berries, finishing their champagne, and getting ready for bed, they held each other and whispered their new words of love before blowing out the candles and falling asleep in each other's arms.

Chapter 8

IT was early June, and summer was starting, the air smelled of flowers, and love was in the air, or at least it felt that way for Mark and Tyler. The last couple of weeks had been largely uneventful. Occasionally Mark would experience bouts of sadness, particularly when something would happen and he'd impulsively reach for the phone to call his mother. At those times, he'd turn to his lover for comfort. Mark had made progress on the portrait of his lover and it was now nearly finished. He was pleased and relieved. With Tyler's birthday less than a week away, he had been working hard to make sure the portrait was done in time. However, Mark was having trouble completing the face. It looked like the sketches he'd made, but something wasn't quite right. Sitting in his studio staring at the portrait, he just couldn't put his finger on what was wrong. Putting his sketches aside, he decided to look at the real thing for a while.

Leaving the studio, Mark quietly walked to the front of the store. Being a Wednesday, the store was closed and Tyler was wearing jeans and a T-shirt, working on the store displays. Tyler didn't see Mark as he approached; his attention was focused on a living room display. Mark just stared at Tyler as he worked, watching his muscles flex as he lifted and moved furniture, studying that face he'd come to know so well. Stepping back from the display, Tyler nodded and seemed pleased with the result. Mark saw the moment Tyler realized he was there: his expression changed slightly, his eyes lit up, and a smile burst onto his face. Mark actually said out loud, "God, that's it!" He raced to Tyler, kissed him quickly, and almost ran back to the studio. Tyler just smiled and shook his head. Artists….

Mark had it. He'd been painting Tyler's face from the sketches, getting it technically right, but in his mind he always saw Tyler's face as it was just a minute ago, with that expression of love and joy on his face. Putting the sketches aside, he started to work. The picture in his mind that he wanted for the painting was now bright and vivid. In an hour he had it. The color was perfect; the expression on the face was pure passion and joy. Sighing deeply, he put the painting aside and started work on the portrait of Bill.

Tyler spent his morning in the store, punching up displays and making a few repairs. Late in the morning, he readied some new pieces for display in the store. After about an hour, Tyler was able to get a piece he had been working on for the past week ready for sale. He was pleased. The piece had required a lot of effort, but the finished result was stunning and Tyler knew it would sell quickly. Poking his head into the studio to see how Mark was doing, he called out, "Mark, are you ready for a break?"

"Yes, Ty." The finished portrait had been set aside to dry and cure where Tyler couldn't see it.

Stepping from behind his easel, Mark raced to Tyler, wrapping his arms tightly around him and kissing him hungrily, that lithe body rubbing. Tyler returned the kiss, adding his own passion and heat to Mark's hunger. They kept kissing, and Mark was going wild with desire. Tyler spied a large Empire sofa and he guided Mark toward it, tumbling onto the sofa without breaking their kiss.

Tyler attacked, needed to get to Mark, wanted to feel his skin. His mind clouded with desire, his fingers fumbling, buttons flew and pants were kicked away. The old sofa groaned under their weight, adding to their own whimpers and moans of pleasure.

"Need you."

"Want you."

"Please, Mark, now."

"Love you, Ty."

Brief declarations of love and passion were punctuated by long pleasurable sounds that spoke more clearly than any words. Kissing, tasting, touching, sucking, trying to get enough and realizing that neither could, that it just wasn't possible.

The back room of the store was filled with the sounds of their love and need, the musical sounds of love built and built in a cadence of passion that filled them both. Exhausted and spent, Tyler collapsed onto Mark. Once they were able to catch their breath and move again, Tyler lifted himself off the sofa. Grabbing Mark's torn shirt, Tyler used it to clean them both, and then rejoined Mark on the sofa, snuggling into him.

"You're incredible." Kissing him softly, he sighed, "I love you."

Mark returned the kiss, hugging Tyler tightly. "You're pretty incredible yourself, hot stuff... my hot stuff."

"I love how you love me. Always make me feel on top of the world."

"You are on top of the world. My world." The kisses began again. Slow, deep, long kisses. Mark loved those kisses; they penetrated him and he could feel them deep inside, warming him, filling him with Tyler's love.

As they started to get up from the sofa, Tyler laughed. "Looks like I'll have to get that sofa reupholstered now." In their haste to get out of their clothes, they had torn the old fabric on the seat of the sofa.

Hugging Mark as he tried to get dressed, Tyler asked, "What do you have planned for this afternoon?"

"Well, I finished what I wanted to do. What did you have in mind?" Mark pulled on his pants, throwing his shirt in the trash.

Tyler pulled on his own pants and slipped his T-shirt over his head. "Would you like to get some lunch and then go to the art museum? I'd love the artist's tour." Tyler saw Mark's eyes light up.

"Really? Yeah. There are some things I'd really like to show you." Mark had finished dressing and was heading upstairs to get a shirt. Tyler turned out the lights in the store, set the alarm, and followed Mark upstairs.

They had lunch at a café downtown and walked to the art museum. Mark was practically bouncing as they walked from the café to the museum. Tyler could only smile; he loved to see Mark happy and full of energy. Crossing the bridge that led to the main entrance, Tyler couldn't help but marvel at the building. The museum addition had been completed a few years earlier. The building was white and shaped like a ship, complete with a mast. The sail was a sun shade that could be raised and lowered to shield the main atrium windows. The bridge to the main entrance looked like a ship's boarding ramp. The overall effect was awe-inspiring.

Entering the building, Tyler paid the admission and Mark led him into one of the main galleries and directly to the Monet. "This is my favorite painting in the museum."

Tyler was a bit surprised; it seemed so conventional. "Tell me why."

"It's not so much what is in the painting, as what isn't." Tyler was confused, but kept quiet. "Look at all the color and detail in the painting. The people, their clothes, the buildings." Tyler complied. "Now, walk up to the painting and look closely." Tyler got within a foot of the painting and he could feel Mark right behind him. "Look. The detail isn't there. Your mind put it there. The artist just suggested it was there and your eye and brain filled in the rest. That's why I like it. No two people see that painting the exact same way. Each person's brain fills in those details differently."

Tyler stood and looked; he was amazed. He'd seen that painting a number of times, but now he looked at it with fresh eyes. "Thank you," was all he could whisper.

As they continued to tour the museum, Tyler marveled at the knowledge and depth of understanding that Mark possessed for art. Modern art had never appealed to Tyler. He was always more traditional, but after spending time with Mark, he was able to appreciate some of the works on display. After wandering through the galleries, they found themselves on the lowest floor. The back of the museum faced Lake Michigan, and the ground floor was all windows. As they stood looking out of those windows, Tyler pressed his body to Mark's back, wrapped his arms around his chest, and nuzzled Mark's ear and cheek.

When they were ready to move on, Tyler led Mark to the decorative arts section. The museum had a large collection of these objects, including American furniture pieces ranging from the early Colonial period to the present day. As they wandered through, Tyler explained the important pieces and how they related to their time periods. Mark was fascinated, particularly with how Tyler explained each piece as a work of art.

"What you're telling me is that these are one-of-a-kind pieces made by skilled artists." Mark was fascinated; he had never really considered that furniture could be art.

Tyler smiled brightly. He had always been unsure how to explain his love of antiques to Mark. "Exactly. These artists worked in wood, brass, and finishes instead of canvas and paint."

"Now I understand why you love what you do. You're not selling old furniture; you're selling art in the form of furniture." Tyler nodded his head silently, leaned over, and kissed Mark sweetly. "Let's head home. I want you alone." Mark nodded and they left the museum and headed back to the apartment.

Walking up the sidewalk to the store, Tyler noticed that the mail had come and suggested that they enter through the store so he could pick it up. After unlocking the door and turning off the alarm, he picked up the mail and started sorting it. On top of the pile was an envelope with no stamp or address. Tyler opened the enveloped carefully. Inside was a single piece of paper. Unfolding the paper, Tyler started to read.

Mark saw Tyler's face turn white and then he dropped the paper on the counter. "What is it, Ty?"

"It's a piece of hate mail. Don't touch it. I'm calling Officer Davis." Tyler picked up the telephone and dialed the police station. When the switchboard answered, he was told that Officer Davis was on patrol.

"Could you radio him, please? I see him all the time in my neighborhood." The officer said that she'd try. Tyler was a little impatient, but decided to wait. They left the letter where it was and sat together in the store. Sam arrived a few minutes later.

"The station radioed that you had called, asking for me. What's up?"

Pointing to the letter, Tyler explained, "We received this through the mail slot in the store. I did touch it, but we put it on the counter as soon as I realized what it was."

Sam put on a pair of rubber gloves and picked up the letter. It was typed and printed on a computer in a large font.

Faggots

Beware.

All faggots should die.

We are watching you.

You should do what you're told.

Sam read the letter, showed it to Tyler and Mark, and put it in a plastic bag. "I'll have the lab check to see if they can get any fingerprints. Tyler, I'll need you to come with me so we can get your fingerprints. That way we can eliminate yours from the analysis."

"Okay. Do you want to stay here?" When Tyler looked at Mark it was like he'd seen a ghost. He was white and shaking. Tyler scooped him into his arms to comfort him, whispering, "I know what you're thinking, but please don't jump to conclusions. You're safe and nothing's going to happen to you."

Mark's response startled Tyler. "I'm not worried about me. What if something happens to you?"

Tyler could understand Mark's concern but he didn't want to overreact. "We can't let things like this dictate our lives or make us scared. Okay? Let's go to the police station so we can help them find out who did this." Turning to Sam, he asked, "How do you want to do this?"

"Why don't I meet you at the station in fifteen minutes? I'll personally walk you through the process." He gently squeezed Mark's shoulder and left the store.

Mark continued to shake, finally finding his voice. "I know it was Roger who did this!"

"I think so too, but we need to prove it. Look, I think we should say nothing of this to anyone. If Roger did this, then he'll slip up. Okay?"

Mark nodded. "Yeah. Let's go and meet Sam at the station."

Just before leaving the store, Tyler remembered that he'd thrown the envelope away. He gently picked it out of the trash and wrapped it in a blank piece of paper. They locked the store and headed to the police station.

At the station, Sam arranged for Tyler to be fingerprinted and he took a statement. Tyler gave him the envelope, which, unfortunately, hadn't been licked.

Mark looked confused. "Licked?"

Sam explained. "If an envelope has been licked, there may be traces of saliva containing DNA, which can be used to identify the person who licked the envelope." Sam put the envelope with the letter. "Thank you both. If we find anything, we'll let you know and please call us right away if anything else happens."

When Mark and Tyler got home they were drained. They spent the next hour making a light dinner, the regular routine soothing rattled nerves. After dinner, they were cuddled on the sofa watching TV when the phone rang. Tyler answered.

"Hello, Tyler? It's Amy. Can I speak to Mark?"

"Sure, Amy. Hold on." Covering the phone with his hand, he whispered, "Say nothing to her." Mark nodded and Tyler handed him the phone. They talked for quite a while. When he hung up, Mark felt better.

"It was good to hear from her. Mostly we just talked. She did ask what happened with Roger. He had called her after he left here the other day. When I told her what you said, she started to laugh and said it was time someone stood up to him."

"Well, I'm glad she called."

"Me too. It was good to talk to her. Say, I was thinking, would it be okay to have her over for dinner sometime?"

"That's a great idea. The next time you talk to her, set something up." Tyler was smiling. "Has she seen the portrait you did of her?"

"No, I never got a chance to show her. Why?"

"Well, I was thinking that I don't want you to sell it, at least not right now. I'd like to hang it here in the living room, maybe fill these empty walls with art—your art." They were still cuddling on the sofa, and Tyler gently kissed Mark on the lips, slowly moving to kiss and nuzzle his neck. "I like this spot right here," Tyler whispered into Mark's neck as he nuzzled Mark's shoulder.

"Oh, that's nice, Ty. Like it some more." Mark arched his back and closed his eyes as he reveled in the feel of Tyler's lips on his body. Tyler slipped his hands beneath Mark's shirt, gently rubbing and running his fingers through the soft hair on Mark's chest.

"Mark, let's go to bed. I need you." Mark made no effort to move. The feel of Tyler's hands and lips had him glued to the spot.

"Mmmm, I need you too." Mark stroked Tyler's leg and inner thigh, feeling Tyler's pants stretch and fill. Slowly, Mark raised himself from the sofa, took Tyler's hand, and quietly led him to the bedroom.

Chapter 9

MARK was working diligently, making sure that everything was ready for Tyler's birthday. The table had been set, dinner was cooking, guests had been invited, and Tyler's present had been hidden under the bed and would be hung after Tyler got dressed for the evening. The hook for the painting was already in place on the wall. Three of his paintings had been hung in the living room: the portrait of Amy, and the two landscapes. This afternoon he had also hung two of the paintings that he'd found while cleaning out the storage room. Mark had cleaned the paintings as well as the frames. He figured that Tyler would think that was his present.

Mark was currently putting the finishing touches on the birthday cake he'd baked for Tyler. It had been a long time since he'd baked anything, but the cake had turned out quite well. Finishing the cake and putting it in the refrigerator to chill, he heard Tyler on the stairs.

Meeting Tyler at the door with a kiss and a smile, Mark exclaimed, "Happy birthday, Ty!"

Tyler hugged Mark tightly. "Thank you." Tyler returned the kiss, hoping for more. He then looked around the apartment and saw the table set for nine. "I take it we're having company for dinner." Raising his eyebrows, he asked, "Do we have time?"

"Sorry, Ty. The guests will be arriving soon and you need to get ready. You'll get yours later." Tyler certainly hoped so.

Tyler took a shower, got dressed for the evening, and joined Mark in the kitchen. "Can I help?"

"Would you set up the stereo for some soft music?" As he went into the living room, he saw the two paintings hanging on the walls. "Mark, what are these?"

Mark stuck his head into the living room. "Those are two of the paintings I found when cleaning out the storage room. I cleaned and re-varnished the paintings and repaired the frames. Happy birthday!"

Tyler was speechless. He hadn't seen those paintings since he'd cleaned out his grandmother's house years before. He felt tears run down his cheeks as the memories of his grandmother and Mark's thoughtfulness and love just overwhelmed his emotions. Mark joined him in the living room and he thanked him with a deep, long kiss.

Holding Tyler tightly, Mark said, "I'm glad you like them. I thought they might bring back memories for you."

Wiping away the tears, Tyler swallowed hard. "So who's coming for dinner, or is that a surprise too?"

"I invited Tom and Bill, Steve, Peter, Sam, Gladys, and my sister Amy. They all accepted and are expected any time." Just then the doorbell rang. Mark went down to answer the door while Tyler continued to stare at the paintings.

Almost everyone arrived at once. Everyone except Amy was waiting for Mark at the door. Mark ushered them up to the apartment and got everyone a drink. Once drinks had been served, the bell announced that Amy had arrived. Everyone was having a wonderful time talking and meeting each other. Mark went down and brought Amy up to the apartment, introduced her to everyone, and got her a drink. He then placed hors d'oeuvres on the coffee table and went to finish preparing dinner.

Dinner was a huge success and everyone enjoyed the meal. The dinner dishes were cleared and the dessert plates were brought to the table. Mark dimmed the lights and brought in the cake. Tyler saw that there were indeed thirty candles on the cake and only hoped the house didn't go up in flames. Everyone sang "Happy Birthday", Tyler blew out the candles, and Mark served the cake.

People moved from the table to the living room and after-dinner drinks were served. Everyone seemed to be admiring the paintings. Amy approached and gushed, "Mark, honey, that portrait of me is stunning. I look so beautiful." She was almost crying.

Mark smiled. "That's what I see when I look at you. I painted it months ago. It was one of the paintings I took out of the house." Mark's expression turned sad. "I was starting a portrait of Mom, but I destroyed all the sketches." Working on the painting had been too painful, so he decided not to continue.

"Are all these paintings yours?" She gestured toward the walls.

"No. Those two are from Tyler's family. The rest of them I painted." Peter had joined their conversation and was listening intently. "Hey, Peter, are you having a good time?"

"Wonderful time, thank you, Mark. Umm… is it true the portrait is your work?" He indicated the portrait of Amy.

"Yes, I painted it months ago."

"The landscapes as well?"

Mark nodded his head. "Yes." The expression told Mark that Peter had more he wanted to ask. Whispering softly, Mark said, "There is one other painting, if you'll follow me." Mark quietly led Peter to the bedroom, pulled the portrait from under the bed, and hung it on the hook he'd already set in the wall. "This is Tyler's birthday present. He hasn't seen it yet."

Peter was stunned. He stood in front of the painting and stared. Finally Peter found his voice. "Mark, this is marvelous. I have never seen anything like it. The composition is perfect, but the facial expression is incredible—pure love and passion. That face says love, pure and simple." Peter stopped talking and stared at the portrait. "The picture of your sister is wonderful, too, particularly after meeting her. The portrait captures her personality." His attention never wavered from the portrait of Tyler.

Mark led Peter back to the party where Tyler corralled him, whispering, "Did Mark tell you about his commissions and the landscape he sold?"

"No, he didn't." Tyler could tell that something was going on in Peter's mind and Tyler slowly drifted to other conversations going on through the room. Everyone seemed to be having a great time and Tyler was very happy.

Mark snuck up behind him and gave him a kiss on the neck. "So, birthday boy, are you having a good time?"

Tyler turned around and kissed Mark long and hard. "It's the best birthday I can remember in a very long time. Thank you." Tom and Bill wandered over and ribbed Tyler. "Tyler, man, you're getting old now. Soon that arthritis will start to catch up with you." They were both laughing.

Tyler joined them, laughing heartily, particularly since they were both almost fifteen years older than he was. "I'll reserve my room in the nursing home next week."

The conversation drifted on as Tyler excused himself and slipped over to speak with Gladys and Steve. "Steve, are you having a good time?"

"Yeah, it's a nice party." Steve was holding a beer and Tyler knew he was happy.

Tyler turned to Gladys, gave her a hug, and asked how she was doing. "I'd like to come back to work in about a week, if that's okay with you."

Smiling broadly, he said, "That's wonderful. I'll be glad to have you back. I've missed you."

Hugging Tyler, Gladys replied, "I've missed you too. I really missed our talks." Gladys winked. "It looks like you've found yourself a nice young man. I'm so pleased for you. I've worried about you being alone and it's good to see you happy."

He kissed Gladys on the cheek. "It's nice to be happy."

At about ten, the party started to break up and most people left. Amy stayed, helping Mark and Tyler clean up, and then joined them in the living room. Mark was sitting on the sofa with Tyler curled up next to him. Mark gently kissed him on the cheek.

"Mark, it was a wonderful evening. Thank you for inviting me." Amy looked a little uncomfortable and Tyler noticed her discomfort.

"Amy, we're glad you came…. I'm glad you came. It means a lot to both of us." Tyler looked at Mark, the love showing on his face. "Amy, there is something that I want you to know. Something that's important you understand. I love Mark."

Amy swallowed hard. "I can see you do. It shows in your face and eyes whenever you look at him. I've just never seem him that affectionate before." Tyler sat up on the sofa and moved away from Mark but Amy stopped him. "Tyler, don't get me wrong. I think it's wonderful." Tyler settled back next to Mark.

They talked and chatted for almost an hour, laughing, joking, and telling stories. Amy talked about her sons and asked Tyler if he had any nieces and nephews.

"No, I was an only child." A cloud briefly passed in front of Tyler's face. Mark saw his reaction.

"Amy, Ty hasn't seen his family since he told them he was gay. They did the same thing to him that Mom and Roger did to me."

The look on Amy's face was a combination of shock, surprise, and anger. "Then think of us as your family. I'd love for you to meet John and the kids… soon."

Finishing her drink, she got up to leave. They both saw her to her car. Amy hugged Mark tightly. "Marky, I am so happy for you. I can see you're happy and no matter what, I love you. I told you the other day it didn't matter who you fell in love with. Well, I was wrong. It does matter. It matters a great deal that you're happy and that he loves you back." Then she shocked them both and gave Tyler a hug, kissed him on the cheek, wished him a happy birthday, and said that she'd have them to dinner soon.

Heading back up to the apartment, Mark slipped his arm around Tyler's waist. "Let's clean up and go to bed. I have one more surprise for you." Tyler raised his eyebrows but said nothing. While Mark finished cleaning up, Tyler turned off the lights and locked the doors. "Let's go to bed, Ty." Mark led Tyler to the bedroom.

When Tyler saw the portrait, he was stunned, tears running down his face. Mark gently wrapped his arms around Tyler's chest, pressing his body into his back. "Happy birthday, Ty." Tyler was speechless and couldn't move. He just stood in front of the portrait and cried tears of joy.

Finally, he was able to speak. "Is that how you see me?"

Mark kissed his neck gently. "Oh, yes." Mark continued to kiss Tyler's neck and shoulders, using his hands to slowly open the buttons of Tyler's shirt. After removing Tyler's shirt, Mark gently unfastened his pants. They fell to the floor, and still Tyler hadn't moved. Mark continued kissing his neck and shoulders, occasionally nibbling on his ear. "Ty, come to bed." Tyler finally looked away from the portrait, stepped out of his pants, and joined Mark on the bed. Mark had already undressed and both men were wearing only white briefs.

"Mark, I have to know: Is that how you really see me? Am I really that sexy?"

Mark maintained a serious face. "No, Ty... you're sexier. The painting was only the best I could do." Mark gently shifted Tyler's gaze from the painting to himself. "Definitely sexier." They kissed gently at first, but soon their kisses became more urgent. Those kisses. Tyler's kisses. Building his need, filling him with love. "Love your kisses, Ty."

Lifting his eyebrows, Tyler queried, "Yeah?"

"Oh, yeah. Don't stop. Don't ever stop." Mark took his mouth, kissing him hard, proving just how much he loved those kisses.

Passion, need, and heat took over, threatening to overwhelm them. Tyler was lying on his back on the bed and he let Mark take control. Soon Mark was nibbling and sucking on his nipples, driving his desire, and making him beg for more. "Mark, please... need you...

more... love you!" He felt Mark's hand on the bulge in his briefs, rubbing him, teasing him, increasing his want to need.

Suddenly, Mark's lips and hands were gone. They returned rubbing, sucking, and licking his calf, his knee, his inner thigh, nuzzling him through the briefs. Tyler's voice was almost a squeal. "Oh, god... oh, please, I need... I want... you... please..." The other leg got the same treatment: calf, knee, inner thigh. Tyler was completely incomprehensible, his words gibberish, driven by desire, as Mark sucked his balls through the fabric, his hands at the waistband of his briefs, teasing, tantalizing. "Maarrk, need you... love... so... good...." Tyler's fists gripped the sheets, his legs shifting and shaking uncontrollably.

Tyler continued to beg, "Oh god... Mark... I need you... I want you...." Mark stood up, removed his briefs, lubed his finger, and reached to his butt. "No, Mark. I want you inside me. I need you...."

The thought of himself inside Tyler was almost too much. A deep moan swelled from within Mark, his breath ragged, his desire almost uncontrolled. "Ty, are you sure?"

Tyler nodded vigorously. "Never wanted anything so much. I need you, Mark!"

He forced himself to slowly remove Tyler's briefs rather than rip them from his body. Tyler's legs spread almost involuntarily and Mark gently lifted them toward his chest. Lubing his finger, Mark felt for his entrance, but... there was something in the way.

Mark looked quizzically at Tyler. "Mark, it's a butt plug. I used it to help get me ready for you." The sight of the clear plug in Tyler's butt was so hot. Mark felt his balls contract and he nearly came from the view. Closing his eyes, Mark forced himself to think about something else to help cool himself down.

Mark was fascinated, and he slowly started to work the plug out of Tyler's butt. As he removed it, Tyler made the most wonderful noises. "Oh, Mark... good...." So he reinserted it and removed it again, and the noises continued and actually got more insistent. "Need you... now... more, all of you...!" Putting the plug aside, Mark lubed his cock and pressed it to Tyler's entrance.

As Mark pressed into him, Tyler could feel himself being stretched beyond what the plug had done. "Yeah, Mark, that's it."

The burn hurt for a second, but soon the pain was gone and Tyler felt himself being filled by Mark. Slowly, as Mark pressed into him, he could feel each and every inch, slowly entering him, filling him, completing him. Tyler felt Mark's pubic hair tickle his scrotum and he knew Mark was buried deep inside him. "Oh, Mark. So full, so deep!"

"So hot, so tight, can feel your heart beat." Mark threw back his head as Tyler clenched his muscles. "Oh, that's so good." Mark looked down at Tyler filled with him. "So sexy, so damn sexy." They both held very still, enjoying the new feelings and sensations.

Relaxing his muscles, Tyler slowly started to rock against Mark, signaling that he was ready. In return, Mark slowly started to move, using short, slow strokes. With each stroke, the length extended and the speed increased slightly. Soon Mark was moving inside him with long, deliberate strokes, hitting his pleasure center almost every time. Whimpering and moaning, Tyler begged for more. "Mark, feels so good… so hot… so big… so full."

Mark picked up the pace of his thrusting. He was almost pounding into Tyler. The bed was rocking. Tyler was flying, his head ready rocking back and forth on the pillow, his words completely incomprehensible, just sounds and moans, his eyes rolled back into his head as he rode the waves of passion.

Tyler reached to stroke his cock, but Mark batted his hand away gently. He felt Mark's hand on his cock, pulling, stroking, sliding his foreskin across the head. Tyler grabbed the bed with his fists and allowed the sensations of pleasure to flow over him. He knew he was close, and Mark must have felt it too, because he picked up his speed one last time and pounded into Tyler at a furious pace. Tyler started shooting before he realized he was climaxing, then the wave of pleasure hit him and he shot hard, onto his chest and face, and even into his hair. "Oh, Mark! Love…!"

Tyler then felt Mark explode into him. He felt each throbbing wave of Mark's climax as it gushed into him. "Ty…." Mark kept moving inside him, each stroke slowing.

Mark collapsed onto him, breathing heavily, kissing lovingly, softly caressing, and petting. Tyler felt that Mark had yet to go soft. He could still feel Mark's cock pulsing inside of him. Gradually, the pulsing diminished and Mark carefully and slowly withdrew, kissing him deeply.

As their breathing began to return to normal, Mark slowly led Tyler to the bathroom, started the shower, continually kissing until the water warmed. "Ty, so sexy, so hot, so giving…. Love you so."

"Love you so much, need to give… what you… gave me." Tyler's breathing was still deep.

"You gave me more."

Tyler was so drained that he was finding it difficult to stand. Mark guided him into the shower and gently washed his hair and body before washing himself. After using the big fluffy towels to dry Tyler, Mark dried himself and guided Tyler back to the bedroom and the bed. When Mark walked into the bedroom he smiled and almost laughed, went back into the bathroom and grabbed a towel. Tyler had climaxed so violently that Mark needed to clean the headboard. Mark and Tyler both laughed as Mark cleaned the come off the headboard, threw the towel into the bathroom, and joined Tyler in bed.

Tyler snuggled next to Mark, wrapping his arm around his chest. "Mark, you were amazing." Tyler looked at Mark and saw that he had tears in his eyes. "What's wrong?"

Mark wiped his eyes. "Nothing's wrong. I just never thought I'd get to do that."

Tyler was a little confused. "Do what?" Understanding flooded over Tyler. "Are you telling me you've never topped like that before?"

"No." Mark was looking away like he was embarrassed. "My previous boyfriend wouldn't let me. He said I was too big." Tyler felt for Mark.

"Mark, sweetheart," he said, turning Mark's head gently to face him, "he didn't know what he was missing. You were incredible. You filled me in a way no else has ever done. That was the perfect way to cap a perfect birthday. Thank you for everything."

Soon Mark heard Tyler's breathing soften as he fell asleep. Mark spooned into Tyler's back and he fell asleep as well.

Chapter 10

THE Tuesday morning after his birthday, Tyler was awakened by the sound of an angry telephone. Looking at the clock by the bed, he saw that it was only six-thirty. The bed was already empty. Tyler figured Mark had to work early and was reading the paper. Reaching for the phone, Tyler answered in a groggy voice.

"Tyler, it's Amy. I need to speak to Mark." Tyler could tell she was upset and had been crying.

"Amy, what's wrong?"

"Mom died yesterday morning. I need to tell Mark right away. Roger jumped the gun and the obituary is in today's paper. I need to…." Tyler heard a mournful wail coming from the kitchen.

"Amy, oh god…. I think it's too late. Look, we'll call you later and you can tell us what happened." Tyler hung up the phone and rushed to Mark. Mark was sitting on the kitchen floor, curled into a ball sobbing, moaning, and rocking back and forth. He couldn't form any words, just deep sobs. Tyler scooped Mark into his arms, hugging and comforting him. After a few minutes he seemed to calm down. Tyler picked up the newspaper; the obituary for Mark's mother was right on top. Setting the paper on the table, Tyler helped Mark get up from the floor and guided him to the bedroom.

Mark lay on the bed, crying and shivering. Tyler got into bed with him, pulled up the covers, wrapped his arms around him, and pulled him to his body. Tyler just let him cry, figuring it was best to let him get it out of his system. Finally, Mark seemed to truly calm down and seemed able to talk.

"Mark, the phone call was from Amy. She was trying to tell you before you saw it in the paper. She said that your mom died yesterday. Roger got the obituary in the paper right away. How, I don't know. When you're ready we need to call Amy to find out the details." Tyler was still holding Mark tightly. After a while, Mark was able to dry his tears.

Once he calmed down, Mark started to sniffle. "I bet Roger did this deliberately."

Tyler took and released a deep breath. "I'm afraid it looks that way. Mark, let's get dressed. I think we need to call and talk to Amy. There's a speaker phone down in the store. I'd like to hear what she has to say about this." Tyler was wondering why Amy hadn't called them yesterday.

"Thank you, Ty," was all Mark could manage. Tyler dressed quickly, and while Mark was dressing, he glanced at the obituary. As he read it, he got angry—really angry. The bastard had not listed Mark as next of kin. Only Roger and Amy were listed. Tyler stuffed the paper in the trash.

In the store, Tyler dialed Amy's number. When she answered, Mark found he was unable to talk and started to cry again, so Tyler spoke for him. "Amy, what happened?"

"Mom died yesterday morning at the house. Roger found her on his way to work. We were out of town and didn't have cell phone service. We got back home late last night and went right to bed. I didn't get Roger's messages until this morning. I called him as soon as I got the message and he told me that he had already called the funeral home and answered all their questions. He gave them the okay to run the obituary. When I hung up with Roger I called you right away." Amy was now crying as well. Finally she choked out, "Marky, I'm sorry I wasn't in time." Then she was sobbing.

Finally Mark found his own voice. "It's okay, Amy. You tried." He was breathing more normally now. "When's the funeral?"

"It's Thursday morning. Saint Thomas's at eleven o'clock. Mom had already prearranged for almost everything."

"Yeah, I know...." Mark stopped talking in the middle of his thought and a wicked little grin momentarily crossed his face. Tears were still streaming down his face. "Amy, I'll call you later to touch base. I've got to make a few calls. Thank you for caring. I love you."

"I love you too, Marky. Bye." She was still sniffling when Mark hung up.

Mark shook with rage when he hung up the phone. "That bastard! That mean, cruel bastard!" His anger overflowed and he spent the next few minutes pacing back and forth, calling Roger every name in the book. After the anger was out of his system, he seemed to calm down a little. "When it comes to Roger, no more Mr. Nice Guy."

Tyler was at the front door of the store putting up a sign.

Mark asked, "What are you doing?"

"Mark, you need me. I'm putting up a sign that we will be closed until Friday due to a death in the family." Mark ran to Tyler and hugged him tightly and led Mark back upstairs.

Mark spent the next few minutes letting Peter know what had happened. Peter was wonderful and told Mark to take the time he needed. He also asked him to see him on Friday morning. Next, Mark called his mother's lawyer. They talked for quite a while. When Mark hung up the phone, that wicked little grin was back.

"All right. Why the grin?" Tyler was trying to figure out what was going on in Mark's mind. He was a little worried.

"I spoke with Mom's lawyer. Mom didn't change her will in the last few weeks."

"So...." Tyler was confused.

"So that means that I'm sole executor of her estate. Her lawyer confirmed that fact a few minutes ago and Roger doesn't know it. I had the lawyer call a locksmith and he's having the locks on her house changed. The keys will be sent to me by messenger. He's going over to the house himself, and if Roger's there, the lawyer will have him leave. If he's removing things, the police will be called."

"You sneaky little devil."

"If he's not there, the lawyer is going to call him and make sure he knows that he must stay away from the house unless he gets specific permission from me."

"Mark, are you okay with all this? It seems overwhelming." Tyler was a little worried, not just about the work involved, but about Mark's sudden changes in mood.

"Actually, it feels good to be doing something. I think I'll call Amy and see if she wants to meet us at the house." Mark looked at Tyler. "I'm sorry. I should have asked you to come, not just assumed you would."

"Of course I'll go. You can always assume that I will be there for you, because I always will. Go call Amy."

Later that morning, the lawyer called to say that the locks had been changed. He'd met the locksmith at the house and it didn't look as though anyone had been there. The house keys arrived by bicycle messenger just after they hung up with the lawyer. Mark had arranged to meet Amy at the house the next day at one. After all the activity, Mark was drained. Tyler, however, was conflicted. He was sure that Mark had not read the entire obituary and did not realize that Roger had excluded him from the list of next of kin.

"Mark, I need to ask you a question." Mark nodded and looked at Tyler. "Did you read the entire obituary, or did you just see the name?"

Mark looked quizzical. "I just saw the name. Why?" Tyler didn't know exactly what to say, so he just plowed ahead.

Tyler hugged Mark tightly and told him, "Mark, I read the obituary and Roger didn't list you as next of kin. He only listed himself and Amy." The look on Mark's face was surprise and then sadness.

"How petty can he get?" Shaking his head, he sighed, "That's Roger. Always trying to be mean. Well, he can't hurt me; not if I don't let him…." Mark lifted his face, shouting at the ceiling, "And I don't!"

Later that afternoon, they were sitting on the couch. "Tyler, I feel really weird. Not like I expected to feel. This morning I was more upset that Amy hadn't told me than about Mom's actual death. I felt a huge relief that she was out of town and didn't know either."

"I know. The grief will overtake you at the most unexpected time. Just let it out when it does; don't hold it in. I'll be here for you and I'll understand."

That evening, they watched television and went to bed early. Tyler held Mark close, kissing him gently. "I wish I could help you more."

"Just being here is a help, Ty. Good night. I love you."

"I love you too." Mark slept on and off all night. Each time he woke up, Tyler was there to comfort and hold him. Eventually he fell into a deep sleep.

The following day, they met Amy at one. When they arrived at Mark's mother's house, she was waiting for them. They were just walking into the house when Roger showed up. Mark turned. "Amy, let me handle this,"

Roger stormed up the walk, yelling the entire way. "How dare you!" He was pointing his finger at Mark and visibly shaking with rage.

"How dare I what?" Mark's voice sounded completely innocent.

"You can't keep me out of the house!" Roger was still yelling, his rage obviously getting the better of him.

Mark just looked at Roger, shook his head, and spoke very calmly. "As executor of Mom's estate, it's fully within my rights. Now I suggest you calm down. I intend to be completely fair. I know there are things in the house that you'd like to have." Roger shook his head. He was still angry, but seemed to be calming down. "If you calm down, I will let you in the house for thirty minutes to compile your list. You can't take anything until I see the list and approve each item. Do you agree or do you go home?"

Roger seemed mollified for the time being and agreed.

"Go in the house and start making your list, but don't be greedy or everything will be sold and you'll get nothing!" Roger walked into the house, found a piece of paper, and started his list.

Tyler hugged Mark tightly and whispered, "You did great. I'm so proud of you."

Amy followed Roger into the house and kept an eye on him. After about half an hour, Roger came out, thrust the list into Mark's hands, and strode to his car. "If you don't give me what I want, I'll contest the will."

"Roger, I asked the lawyer about that. He said that if you do, you'll just tie the estate up for years and you could get nothing at all. So don't threaten me." Mark watched as Roger drove away. "That was too easy."

Amy shook her head. "I agree. He's up to something."

"Yeah." Mark's mind was working overtime. "Tyler, would you take the car home and bring the truck and trailer back? We may need it." Tyler went to the car and headed back to the store to get the truck. Mark and Amy went into the house. "Amy, are there things you want?"

"Yes, there are a few things." She was looking around rather blankly.

"Look, Amy, I know this is hard and fast." He looked at Roger's list. "Amy, look at this list." The items on Roger's list were all the items he thought Amy or Mark might want. "Screw him. Amy, go upstairs and get Mom's jewelry box. Take it home. It's yours, all of it." Amy wandered through the house and took the jewelry box and a few other pieces. "Is this all you want?" Amy nodded her head. "I took what I wanted and a few things for each of the kids. We don't really need much."

"Okay, I'll get some boxes and pack up the rest of the things Roger wanted." He had finished packing when Roger barged through the door. Mark just jammed the boxes into his hands and told him to take the stuff and go. He loaded the boxes into his car and started to look through them. Coming back to the door, he yelled, "Hey, where is the rest of it?"

"Roger, Amy took some of the other items. You got greedy and mean. Other than the jewelry, most of the items are there. Now I suggest you go. Everything else will be sold and the money split evenly. If you want anything else, you can buy it from the estate."

"Well, what are you taking?" He sneered.

"Nothing, Roger. There is nothing here I want, except to be rid of it all." The pain was clear on his face and it surprised Roger. "Go home, Roger. Go home to your family. They need you." Mark then turned and went back into the house. A few minutes later, Tyler arrived with the truck.

"Mark, what do you want to do with the truck?" Mark was getting tired and it showed in his entire body.

"I want you to go through the house. I want to make sure that the most valuable items are safeguarded. We can take them to storage for the time being if we have to. I just don't trust Roger."

"We can put them in the back room of the store until you decide what you want to do with them."

They started upstairs, going through each room. Most of the items in the bedrooms were ordinary. The living room still had a large number of paintings and relatively small antique pieces. These were packed and loaded into the truck. The dining room was full of silver, porcelain, and other items. These too were carefully packed and loaded into the truck.

For the next few hours, they set up an efficient production line. Tyler would bring the items to Mark and Amy. They would then pack, inventory, and load them into the truck. Once they were convinced that the most valuable items were loaded, they locked up the house, said goodbye to Amy, and headed back to the store.

Arriving at the store, they unloaded the truck into the storage area and headed to the apartment. Tyler fixed dinner as Mark tried to relax on the sofa. It had been an exhausting day and tomorrow was the funeral, but Mark was jittery and full of energy despite all the work they'd done during the day.

As Tyler was cleaning up, Mark slipped his arms around his waist. "Ty, I need to paint. It's the one way I can work through these feelings. Please don't wait up for me. I'll come up later."

At about eleven, Tyler went to bed. Mark hadn't come up yet, but he knew he had things to work through. Tyler fell asleep and later woke to Mark getting into bed with him. He curled up to Mark and fell back to sleep.

Chapter 11

THE next morning—Thursday—Tyler work up to an empty bed. Mark had joined him during the night, but Tyler didn't know when he'd gotten up again. He went to the bathroom to get cleaned up, put on his robe, and went to find Mark. Tyler figured he was in the studio, and he was right. Mark was already hard at work at his easel. He barely looked up when Tyler stood in the door.

"Ty, I'm almost done. I'll be up in a minute and explain then. Okay?" He went right back to work and Tyler went back upstairs to finish dressing and lay out clothes for the funeral. Once he was dressed, he started making a light breakfast. Mark joined him in the kitchen a few minutes later. "Did you get much sleep last night?"

"No, I came to bed late and I couldn't sleep. My mind wouldn't shut off. I lay next to you and must have dozed off for a while. I woke up again about six and went back to work." Tyler had a worried look on his face. "Ty, sometimes it's like this. I get a picture in my mind and I have to get it on canvas. I don't want you to worry. This happens sometimes and I just need to go with it."

Mark ate some breakfast, but he seemed anxious. "Ty, I need you to come with me. I need to show you something." Mark practically dragged Tyler down to the studio. There was a painting on the easel. Mark turned the easel to reveal the painting. It was a beautiful painting of his mother as she would have looked twenty years earlier. "I got a picture in my mind of how my mom would have looked when I was a child. I wanted to paint her that way, to remember her then, as opposed to now."

"Mark, it's beautiful. How did you do it so fast?"

Mark started talking really quickly. "It's not completely finished yet, but it's a good enough start that I won't lose my vision. I did it using acrylics because they dry relatively fast. Do you really like it?" Mark was a bundle of nerves and energy.

Tyler nodded. "It is beautiful. Just like you." Tyler leaned over and kissed him. Mark reached behind a bench and brought out another canvas.

"Ty, I also started this one. I need to finish it so I don't lose my vision for it. Please give me a few hours and I'll show you this one as well." Mark sat at the easel and started to work again. Tyler quietly left the studio and headed back upstairs. They had plenty of time before the funeral and what Mark was doing seemed to be good for him. Tyler cleaned the apartment, showered, and completed a few other domestic chores. He had to force himself to keep away from the studio.

At about ten Mark raced upstairs and brought Tyler back to the studio. "I started this one last night as well, but I needed to finish the other one first." Mark then turned the easel and showed him the painting. Tyler physically stepped back; the image was like a punch in the gut. It was a portrait of Mark's brother. The likeness was amazing, but the expression was menacing, mean, full of hate, and almost evil. It made Tyler shudder.

"Is that what you see in Roger?" Mark only nodded. "As a work of art, it's probably the most powerful piece I have ever seen in my life. It really gives me the creeps."

"Try living with him. He was always mean, bullying, and pushy. Until I started painting, I didn't realize how much I loathed him." Mark looked at his own work as if staring his pain in the face. "Ty, I never want to see him again if I can help it."

"Well, Mark, I wish I could tell you that you didn't have to, but we need to get ready to go."

Mark went upstairs, showered quickly, and dressed for the funeral. He had to borrow some clothes from Tyler because he didn't have proper clothes.

They drove to the church and arrived about fifteen minutes before the start of the service. Amy met them in front of the massive stone pile of a church.

"The service is going to start soon. Please sit with John and me. We saved you places." Amy led them to the pew and introduced Tyler to John. He seemed like a really nice guy and spoke very nicely to both of them before the service started. Tyler noticed Roger sitting on the other side of the church, glaring at Mark. Amy leaned over to Tyler and told him that Roger had told the rest of the family about Mark. "I just wanted to warn you. Once the funeral is over, take him home. Roger has them all stirred up and he doesn't need or deserve this type of treatment."

"Thanks, Amy. That was the plan anyway. We weren't planning to stay for the grief buffet."

The church was a very beautiful, inspiring building with spectacular windows and intricately carved woodwork. The minister conducted a nice service. During the eulogy, Mark gently clasped Tyler's hand and softly started to cry. Tyler put his arm around Mark and held him close, telling himself, "Screw these people if anyone doesn't like it." Tyler held Mark for the rest of the service. When the service was over, the casket was wheeled out of the church and everyone filed out behind it. Tyler and Mark stayed behind for a few minutes to speak with Amy.

"Tyler and I are going to stop by the house and start the process of getting the large furniture out."

Amy and John asked together, "Can we help?" Mark smiled for the first time that day.

"Thank you. We'll meet you at the house at about two." Mark and Tyler left the church and headed straight for the car, pulled out of the lot, and headed home.

They ate a quick lunch, Mark yawning all through it. After lunch, Tyler led Mark to the bedroom, had him change clothes, and convinced him to lie down. Tyler sat on the bed next to him, rubbing his back and gently stroking his hair.

Mark woke an hour later. Tyler was still on the bed with him, gently caressing his back, just letting him know he was there. "You feeling better?"

"Yes, thank you."

"For what?" Tyler just smiled and gently kissed his lover on the forehead.

"For being there and helping me through this."

"I'll always be there." Tyler got off the bed and got ready to meet Amy and John.

On the ride over, Mark stated, broaching no argument, "Ty, I want you to give me a price for all the items you want in the house as well as the items already at the store. I'm going to sell them to you."

Mark asked if they could stop at the bank before going to the house. Tyler nodded and drove to the bank, where Mark met with the branch manager. Alice's existing bank accounts were closed except for the checking account, and a new estate account was opened. Mark figured that once everything was settled, the money in the account could then be easily divided. Mark thanked the manager for his help and they headed over to the house with the truck and trailer.

When they drove up, one of the neighbors came out to greet Mark. She expressed her condolences and told Mark that she had seen a man peering into the windows. She said that she turned on her lights and made noise and the man got in a car and drove off. Both Tyler and Mark figured it was Roger.

Mark unlocked the house. They systematically went through the house, with Tyler making a list of each item he wanted and the price he was willing to pay. Mark had been very specific. "A fair price is expected; no more." There were still quite a few antiques in the house. When they'd been through the entire house Tyler handed the list to Mark. Mark briefly looked it over and signed the bill of sale. Tyler wrote a check, and they started to load the truck. Amy and John arrived a few minutes later. John helped Tyler load the truck. Mark had Amy sign the bill of sale as well, figuring if Roger tried to make a fuss they'd be covered. Within two hours, the truck was loaded, the house locked, and they were heading down the walk.

Mark hugged Amy and asked if she and John would like to join them for a drink at the apartment. They gladly accepted. Mark and Tyler stopped briefly to deposit Tyler's check. At the store, the four of them unloaded the truck in record time. The back room of the store was getting quite full, so many of the boxes of smaller items were neatly stacked against one wall of the studio. The paintings were taken up to the apartment.

Once everything was unloaded, Amy wandered into Mark's studio. When Amy saw the painting of her mother, she started to cry. "Marky, it's beautiful. When did you do that?" Mark took her in his arms and started to cry as well. They just held each other, tears streaming down their faces. They made little effort to compose themselves, both letting their grief flow.

Mark dried his tears. "Last night and this morning. I got inspired and was up most of the night working on it." Mark put the painting on the easel and ushered Amy out of the studio. He had no intention of showing her the painting of Roger.

The four of them headed upstairs and Tyler got everyone something to drink. The conversation was light but companionable, not the usual type of after-funeral conversation. There was no reminiscing about the good times with their mom, no telling of stories. They all knew that would be too painful, especially for Mark.

After about an hour, Amy and John left to pick up the kids. Tyler started to make dinner, but Mark was really restless and just couldn't seem to settle down. "Mark, I know you've had a tough day. Is there something bothering you? You seem so restless." Tyler left the kitchen, sat on the sofa, and pulled Mark to him. "Tell me what's on your mind."

Mark's face showed a lot of conflicting emotions. "Why did she hate me so much?"

Tyler knew the question was rhetorical but he tried to answer anyway. "I've thought about that question for years in relation to my parents and I still don't have my answer." Tyler held Mark's hand as he talked. "However, I think that your mom didn't hate you; she just couldn't reconcile your being gay with her other beliefs. So she threw out what didn't fit." Mark seemed to understand so Tyler continued. "I believe that she may have come around in time, if she had lived longer. The important thing to remember is that she did love you." Mark hugged Tyler and yawned.

They were eating a late dinner when Tyler remembered something he wanted to ask Mark. "The last weekend in July, there's a large antique show in Chicago. It's the only show I usually do. I was wondering if you'd like to go with me. I could use your help and we could get a hotel in Chicago and spend the evenings seeing the sights."

Mark's face lit up. "That would be fun. I'd love to go with you. I'll arrange to get the time off work."

"Good. I'll make hotel arrangements and you can decide how to spend our evenings. We'll have Friday and Saturday." Tyler was happy to see Mark smile.

After dinner, Mark went to bed early while Tyler finished the dishes and quietly watched television. Mark didn't stir when Tyler came to bed.

Over the next week, Mark, Tyler, and sometimes Amy spent evenings packing up Mark's mother's house. A lot of the items were donated to the resale shop of a local AIDS charity. As they worked, Mark found items that he knew Amy or Roger would like. He started a box for each of them and he gave the boxes to Amy when she came one evening to help.

On Wednesday, while Amy and Mark were working to clean out their mother's house, the phone rang. Mark answered it.

"Mark?"

"Yes."

"This is your Aunt Phyllis."

"Aunt Phyllis, how are you? I haven't seen you in a while. It's so good to hear from you."

"I called to tell you how awful I think you're being to your brother. Not letting him in the house and cheating him out of some of his mom's things." Mark didn't hear a word after that; he just handed the phone to Amy. All Mark could think was that Roger had set the rest of the family against him. After a few minutes he heard Amy's voice and she was annoyed.

"Did Roger tell you he hit Mark? I didn't think so…. Did he also tell you he threatened him? I didn't think so…. Mom sold the items before she died; Mark had nothing to do with that…. Listen… you better…. Mark was named executor and I am helping him…. Roger is a bully… you believed him…. Yes, I think you do…." Amy handed the phone back to Mark and winked at him.

"Mark, I'm sorry. Roger told me things that obviously aren't true. I'm sorry I believed him without hearing the whole story."

Mark was finding this hard to believe. "Thank you."

"Mark," Phyllis demurred, obviously backpedaling, "would you please come to see me soon and bring your young man? I saw the two of you at the funeral and I'd like to meet him." Mark was absolutely shocked.

"All right. We'll stop by soon. Goodbye." Mark was completely stunned and Amy was smiling at him.

AT the end of the week, Mark contacted a realtor and the house was put up for sale. Once he had signed the listing papers, he felt like a big weight had been lifted off his shoulders. There was finally light at the end of the tunnel. The estate account had become quite large as Mark liquidated his mother's assets.

Tyler heard Mark arrive home from the realtor's office. There were customers in the store so he wasn't able to ask Mark how things went. At five o'clock Tyler closed the store, locked up for the evening, and headed up to the apartment. The door to the apartment opened as he was coming up the stairs, and Mark stepped out onto the landing wearing only a towel. Tyler's body reacted immediately. "Now that's a beautiful sight!" He bounded up the remaining stairs and pressed Mark into the wall, kissing him hard, his need transmitted with each kiss. "Oh god, Mark, I missed this, missed the feel of your body."

"Ty, I need you... waited all day for you."

Tyler guided Mark back into the apartment and into the bedroom, discarding his clothing as they went. "Mark, I want you so bad. Need to be in you."

"Need you inside me, need you to fill me, Ty. Need you to love me."

In the bedroom, Tyler pulled away Mark's towel. A low deep sound, almost a growl, emanated from Tyler when he saw Mark's naked body. Tyler removed his pants, pushed Mark onto the bed, and pounced on top of him.

Tyler kissed Mark frantically, pulling on his lips and thrusting his tongue. Mark returned the kisses, adding his own pent-up desire. Mark's sounds of pleasure started almost immediately as their rigid cocks rubbed against each other, their hips thrusting frantically.

"Love your kisses, Ty. Need more." Mark's legs throbbed against the sheets as the heat from Tyler's kisses shot up and down his spine like an electric charge. "Oh, yeah, that's it." Tyler pulled on Mark's lips, making them red.

"Mark, I'm on fire." Tyler's cock strained, he was so hard; each heartbeat made him throb.

"Mmmmm, me too. Don't stop!" Tyler had no intention. He couldn't if he tried.

Pulling back from those sweet lips, Tyler took Mark into his mouth. Mark bucked and whimpered as Tyler worked him. "Oh... good... oh... god...."

Tyler moaned around Mark, "Mmmmmm, aaahhhhh," as he worked the head and shaft with his tongue before using it to tickle the slit.

Mark pounded the bed with his fists, his legs spreading wide on their own. "Oh… need… you… not… going … to… last…."

Without releasing Mark's cock, he lifted his legs to his chest and slipped a lubed finger into Mark. The bucking and whimpering continued. "Tyler, I need you, please…."

"Mark, so sexy, so hot." Adding a second finger made the begging turn to pleading. "This what you want?"

"Oh, god, yes!" Mark was pounding the bed with his hands. "More, want you… now!" Tyler twisted his fingers as he removed them, pulling a deep moan out of Mark.

Shifting position, Tyler lubed his cock and pressed it to Mark's butt, entering Mark as slowly as he could. "Oh, Ty, yeah, that's it. Need more. Need all of you!"

He started moving almost immediately, pounding into Mark with nearly frantic strokes. Mark was taking it and loving it. "Oh god, Tyler. More, faster, need you so bad."

"Oh, yeah, Mark. Been too long, need you, missed this."

Leaning forward, Tyler kissed Mark deeply, working his tongue in his mouth as he fucked his butt. Mark just moaned as Tyler picked up his pace and stroked Mark's cock. "Yeah, that's it. Way too long. Need you, love you. More!"

Knowing Mark wouldn't last much longer, Tyler increased the pace of his hand on Mark's cock. Soon Mark came in great spurts, shooting onto his hand and chest. "Oh, Ty, love you so much!"

Mark clenched tightly as he came, sending Tyler soaring over the edge. Tyler moaned, "Mark, love you," as he came violently, deep in Mark.

Tyler didn't pull out right away. He said softly, "Love the way you feel."

Slowly withdrawing, Tyler kissed Mark deeply, collapsing onto him. Mark wrapped his arms around Tyler, kissing him and grabbing his butt.

Getting up from the bed, Tyler went to the bathroom, washed himself, and brought a cloth to clean Mark. After throwing the cloth back into the bathroom, he rejoined Mark on the bed.

Almost immediately, Tyler felt as though Mark had turned into an octopus. His hands were everywhere. The caresses became more urgent, Mark's moans and whimpers more wanton and needy. Tyler just went with it, he was so turned on. He had barely gone soft and now Mark was gripping his cock, stroking it back to life.

Using his weight, Mark rolled them on the bed so that his weight pressed Tyler into the soft bed. Mark slithered down Tyler's body, taking his now erect cock in his mouth. "Ty, you taste like pure sex! I love it!"

Tyler resisted the urge to say that was because he'd come not ten minutes before, and just went with the incredible feeling. Mark was using his magnificent lips and tongue to tease the crown. "Yeah, that's great. Right there… oh yeeeaaahhhhh." Taking all of Tyler into his mouth elicited an almost animalistic cry from Tyler. Mark just smiled as he pulled his head back and repeated the motion, getting another cry in return.

Mark released Tyler's cock with a pop, bringing his lips to Tyler's in a deep, passionate, powerful, long, toe- curling kiss that completely stole Tyler's breath.

Mark continued kissing as he reached between Tyler's legs and worked a lubed finger into that sweet, pulsing butt. "Ty, I want you. I want you bad."

One finger became two and soon Tyler was thrusting his hips and moaning for Mark. "Mark, please take me. I need you too."

Mark was too far gone to be gentle. After lubing his cock generously, he inserted himself into Tyler, trying to take his time, but unable to do so. "Mark, fill me. Love you in me." Using long strokes, Mark reveled in the feel of Tyler. Even though he had come twenty minutes earlier, the pressure was already building; his need for his lover was just too great.

Mark stroked Tyler in time with his own deep thrusts. "Mark, yeah, that's so good." Mark kept stroking. "Yeah, that's it. Don't stop."

With each stroke, Tyler moaned like the soundtrack of a porno movie. Mark felt his balls contract and he shot into Tyler, his cock pulsing deep inside him. Tyler came a minute later, pumping the contents of his balls onto his stomach.

Mark collapsed on top of Tyler; they were both completely spent. It took them a while before they had the energy to move, which was fine with them. They hugged, kissed, and petted until they were ready to get cleaned up and have dinner.

Chapter 12

IN the morning, they were leaving for the antique show in Chicago. Mark and Tyler had spent the entire evening loading the truck, trailer, and car. Mark couldn't believe all the stuff Tyler was taking, but he figured he knew what he was doing. The front of the store was largely empty, because, in addition to taking items to the show, Tyler had insisted on getting the store ready for new displays that would be done when they got back. Tyler had explained that he used this show to move older merchandise that had been in the store for a while as well as to show off and get top price for unique or special items.

The past few weeks had been quiet and relatively peaceful for both of them. Mark went back to work and he continued working on the commissioned portraits of Tom and Bill. He was finding it more difficult than he had thought it would be. Working full time, combined with spending time with Tyler, he didn't have as much time as he'd like and inspiration seemed to strike when he was at work. But, he was making slow and steady progress. To add to the progress, Mark's mother's house had sold quickly and now they were waiting on inspections and appraisals. Mark was thrilled that a young family with kids was buying the house.

At six in the morning Steve had joined them in the back of the store. Steve would drive the truck to the show for Tyler, help them unload, and then drive the truck home. He would then drive the truck back to the show on Sunday and help them load what was left for the trip home. Tyler and Mark were riding together in the car and would follow Steve in case there was a problem. This would give Mark and Tyler the car to use in the evenings. By six-fifteen they were on their way to Chicago.

"Mark, once we set up, why don't you wander through the show and look around? There will be a number of booths with paintings and sculpture. Enjoy yourself." Mark nodded excitedly. "I've booked us into a wonderful art deco hotel downtown. The show opens at noon and closes at six this evening. After closing, we'll go to the hotel, check in, and then go to dinner. I already made a reservation for tonight at a wonderful restaurant." Tyler reached across the seat and squeezed Mark's leg playfully.

They arrived at the convention center before eight o'clock. Most of the other vendors were unloading as well. Tyler opened the back of the truck and they all started the process of unloading the truck. Tyler checked in and directed Steve and Mark to their booth for the show. It was a great corner booth. Steve and Mark unloaded the truck, while Tyler placed each item in the booth as it was unloaded. When they were finished, Tyler had created a fascinating display of antiques. The antique show was immense, with aisle after aisle of booths containing antiques of every style, age, description, and price. This was the premier antique show in this area of the country.

"Why don't you bring any of the paintings or art works?" Mark asked curiously.

"I try to keep to furniture and decorative arts mainly because of space and my own expertise." Tyler had used each of the furniture pieces to display other items. He had brought two bookcases and they were being used as cabinets for smaller items. The booth was a study in efficiency and creative display. Mark had to admit that Tyler was very artistic. His ability to take a group of largely unrelated items and create a stunning display was amazing.

Just before the show opened, Tyler sat in a chair and started to get himself prepared for business. "Why don't you look around? If you see something interesting, let me know the booth number and what the item is and I'll take a look." Mark smiled, kissed Tyler, and headed off into the show.

Mark wandered through the show looking at various booths and the items for sale. Most things didn't interest him, but in a booth on the end of one of the aisles, a painting caught his eye. He'd seen something similar when he first started working for Peter. The painting's tag said it was a late nineteenth-century unsigned oil painting. It was beautiful and Mark thought the landscape was stunning. Looking in the lower right corner, he saw a design half incorporated into the painting. Mark practically jumped for joy, but didn't want to give himself away. That small symbol was the signature. This painting had been done by a famous Scottish artist. They didn't know his name, but they knew his symbol. Mark casually left the booth and walked back to Tyler as fast as he could.

Reaching the booth breathless, Mark asked, "Tyler, is Steve still here?"

Tyler nodded. "Steve's leaving in ten minutes when the show opens. Why?"

He quietly leaned over to Tyler. "I found a masterpiece. Please have Steve man the booth. We need to buy this painting right now!"

"Steve, would you mind? Tell people I'll be back in a few minutes." Mark could barely contain his excitement. When they got to the booth, Mark had calmed down and showed Tyler the painting. When the booth owner wasn't looking he showed Tyler the signature mark on the painting. "Are you sure?"

Mark whispered to Tyler. "Peter had one of his works when I started working for him. It sold for almost a hundred thousand dollars and it wasn't this interesting. Please buy it."

Tyler negotiated a price, wrote a check, and carried the painting back to the booth. Mark could hardly believe what he'd found. When they got back to the booth, Tyler was able to look over the painting carefully. It was indeed a good quality painting and he figured he had paid a fair price for it regardless.

"Mark, would you have wanted the painting if it hadn't been by a famous person? Do you like the painting itself?"

"Yes, I like the painting and would hang it in the living room regardless, but I'm not wrong about this." Mark looked perplexed.

Tyler explained. "Mark, I'm not saying you're wrong, or questioning your expertise, but the fastest way to get burned is to buy something just because you think it's valuable. You should always like the items you buy. If you like it, someone else will like it." Mark nodded. "I have an idea. Give Peter a call and tell him what you found. He may be able to help you."

Mark smiled and kissed Tyler gently. "I understand." He then called Peter and they talked for a while. "Ty, he said it sounds promising. He asked me to bring it by the gallery when we get back."

"Excellent. Do you want to finish looking around?" Mark nodded and went to see the rest of the show. When he got back, he told Tyler that there were a number of interesting things. "It was quite an education, seeing all these incredible things that I never paid any attention to before." Tyler could only smile.

The rest of the day was spent working with customers and helping people with their purchases. At closing time, Tyler drove them to their hotel. After checking in, they headed to the room with their luggage and the painting. Their room was an art deco masterpiece. Mark loved it. Once they were settled, Tyler sat on the edge of the bed. "Do you want to sell the painting or keep it?"

Mark looked confused. "I assumed that we would sell it, since you bought it." Mark had already resigned himself to the fact that his find would be sold.

"Well, I paid for the painting with a personal check and we paid sales tax, so if you want to keep it, it's yours, love." Mark leapt at Tyler, throwing his arms around him, pressing him back onto the bed, and started to remove his clothes.

Tyler stopped him. "We need to get ready to go to dinner. I promise we'll pick this up later." They changed clothes and headed to dinner. Tyler had chosen a small intimate restaurant where they could talk, hold hands, and kiss if they wanted, and they did. After dinner Mark suggested a walk, so Tyler drove to Navy Pier where they people-watched and just enjoyed each other's company as they walked along. Passing the large Ferris wheel, Mark asked if they could ride. Tyler bought tickets and they got in line.

They had the car all to themselves. Settling onto a seat, Mark pulled Tyler closer. His kiss started gently, but quickly escalated into more. Tyler returned the kiss, using his tongue to explore Mark's mouth and lips. As the ride came to an end, their clothes were a little disheveled, their lips puffy, hair mussed. It was definitely time to go back to the hotel.

Tyler drove, and once in the room, Tyler told Mark to lie on the bed and relax. After getting a few things ready, Tyler slowly removed Mark's clothing, kissing the newly exposed skin. Tyler knew what Mark liked and paid special attention to his nipples, that spot on his neck, and his ears. With each touch, Mark made happy pleasure noises. "Oh, Ty, yeah… that's so good."

Once Mark was naked, Tyler slowly got up, removed his clothing, and rejoined Mark in bed. Teasingly, Tyler took the head of Mark's cock into his mouth, gently tickling the underside. Mark started making those wonderful pleasure noises that always drove Tyler wild. "You like that?"

Whimpering, Mark moaned, "Uh-huh."

Slowly, he pushed his lips down, taking more of Mark into his mouth. When he had taken Mark to the root, he gently lifted his legs toward his chest. Reaching under the bed, he took the medium-sized glass butt plug he'd lubed earlier, and slowly inserted it into Mark. The pleasure noises increased as Mark's body reacted to being sucked by Tyler and fucked by the plug at the same time. Releasing Mark's cock, Tyler whispered, "It's one of the butt plugs. Do you like it?" Mark could only nod and moan as Tyler gently removed the plug and reinserted it.

"Ty, please… I need you… please…." Tyler loved it when Mark begged, begged for him. There was nothing sexier in the world than Mark naked and pleading for him.

Tyler slowly removed the plug. "Are you ready for me?"

"Oh, god, yes, please fill me." Tyler generously lubed himself and pressed into Mark. He went as slow as he could but his body had other ideas and he quickly buried himself to the root, nearly knocking the breath out of Mark. "More, Ty… don't stop…." Adjusting the angle slightly sent visible waves of pleasure through Mark. "Oh, Ty, that's it, right there." Tyler saw Mark reach for his cock, but he gently pushed his hand away. Leaning forward, Tyler kissed Mark, pushing his tongue deep into Mark's mouth, fucking his mouth with his tongue as he fucked his ass with his cock. Mark was in absolute heaven and still Tyler wouldn't let Mark touch himself. Mark was really begging for it. "Oh, Ty, please…. I need… so bad!"

Reaching to Mark's chest, Tyler tweaked his nipples, sending Mark over the edge. He bucked and writhed beneath him, coming in huge waves onto his stomach and chest without having touched himself. "Ty, I'm seeing stars." The sight was too much for Tyler and he filled Mark again and again, crying out Mark's name.

Withdrawing, Tyler lowered himself onto Mark as he felt his body being wrapped in Mark's arms. "Mark, you're so incredible." Tyler gently kissed Mark's lips, their tongues exploring languidly. Hands gently stroking, maintaining contact, Tyler felt Mark's hand rest at the center of his chest as though he were trying to touch his heart.

Slowly, Tyler felt his need return; it didn't matter that Mark had just blown his mind. Mark seemed to read his mind, because soon the kisses that had started slow and deep became harder and more insistent, signaling rekindled passion and pure wanton need and lust. "Ty, I want you. I need you."

Nodding, Tyler purred, "Mark, you're going to kill me." Tyler's eyes danced through a haze of need. "God, I want you inside me, need you too."

Using his weight, Mark rolled Tyler onto his back and pressed him into the bed. His chest hair tickled against Tyler's chest. Mark lifted Tyler's legs, pressing two fingers into his body. "Oh, that feels so good."

"Yeah, so hot, so sexy." Mark stroked slowly, opening Tyler for him, getting him ready. "Ty, I need you so bad."

"Want you now, Mark. Ready… more."

Mark entered Tyler's body in one long, fluid movement. Tyler was now hard as well, meeting Mark with every stroke. Now it was Tyler's turn to make those happy pleasure noises. "Oh, mmmmm, Mark… that's it, yeah." Mark had an almost innate sense of how to hit

Tyler's pleasure center and he did with almost every stroke. "Right, there, yeah… oh yeah…." Mark started stroking Tyler in rhythm to his thrusting. Tyler's hands grabbed the sheets, as wave after wave of pleasure coursed though his body. His arms and legs were tingling as Tyler felt Mark's orgasm release inside him, and he came onto his stomach. "Oh, Mark… yeah…." Mark collapsed onto Tyler and it took a while before either of them had the energy for anything other than kissing, stroking, and loving.

"Did you like the surprise?"

Mark nodded enthusiastically. "Oh yeah, that was wonderful."

The shower felt hot and soothing on their worn-out and satiated bodies. After drying themselves, they fell into bed, cuddling together in the air-conditioned room, each quickly falling into a deep sleep.

IN the morning, they were up, dressed, and having breakfast by eight, and at the antique show by nine-thirty. After making sure the booth looked right, they were ready for business. Tyler had a very successful day. Many of the furniture items sold, along with most of the other items. As they were getting ready to leave, Mark asked Tyler what they were doing that evening. "I thought we could grab a quick dinner, change clothes, and go to a gallery opening. Peter got us invited." Mark jumped into Tyler's arms, kissing him deeply. "I'll take that as a yes."

Dinner was indeed quick, and after changing clothes, Tyler drove to the gallery, where they showed their invitations and entered. Tyler looked around and asked Mark to stay close. All of the art was modern, and he was completely out of his element. Mark explained some of the pieces as they toured the gallery together. During the course of the evening, they met the artist. He and Mark talked shop while Tyler got champagne.

"What do you think?" the artist, who introduced himself as Samban, asked with a wink.

"Your work shows a certain power and intensity, but I must confess, I'm not sure what your message is." Mark was trying to be polite. He thought the art on display was basically crude and unpolished and that the artist was probably just trying to make a quick buck.

Samban went into all kinds of art-speak explanations about his work. Mark admitted to himself that he talked a good game, but Mark knew bullshit when he heard it and he knew flashy, soulless art when he saw it. After his in-depth explanation, Samban whispered to Mark, "I've got a great hotel room. Would you like to join me for some fun?" He leered as his eyes wandered to Mark's crotch.

Mark was shocked and, he had to admit to himself, a little flattered. He swallowed, trying to keep his voice even. "I'm here with my boyfriend."

"Why don't you both join me? If he's anything like you, we could have a lot of fun." The artist continued leering at Mark.

Mark was decidedly uncomfortable and was trying to figure out how to make a graceful exit without causing a scene. His first thought was "What a pig." His expression, however, remained bland. "No, thanks. We don't...." Mark wasn't sure how to phrase it. "It's just us. We don't play around."

Fortunately for Mark, he saw Tyler heading his way and he excused himself. Samban shrugged and looked around the room. Mark thought to himself as Tyler approached, "Probably looking for another couple to break up."

Mark took the champagne from Tyler and downed the contents in one large gulp. Tyler raised his eyebrows as he watched. Mark smirked as he looked at the artist. "What a pig."

Tyler looked at Mark a little confused; he'd obviously missed something. Mark filled him in as they wandered around. "He asked if I'd like to go back to his hotel room. When I told him I was with my boyfriend, he invited both of us." Tyler was watching Mark closely. "I told him no." Tyler could sense Mark was unsure of himself. "You don't want to go with him, do you?" Tyler was relieved that Mark had turned down the offer. Before he could say anything more, they were separated while passing through the crowd. When Tyler found Mark again, a pressing thought entered his mind.

"Mark, we need to see the gallery manager. Peter called him about you." They weaved through the crowd until they came to a gallery employee who directed them to the manager.

Approaching the manager, Tyler introduced himself and Mark. "Oh, you're the artist Peter was telling me about. He said you had done some stunning portraits. I'd love to see them." He gave Mark a business card and Mark gave him his contact information. "I'll be in Milwaukee in a few weeks. I'll call you and arrange to see your work." After shaking hands, he joined another group.

Mark was getting tired. "Ty, we can go now. I think I need to be alone with you."

They were in the car driving back to the hotel when Tyler asked, "Did you have a good time?"

Mark nodded. "Yes, very much. I know it's not really your thing, so thank you for taking me. I really did enjoy myself."

Tyler smiled and squeezed Mark's leg. "I enjoyed myself as well. Being with you is always my thing." Tyler put both hands back on the wheel and continued driving. Mark beamed, rubbing Tyler's leg gently as he drove through the light late-evening traffic.

"Mark, I didn't get a chance to tell you in the gallery, but I was very relieved when you turned down the offer to play." Tyler's voice was soft, meant to reassure that he was his and his alone.

Mark leaned the seat back and smiled. "You were? I was afraid you might want to."

Tyler shook his head gently. "You're more than enough man for me. I don't need someone else to spice things up. We do that on our own just fine."

Mark's head rolled lazily to face Tyler. "I feel the same way." Soft music was playing on the radio and they both felt mellow and contented as they drove back to the hotel.

In the lobby, Tyler suggested a drink in the bar before they went up to the room. This seemed out of character, but Mark agreed. They entered the hotel bar and Tyler ordered champagne.

"Are we celebrating?" Mark looked curious.

"Yes, we are. The gallery owner wants to see your work. That is fantastic news. Definitely worth celebrating."

Mark looked dubious. "What if he doesn't like my work?"

Tyler just shook his head. "Mark, your work has captivated everyone who sees it; he will be no exception. Besides, my faith in the art world was restored tonight when I noticed that the art wasn't flying off the shelves in there." Tyler was being catty and he knew it.

Mark laughed. "Well, the art was fairly uninteresting, but the event was a lot of fun." After finishing their drinks, Tyler took what was left in the bottle with them to their room along with the glasses.

Tyler put soft music into the CD player, poured each of them a second glass of champagne, made sure everything was ready for the evening, and headed into the bathroom. Mark was sitting on the edge of the bed enjoying his champagne when Tyler emerged naked. Standing in front of Mark, placing his hands on his knees, leaning close, he whispered, "Mark, I want you long and slow." His voice was deep with passion and lust. "I want to feel every inch of you pressing into me over and over again, filling me with your love."

Mark's eyes were wide and a moan emanated from deep in his chest. Gently lifting Mark from the bed, Tyler undressed him completely, and then crawled on the bed. He lay on his stomach, offering himself fully to Mark.

The room filled with the sounds of love as they expressed their happiness and reinforced the commitment they'd just made to each other. As the sounds built, so did their passion. Whimpers and moans replaced words. Mark took the lead, filling his lover completely, his movements languid, rock steady, meant to slowly build their passion, and build it did to heights nearly unimagined by either, culminating in ecstasy, punctuated by words of care, devotion, and, most importantly, love.

"I love you, Ty."

"And I love you."

They crawled back into bed. "Mark, you were amazing. You're always amazing." Tyler curled up against Mark, stroking the hair on his chest and smiling.

"What?"

"The man I always dreamed about had a hairy chest just like yours. This is so sexy." Kissing Mark gently, he continued to stroke and fondle Mark's chest. "Good night, sexy."

Smiling, Mark said, "Good night, Ty. Thank you for a wonderful weekend." He reached to turn out the light.

Chapter 13

THE last day of the antique show was a success. In the morning, Tyler reduced the price of the furniture items that he really wanted to sell and most of those items sold. Mark spent part of the afternoon packing the painting they'd purchased. Most of the day was spent talking, laughing, and helping customers. Hours before the show closed, Tyler's booth looked quite empty. Tyler was absolutely thrilled and declared the show a huge success. Steve walked in about an hour before the show closed and the three of them started packing up. There were very few customers left and Tyler was anxious to head home.

Shortly after the show closed at four, everything was packed and they headed to the truck. Steve and Mark loaded the truck while Tyler made sure that each item was properly secured. All the items were loaded and they were on the highway before five.

"I had a great time this weekend. Thank you for everything." Mark was all smiles.

"I had a wonderful time as well. You were a big help, loving company... oh, and the show was a big success as well." Tyler was grinning. "You know, we should plan a proper vacation. I haven't had one in years and I'd love to have you all to myself for a whole week."

Mark reached over to squeeze Tyler's leg. "I'd love that too."

"Say, why don't you think about where you'd like to go. We can plan a vacation for September."

Taking a deep breath, Mark cooed, "That would be heavenly."

The music on the radio was soothing and soon they were relaxed and contented, enjoying the ride home and each other's company. Arriving back in town, they were both looking forward to getting home. Turning the corner, they saw their street blocked by police cars and fire trucks. Tyler looked concerned. Mark patted Tyler's hand gently. "Ty, I'll see what's going on." Mark got out of the car and found a police officer. After talking to him for a minute, he returned to their car.

"Ty, you should park the car. There's been a fire at the store." Tyler turned almost completely white and didn't move. Mark coaxed Tyler into parking the car, but once it was parked he just stayed behind the wheel. Mark figured he was in shock. A few minutes later, Mark saw Steve pull up in the truck and trailer. Flagging him down, Mark told him what had happened. "Steve, there's been a fire in the store."

Steve nodded. "I'll park the truck at the deli. It'll be safe." Mark thanked him and went back to the car. Tyler had gotten out of the car, and Mark was able to find a fireman who could speak with them. Mark did the talking, since Tyler didn't seem to want to talk at all.

"What happened?"

"There was a fire in the front of the store. When we arrived, the store was full of smoke. We were able to put the fire out, but we don't yet know the cause and no one can go inside until the building is checked to make sure it's structurally sound. I can tell you that part of the ceiling collapsed." The information was imparted with no emotion whatsoever.

"But we live above the store!"

He continued in a very automatic tone of voice, showing little emotion or understanding. "I'm sorry. I suggest you find a hotel for the next few days until the building can be inspected and we can determine the cause of the fire."

"How bad is it?" Mark was trying to get any useful information he could.

"I'm sorry. I really don't know. The building is being secured right now. I can tell you the fire looks suspicious and it could be arson. The police will want to talk to you. We'll call you in a few days once our investigation is complete." He took contact information from Mark and went back to work.

Soon, they were joined by a police officer, who told them he had a few questions. Mark said he'd answer them as best he could. "Can you tell me where you were for the last few hours?" Mark answered. Tyler was still largely unresponsive and Mark was starting to worry. Tyler stood silently through the exchange, saying nothing.

"We were at an antique show in Chicago all weekend. Tyler is an antique dealer. It was his store that burned." The officer took notes and asked for general information. He tried to ask Tyler questions, but Tyler just shook his head. "I think he's still in shock." Mark answered all the officer's questions. "Look, I'm going to check us into a hotel for the night. You can contact us on the cell phone and we'll gladly answer any questions you might have." Steve joined them and told them that he had been by the front of the store before he left for Chicago and everything was fine then. Mark got Tyler back into the car and headed for a hotel.

Once Mark found one and got checked in, he escorted Tyler into the room. He just sat on the edge of the bed and stared at the wall. Tyler offered no resistance, just staring at the walls without speaking. Using the cell phone, Mark called Peter and told him what happened. Peter understood and told him to stop by the gallery later in the week. "You two have had a heck of a couple of months, haven't you?"

"Yes, we have. Thank you for understanding. It can only get better." Mark ordered room service, hoping some food might help. Mark called Tom and told him what happened and how Tyler was reacting. Tom said he'd be right over.

Tom arrived about a half-hour later, just as the room service arrived. Tyler ate a little but continued to stare at the walls. Mark and Tom went into the hall. "I don't know what to do. He's been like that since we found out about the fire."

"I think he's in shock. The store has been his life for years and without it he feels completely lost. All you can do is be there for him. If this continues, you can take him to the hospital." Tom also looked concerned.

"There's another thing. The fireman said it could be arson. We've received threatening notes that I think are from my brother. He may have set the fire somehow. I'm wondering if Tyler would be safer without me around right now." Just the thought nearly broke Mark's heart, but he needed Tyler to be safe.

Tom shook his head. "Do you love him?"

Mark nodded. "So much it hurts."

"Then you need to be here for him." His tone was authoritative, definite.

"But what if he'll be safer without me?" There was a pleading, almost defeated tone in Mark's voice.

"Mark, your job is to love and be there for him. Protect him by doing that. If you leave even for a while he'll completely fall apart and you'll both be without each other. Mark, take it from me: love stays, no matter what, and love is always worth fighting for, no matter what."

Mark needed to hear that. He gave Tom a big hug. "Thank you."

"Do you need anything?"

Mark thought for a minute. "I don't think so. The store is secured, the truck is being parked and locked, and we do have our clothes from this weekend. I just hope they let us in the building soon. I can only hope that he's assuming the worst and once he sees the store, he'll be able to deal with the problem."

They went back into the room. Tyler hadn't moved at all. Tom said goodbye and told them to call him or Bill if they needed anything. Mark sat next to Tyler, hugging him tightly. After a long time, Tyler hugged him back. Mark felt he'd won a huge victory.

Just before bedtime, the cell phone rang. Mark answered.

"Mark? It's Roger. I just heard about the fire. I'm sorry; that's a real shame." Mark wasn't sure if he was being sarcastic or not. "The reason I called is I was wondering when the money from Mom's estate would be distributed? I know this is a bad time, but I really need to know."

"Roger, the house closes in a few weeks. Most of the money will be distributed then. The last of it will be distributed once the lawyer and I are sure everything has been paid. I'll let you know." Mark was trying to keep from being short, particularly since Roger actually seemed to be civil.

"The reason I'm asking is I was wondering if the large table that was in storage and the small desk had been sold."

"No, I don't think they were sold."

"If they survived the fire, I'd like to use some of the money from Mom to buy them. Would you ask Tyler to give me first chance? Please?" Mark was wondering why Roger was being so nice.

"I'll ask him when we see what survived." Mark shook his head, thinking, *what nerve he has.*

"Thanks, Mark. Say, don't fires sometimes have a tendency to restart? I sure hope that doesn't happen." All Mark heard was a dial tone. Mark was now very frightened that Roger had started the fire in the store, but he said nothing. Mark again tried to comfort Tyler, but he was barely responding. At bedtime, they cleaned up and got into bed. Mark hugged him close, determined to let Tyler know that he was there for him.

After two nights in the hotel, they finally heard from the fire department that the building was sound and that the fire appeared to have been caused by a short in some old wiring. Arson had been suspected because of where the fire had started, but that had been ruled out. The fire department did say that the building would need to be rewired before anyone could live there, but they could now go into the building. Mark was relieved that Roger hadn't started the fire, but he still wondered what he was up to.

Tyler had not spoken much over the past two days and had spent most of his time staring at the TV. Mark convinced Tyler to get dressed and get into the car and Mark drove to the store. The front windows and door had been boarded up, so they went around to the back. Opening the door, the air smelled slightly of smoke. The large rear doors to the store were closed. Looking around, the back room seemed pretty much untouched. That was a huge relief, because a lot of Tyler's recent purchases were undamaged. Mark, followed by Tyler, opened the doors to the store. The smell of smoke, charred wood, and dampness was overpowering. They walked through the store, surveying the damage. The back of the store wasn't too bad. The items had been sprayed slightly, but weren't too damaged, other than any piece with fabric, which would need to be reupholstered. The front of the store was another story. The walls and floor were charred, the windows broken, and the ceiling had collapsed, but the floor above seemed to be intact. Everything in the first third of the store was destroyed. Thank goodness Tyler had insisted on getting the front of the store ready for new displays before they left.

Heading out of the store, Mark quickly checked his studio. The door had been closed and everything seemed all right. The room didn't even smell like smoke. He made a note to pack all his work into the car before they left and take it to Peter's. He knew he'd store it for him. Before heading up to the apartment, Mark craned his head, but he couldn't see Tyler. Looking around, Mark could see that the door to the apartment was open. Mark hurried inside. He couldn't see Tyler, but he heard sniffling coming from the bedroom. Racing to the bedroom, he saw Tyler curled up on the bed with tears running down his face. He was staring at the portrait Mark had given him for his birthday. Mark gently climbed onto the bed with him, wrapping him in his arms. His sniffles turned to absolute sobs as Tyler just cried his eyes out. Mark held him tightly and rocked him gently, just like Tyler had done for him months before. Slowly the sobbing subsided and the worst of the worry, despair, and hopelessness went with them. Mark just held Tyler and waited.

"I was so worried about the store, but when I came in here, I saw our bed and the painting. I realized what was important, what can be replaced and what can't." He started to sniffle again.

"Tyler, I'm not going anyplace but where you are. You're stuck with me." Tyler hugged Mark tightly and started to breathe normally.

Tyler finally straightened up and took a deep breath. "Where do we start?"

Mark smiled. "I think we already have." Mark was so relieved that he wanted to cry now. He was finally able to look around the apartment. It smelled of smoke, but other than that there didn't seem to be any damage. "The fire department said that no one could live here until the entire building was rewired. So I think we need to call the insurance company, get them started, and find a place for us to live."

Something in Tyler clicked and soon he was in action. He called his insurance agent and got the claim moving. He explained that he had stellar coverage on the store and the apartment. They heard a voice at the base of the stairs. Mark looked, saw that it was Steve, and motioned for him to come up. They were starting to formulate a plan when the insurance adjustor called. Tyler explained things and he said he'd be right over. Steve brought over lunch as they waited for the insurance adjustor. He arrived just after lunch, looked all around the building, took pictures of everything, and gave them some basic information.

"We have a deal with East Side Terrace. They have furnished apartments they rent to business people. I called on my way over and they have an apartment waiting for you. They'll bill us directly. I'll estimate the cost to repair and clean the building and we'll send you a check. Please make a list of all contents that were destroyed or damaged. You have replacement value on all contents. Here's a form that will help you."

Mark and Tyler were impressed. He really seemed to know what they needed.

"There are a number of other clauses in the policy that will take effect, including the business continuity clause. Can you tell me who your accountant is? I can work directly with them."

Tyler gave him the information. The adjustor asked a few more questions, shook hands, and left.

Mark spoke up. "Tyler, I have an idea. Why don't you get on the phone and find a climate-controlled storage facility, and rent storage? We can put all the undamaged items there. That'll free up space and ensure they don't get damaged during the cleanup. Then we can start sorting the other items and determine what was destroyed and what's repairable."

Kissing Mark, Tyler exclaimed, "You're a genius." Tyler got on the phone and soon had a large storage area reserved, and Steve brought around the truck. They loaded the trailer, inventorying the items as they were loaded. Steve was going to load a small desk when Mark stopped him. "This needs to stay. Please put it in the apartment for now." Tyler looked confused but didn't argue.

The loaded truck and trailer were driven to the storage facility and unloaded into the large storage unit Tyler had rented. "Tyler, isn't this too big?" Mark's voice echoed through the empty space.

Smiling broadly, Tyler said, "Mark, if I'm going to reopen, I'll need a place to store inventory until the repairs are finished, so I rented the biggest room they have. If we fill it, I'll rent another." Mark was thrilled to see the Tyler he loved starting to show himself again. They continued taking loads of undamaged items to storage for the rest of the day. At the end of the day, Mark loaded his art supplies and all the paintings in the apartment, shop, and studio into the car.

"I called Peter and he said to bring all the artwork to his gallery, where he'll store them for us." After finishing work for the day, they said goodbye to Steve, who took some beer, and they headed to Peter's gallery. Peter was happy to see them and showed them where all their paintings could be stored.

As they were unloading, Tyler stopped Mark when he unloaded the portrait of him. "This goes with us." Mark put it carefully into the car.

When they unloaded the painting they had bought in Chicago, Peter stopped them as they got in the door, took the painting, and went into his office. When all the paintings were stored, they joined him. "Well, Mark, this is an exceptional find. It's authentic all right. Do you want to sell it? I'll be glad to broker the sale. The last of his works to sell brought a quarter-million, but it wasn't this nice. This could bring more."

Mark was stunned and Tyler almost choked. "Did you say a quarter-million dollars?" Peter nodded. "We intend to keep it for now. Would you please put it in the vault for us?" Peter led them to the painting vault, carefully wrapped the painting, and stowed it on one of the padded racks. "Thank you for all your help. We really appreciate it."

"It's not a problem. I'm just glad I can help." Peter looked at Mark. "I have a business proposition for you, but I want to talk to you when you're less rushed. Take the week off and get things in order. Come to see me later in the week and we'll talk. Okay?"

"Sure, I'll see you later in the week." Mark was a little curious, but he knew Peter wouldn't be rushed. They thanked Peter again and headed to the hotel. They would move to the apartment tomorrow. Tyler called East Side Terrace to let them know that they'd be by in the morning to get into the apartment. When they got back to the hotel, they informed them they'd be checking out in the morning, ordered room service, went to their room, and tried to relax for the rest of the evening.

Just as they were going to bed, Mark remembered the conversation with Roger. He recapped it for Tyler. "Look, I think there's something about those pieces that we don't know. Roger is not sentimental. He's greedy and self-centered. That's why I didn't want Steve loading the desk. I want to be able to look at it closely and see if we can figure out if there's anything special about it."

"Not a bad idea. We'll leave both pieces in the apartment and look at them there." Tyler yawned. "Good night, Mark. Thank you for being there. I love you."

"I love you, too, Ty, and I'll always be there." Just like you were for me. They turned out the light.

Chapter 14

ALMOST a week after the fire, Tyler and Mark had accomplished a lot at the store. All undamaged merchandise had been moved to storage. The furniture from the apartment had been cleaned by a fire restoration company and put in separate storage. Lists and forms for the insurance company had been completed, signed, and certified. Contractors had been contacted, but Tyler had yet to authorize any of the repair work on the store. Mark was surprised, because he figured that Tyler would want to get the repairs completed as quickly as possible so he could reopen the store.

Two days before, another threatening note had been slipped under the back door of the store. The note said "God cleanses sinners with fire." Tyler turned it over to the police as he had with the other one. The police had gotten nothing from the first note and they weren't hopeful, but they said they'd try. This second note only made Tyler and Mark more anxious.

The temporary apartment was nice, but it wasn't home. The furniture wasn't theirs, the bed didn't feel right, and Mark hadn't been able to paint since the fire. He missed it, and needed the creative outlet. He and Tyler had even had a fight the night before over nothing and now Mark couldn't sleep. Mark had asked about bringing his painting supplies to the apartment so he could work and Tyler had questioned if that was a good idea. An innocent and appropriate remark had set Mark off. He had said some nasty things that he didn't mean and now it was the middle of the night, he was feeling guilty and miserable, and all he wanted to do was apologize to Tyler, but it was three o'clock on a Saturday morning and Tyler was asleep.

Tyler was lying on his side. Mark spooned his body into Tyler's back, an arm draped over his chest. Mark's body immediately responded to the feel of Tyler's body pressed against his own and soon Mark was hard. He sighed; he should have known. His body always responded to his Ty. Two days earlier, they had been working in the store. It was hot and Tyler had taken off his shirt. Twenty minutes of watching Tyler as he worked without his shirt was all Mark could stand. Mark had pulled Tyler into the studio and stripped him naked before Tyler had known what had happened. They made love on the drop cloths with Mark on his back and Tyler pounding into him. Now in bed together, Mark rolled away so he wouldn't disturb Tyler's sleep.

"Mmmm… where'd you go?" The words were half-slurred with sleep.

"Shhhh. I didn't want to disturb you." The words were soft.

"You didn't. I haven't slept well." Tyler rolled over to face Mark. "Mark…."

Mark cut him off as the words came pouring out. "Ty, I'm sorry. I said some awful things I didn't mean and I feel so bad. I shouldn't have gotten mad at you."

Tyler folded Mark into his body.

"I know you didn't mean those things; it was just anger and frustration. I understand." Tyler kissed him gently. Mark returned the kiss, but added passion and heat. Tyler responded by throwing off the covers, covering Mark's body with his, and pushing his tongue deep into Mark's mouth, his cock rubbing against Mark's. Mark moaned into Tyler's mouth as their hips pressed and thrust against each other. Tyler's kisses became more insistent. Between kisses Mark moaned, "I need you, Ty… now… please."

Mark lifted his legs to his chest as Tyler lubed his fingers, pressing two of them deep into Mark. "Oh, Ty, I need you. That feels so good." Mark pressed his butt against Tyler's fingers, wanting more.

Withdrawing his fingers, Tyler lubed his cock, and entered Mark with a thrust. Using long, powerful strokes, Tyler pressed into Mark, using his entire body. Each thrust was massive, powerful, giving Mark everything he had. "I love you, Mark."

Mark opened himself to Tyler, taking everything he had to give and returning it to Tyler. "I love you, Ty."

Using his hand, Mark worked his cock in rhythm with Tyler's thrusts. Their pleasure noises filled the room. Mark came with a shout as Tyler thrust deeply before his climax surged into Mark.

Tyler got a towel, cleaned them up, and snuggled next to Mark. "I love you, Mark." He kissed Mark gently, hugging him to his body. Makeup sex was so hot.

Mark was almost weeping. "I'm sorry for snapping."

"It's okay, sweetie. I understand." And he did. Tyler knew they needed to make plans for the future. "We'll talk in the morning."

Tyler was making a special Saturday morning breakfast: blueberry pancakes, Mark's favorite. A shower-fresh Mark padded into the kitchen wearing only his underwear, smelling of soap, his hair still damp from the shower. Tyler's body reacted with gusto. "God, you look good." Tyler forced himself to go back to making breakfast. Mark spooned into Tyler's back, pressing himself into Tyler's butt. "Mmmmm, that feels good." Tyler turned his head, kissing his artist good morning. "Breakfast will be ready soon." Mark padded back into the bedroom to get dressed.

Over breakfast, Tyler asked Mark what he had planned. "Well, I would like to stop by the gallery and talk to Peter. He had something he wanted to discuss. Also, we wanted to look at the desk and table that Roger was interested in. I just don't trust him."

"After breakfast, let's head to the gallery to see Peter and then we can go to the store and take a look at those pieces we left in the apartment. But I want to talk to you before we leave." Mark nodded, his eyes glued to Tyler. "I know you've noticed that I haven't started repairs on the building. I've had some ideas running through my head and I wanted to get your input and thoughts."

Tyler had Mark's full attention now. "Okay. What are you thinking you'd like to do?" Tyler served breakfast and they talked as they ate.

"I'd like to completely remodel the building. Turn the first floor into an antique gallery with regular and room-type displays that include furniture, lighting, decorative items, rugs, chandeliers, art, and sculpture. The concept is similar to the current store, but would make the first floor all high-end pieces." Mark nodded; he was following so far. "Expand the store into the second floor with good quality, less expensive items, some in room settings, some not, all displayed properly."

"That sounds wonderful. I like the idea."

"A staircase would be added, along with an elevator, and the apartment would be remodeled out of existence." A quizzical look on Mark's face made Tyler pause. "I'll come to that in a minute." Mark remained quiet, letting Tyler finish his plans. "Here's where you come in. I want you to stop working for Peter and come work with me as the buyer of antique art. It wouldn't be a full-time job, but I would need your expertise." Tyler smiled and took Mark's hand. "Your thoughts so far?"

"I love the idea. It would allow us to work together part of the time and I'd still have time to paint." Mark smiled and Tyler nodded.

"We both need to have separate portions of our lives; we can't live and work together all the time. We'd drive each other crazy. But this way should work well for both of us and you could travel with me on buying trips." The leer Tyler gave him made Mark's cock jump in his pants.

"The second part of the plan would be that we buy a house together. It would be our home and would belong to both of us. Your studio could be either at the house or at the store. That's up to you, and you don't need to decide now."

Mark jumped up from his chair and threw himself at Tyler, nearly knocking him over backward, kissing and hugging him tightly. "Could we get a big old home on the East Side and fill it with antiques and art?"

"I'd love that." He would, too. Those had been his thoughts exactly.

Tyler got up from the chair and headed to the bedroom, but he only made it as far as the sofa before Mark reached him. Mark tore at their clothes, his need to be skin-to-skin with Tyler overpowering. The kisses were ravenous. "Ty, I want you now!" The two of them proved to each other that happy, celebratory sex trumped even makeup sex.

After showering together, they dressed and drove to the gallery. Peter was thrilled to see them, ushering them both into his office. "Mark, I have a proposition for you. I'd like to act as your agent. As your agent I would broker the sale of your art, plan exhibitions of your work, and handle dealings with galleries. I'd like you to work full-time on your art and quit your job here in the gallery." Mark looked at Tyler and smiled; great minds think alike. "I'd also like to schedule a show of your work here in the gallery in six months." Mark was so excited he could barely sit still. "We'll get together and work through the details a little later, but I'd like the show to be your portraits and landscapes; they really speak to people. I'm going to remove from display the pieces currently hanging in the gallery because we may want to use them in the show."

Mark could no longer contain himself. He hugged Tyler, and Peter as well, both of them smiling broadly at Mark's excitement. When Mark sat down, Peter continued, "Mark, a show will require a large number of works. From my memory, there are already eight here in the gallery. I would like eight to ten more if possible." They spent a few minutes talking over details and answering questions. Peter said, "Think about my offer and let me know. I'll then draw up the appropriate paperwork." After saying goodbye, they left the gallery with Mark walking on air, and he talked nonstop on the walk to the store.

Arriving at the store, they immediately headed up to the apartment to look at the desk and table. They opened the windows to let some of the smoky smell dissipate, and decided to start with the desk. It was a relatively small lady's desk—a nice piece, but not particularly valuable in itself.

Tyler looked puzzled. "Sometimes desks have secret compartments, but I looked earlier and didn't find one. We'll have to try again. Look for missing space that can't be explained." They both examined the desk carefully but couldn't find anything. Mark suggested they turn the desk upside down. Laying a sheet on the floor, they carefully tipped the desk over.

"Did you hear that? It sounded like something inside moved." Mark nodded. Turning the desk right side up, the sound repeated. "It's on my side of the desk." Concentrating on that side of the desk, they found a small panel that lifted out on the inside of the desk. Inside was a small space containing a small cloth bag. Tyler removed the bag and carefully poured the contents onto the desk.

Three pieces of jewelry fell out of the bag: a ring, a brooch, and a matching necklace. They sparkled brightly in the light.

Tyler picked up the brooch and examined it closely. Inscribed on the back of the brooch was Tiffany and Co., New York. "Ty, are those what I think they are?"

Tyler nodded. "They're real diamonds and they're huge. All of the pieces are marked Tiffany and Company. They must be worth a fortune."

"Most of my mother's antiques were family pieces. My grandparents were wealthy. I bet Grandma put these in here for safekeeping at some point. The real question is, did Roger know about them or not? Either way, they're yours, Tyler. You bought them when you bought the desk."

"No, they're yours." Tyler put the pieces back in the bag and handed them to Mark. "I can't keep them. I wouldn't feel right. Besides, they should be part of your Mom's estate."

Mark took the bag. "Okay, I'll add them to the estate. Say, let's ask at the jewelry store down the street, see what they can tell us." Leaving the apartment, they walked to the jewelry store a block away. Tyler knew the manager and asked to speak with him. They showed him the pieces and his eyes went wide. After spending a few minutes looking at them he whistled, "These are incredible. The diamonds are of superior color and quality, the settings are platinum. Judging by their cut, these were probably made in the twenties. I would suggest that you sell them at auction, probably in New York." He just shook his head. "Guys, the diamonds together probably weigh between forty and fifty carats." He took a few minutes to measure the stones. "The diamonds in the ring alone are over ten carats. The brooch has almost fifteen carats, and the necklace is just over twenty carats." He gently put the pieces back in the bag and handed it back to Tyler.

Tyler spoke to Mark as they left the store. "The bank is still open and I have a safe-deposit box there. Let's hurry and get these locked up." They made it to the bank five minutes before closing. They didn't want to let Tyler into the vault, but after speaking with the manager, they let Tyler put the jewelry in his safe-deposit box. Leaving the bank, they both felt relieved. After lunch, they headed back to the apartment to look at the table.

"Mark, there's probably not a hidden compartment in the table. So if there is something special, it must revolve around the table itself. When I first saw the table I knew it wasn't an ordinary piece. The quality of construction, the carving, the intricate inlay...." Tyler abruptly stopped talking.

"What is it?"

"Shit... why didn't I think of it before? There was a company that made fabulous pieces of furniture for people like the Vanderbilts. The firm was called Herter Brothers. I never thought of them because their pieces are really rare, particularly in this part of the country. I wonder if this could be one of their pieces." Tyler continued thinking aloud. "We should go to the downtown library. There are books that include pictures of their pieces."

At the library, they checked out a number of reference books on antique furniture, including a book on Herter Brothers. After leaving the library, Mark suggested that they look at neighborhoods to see where they might want to look at houses. Tyler just smiled. He loved Mark's energy. Driving to the east side of town, they started looking at houses, deciding on the styles of homes they both liked. Tyler was driving and Mark was craning his head as they drove up and down streets. The area they both liked best was just off the park.

"Tyler, look at that house. It's beautiful, and it's for sale." Tyler hit the brakes, abruptly stopping the car. "What's wrong? Don't you like it?"

There was a tear rolling down Tyler's face. "That's my grandmother's house."

"Tyler, you're kidding...." He shook his head. "Um... how would you feel if we bought that house?"

"It would be like a dream come true, but how would you feel about it?" Tyler was looking at Mark with tears running down his cheeks.

"I think the house is beautiful." Mark wiped the tears from Tyler's cheeks.

As they were talking, a realtor was coming down the walk with a clipboard. Tyler parked the car and they got out, approaching her.

"Good afternoon. Are you the agent listing the house?"

"Yes, I'm Mary Jackson." She shook both of their hands. "I just listed the house."

"I know this sounds weird, but would you be willing to show us the house now?" Mary said she would be happy to, and led them up the walk. It was a beautiful Queen Anne style Victorian house, complete with a turret painted a soft yellow with light brown trim. From the outside it was stunning. She started describing some of the features of the house. When she opened the front door, Tyler was flooded with memories. The house looked different. A lot of work had been done to restore it. The carpeting he remembered was gone, revealing the house's beautiful inlaid hardwood floors. The woodwork in the entrance hall was just like he remembered, with the large stained-glass window on the landing. The house had a large living room, dining room, office, and kitchen with intact butler's pantry on the first floor as well as four large bedrooms on the second floor. None of the woodwork in the house had ever been painted. The fireplaces were exquisite. The kitchen and bathrooms had been beautifully remodeled. The realtor was surprised when Tyler immediately went up the back stairs from the kitchen and up to the third floor. Mark followed him closely. There was a lot of storage and two finished rooms that had once been servant's quarters. The realtor followed behind them. "I used to play up here as a child." Turning to the real estate agent, he explained, "My grandmother owned this house." As they headed back down to the main floor, Tyler asked for a few minutes alone in the dining room. The realtor said she'd wait in the car.

"Mark, what do you think?" Tyler was almost vibrating with excitement.

"I think it's gorgeous. I'd love to live here."

"Good. Me too. I can't think of a better use for Grandma's money than to buy this house. Can you?" Mark shook his head. "Call the real estate agent you used to sell your mom's house." Tyler handed Mark his cell phone. Mark had called the agent so often that he knew the number by heart. Tyler studied the data sheet on the house.

"He was in the office and told us to stop by now if we'd like." Mark was getting excited and so was Tyler.

They left the house and thanked the realtor. She smiled and went to lock the house. Tyler drove directly to their realtor's office. Mark introduced Tyler to Scott. "Scott, Mark and I have a house we'd like to make an offer on." Tyler explained the house and handed Scott the data sheet from the other realtor.

Scott was surprised by how fast they wanted to move and suggested that they look at other homes first. Tyler explained his history with the house and Scott immediately understood. Scott wrote up the offer and, when he got to the part about a mortgage, he nearly choked when Tyler told him they would pay cash for the house. "My grandmother left me a lot of money when she died. I'm using some of it to buy the house." Scott completed the offer.

"When do you want a response from the seller?"

"Tell them the offer expires at ten tonight. I don't want to get into a bidding war and I don't want anyone else to see the house if we can help it."

They completed the offer and Mark and Tyler signed it. They shook hands with Scott and left the office. "Mark, I'd say we had a full day. Let's head back to the apartment. I need to relax." Driving back to the apartment, Mark couldn't believe the day they'd had. He'd been offered a firm start to his artistic career, they'd found the jewelry in the desk, and they'd found a house. Not just a house, but one that had meaning for Tyler. When they got to the apartment, Mark grabbed the library books from the backseat.

Shortly after they got into the apartment, Tyler's phone rang. Mark still had the phone and answered.

"Hello."

"Mark, it's Roger. I was wondering if the desk and table made it through the fire and if you'd spoken with Tyler about selling them to me?"

"Yes, they made it through the fire just fine. He has agreed to sell you the desk. He is still deciding about the table." Mark could hear Roger starting to get worked up. "Look, Roger, next week, I'll send you the initial distribution from the estate. I'll call you before then with an answer on the table." Roger started to say something more. "Goodbye, Roger." Mark hung up the phone.

An idea struck him. "Ty, that was my brother. He asked about selling him the desk and table. When I told him you'd sell him the desk he really didn't seem interested. I don't think he knew about the jewelry. I think the desk was a smokescreen. He really wants the table. I told him I'd let him know next week. That will give us time to research it."

Mark slipped his arms around Tyler's waist, pressing his body to his back, nibbling on his ear, and gently rubbing his stomach and chest. "I love you, Ty."

"I love you too."

"Ty, do you think that we'll be able to go on vacation next month like we planned?"

Tyler smiled. "I sure hope so. I'm looking forward to getting away with you. Why?"

"I think I'd like to go to New England for the week. Rhode Island, Connecticut, Massachusetts. What do you think?" Tyler turned to face Mark, kissed him deeply, and slowly moved them toward the bedroom. "I'll take that as a yes." They tumbled onto the bed just as the phone rang.

Tyler answered the phone while Mark opened his pants. "Hello." Tyler tried to keep from laughing as Mark slipped off his pants, tickling his legs.

"Is this Mark and Tyler's?"

"Yes."

"This is Scott Keefer. I'm calling to tell you that your offer on the house has been accepted. They asked if closing could be in mid-September." Mark had removed Tyler's underwear and was licking his cock, tickling the head and shaft with his tongue. Tyler tried not to moan into the phone.

"Sure. That's not a problem. Can you arrange for the inspection?" Mark had now taken Tyler to the root and was sucking him like a vacuum cleaner.

"Absolutely. They also need a check for the earnest money." Tyler could barely breathe as Mark used his lips to gently pull and suck his foreskin.

"Okay. We'll drop by with a check tomorrow and we can work through any other details." Still sucking Tyler's cock, Mark was now lifting his legs, and Tyler needed desperately to get off the phone.

"You'll also need to sign the updated offer with the new closing date." Mark had spread Tyler's legs wide, using his tongue to tease his opening as he inserted two fingers deep inside.

"We'll do that when we see you tomorrow." Mark rubbed his fingers over Tyler's gland, sending jolts of pleasure up his spine.

"All right. See you tomorrow." Tyler could barely talk as a tingling sensation ran through his body.

"Bye, Scott." Tyler hung up the phone and moaned loudly. "Oh god, Mark, you almost killed me…. Oh god…." Tyler still had his shirt on and Mark was still fully clothed. Tyler removed his shirt, while Mark continued to work his opening with his tongue and fingers, trying to undress at the same time. Mark managed to get his pants off and his cock lubed before pressing into Tyler and fucking him with complete abandon.

Tyler groaned, moaned, and whimpered as Mark pounded his huge cock into him again and again. "Mark, that's so good. Oh god." Watching Mark fuck him with his shirt still on drove Tyler wild with desire. "You look so hot, so sexy." Soon Tyler was coming, shooting all over himself.

Mark came soon after Tyler, emptying his balls deep inside Tyler. Finally, Mark removed his shirt as he withdrew.

"I take it we got the house?" was all he could say, smiling broadly. Tyler nodded as Mark curled up next to him.

Cuddling turned to utter relaxation. "Mark, I think we should get cleaned up before we stick together."

After showering, they spent the evening making dinner and talking about the house, vacation, and their future.

Chapter 15

THE following Friday was a beautiful day in mid-August. The house purchase was moving along smoothly, the sale of Mark's mother's house had been completed, and checks for Amy and Roger were ready to be sent. Mark was sitting in the kitchen of the temporary apartment while Tyler was in the shower getting cleaned up.

Mark called Amy first. "Amy, it's Mark."

"Hi, Marky. How are you?" He told Amy about the house and Tyler's plans for the store. She was thrilled.

"I'm sending you a check as the initial distribution from the estate. I also have some really good news. We found a secret compartment in Mom's desk. It contained three pieces of jewelry. Very expensive jewelry. Tyler could have kept it— he did buy the desk—but he gave it all back to me. I've decided to sell it at auction and add it to the estate. So there will be more to come later."

"Marky, why don't you divide the proceeds four ways? Tyler deserves a share for his generosity." Mark was surprised, but then Amy always was generous.

"Thank you." Mark beamed into the phone. "I'll tell Tyler."

Mark walked into the bedroom as Tyler was coming out of the bathroom. "I spoke to Amy and we agreed that we're going to split the proceeds of the jewelry sale four ways, with you getting a share as well. Before you argue, it was Amy's idea." Tyler smiled broadly.

"That's very nice of both of you." Tyler hugged Mark kissing him gently. "But not necessary." Mark ignored Tyler's last comment; it was necessary and the right thing to do.

"Tyler, could we visit Aunt Phyllis this afternoon? I promised her we would, and she specifically asked me to bring you."

"Absolutely, I'd like to meet her." Tyler was curious about the aunt who had changed her tune so completely.

"Great. Thank you." Mark's mood changed and he huffed to himself, "Now I have to call Roger, then we need to complete researching the table." Tyler looked a little disappointed. "You'll get yours a little later; don't worry." Mark kissed Tyler sweetly and went to call Roger.

"Roger, it's Mark. I'm calling to let you know that the check for the initial distribution is being sent today." Mark told him the amount and about the jewelry. He also told him how the proceeds were being split. "Roger, Tyler gave the jewelry to me. I am sharing the proceeds with you and Amy. Besides, including Tyler was Amy's idea, not mine."

"Fine. What about the table and desk? Will he sell them to me?"

"Tyler will sell you the desk, but we've decided to keep the table for our house. We both like it and we've decided to keep it." Roger was starting to get angry and Mark just let him sputter for a while. "Do you still want the desk?"

"Yes!" He was still huffy.

"Fine. You can pick it up at the store on Monday at four. I'll meet you at the back door."

"All right!" Roger hung up the phone without another word. Mark could tell he was really angry, but he just didn't care.

"Ty, we really need to determine if there is something about this table." They spent the next hour looking through books. Mark picked up a book about Herter Brothers furniture and started to look at the pictures to see if anything pictured looked similar to the table. As he leafed through the book, he was enthralled by the artistry of the furniture. Checking the cover again, Mark mumbled half to himself, "I've seen this book before. Oh god, at Roger's. He had a copy on his coffee table." Tyler became very interested and started looking over Mark's shoulder as he leafed through the book. "I haven't seen other pieces like our table, but it's of the same quality as the ones in this book." Mark continued to leaf through the book until he got to one of the room pictures. Tyler and Mark saw it at the same time.

"Oh my god, it can't be," was all Tyler could say. The more they looked at the picture, the more they realized that the table they had was the same one pictured in the book. Not only was the table made by Herter Brothers, but it was used by them when they decorated the Red Room of the White House. Tyler whistled.

"Ty, I don't get it. How can this be our table?"

"Furniture from the White House was regularly sold off whenever a room was being redecorated by one of the first ladies. It looks like the table was purchased by your grandparents." Tyler continued to stare at the picture and compare the details pictured to the table. "Mark, this is a find of major importance. This will be worth a fortune at auction."

Mark looked up at Tyler. "I don't care. I'd like to keep it and use it in our home."

Tyler just nodded. "If you'd like. It'll make a great conversation piece."

Mark started to laugh. "I'm glad I told Roger you didn't want to sell it. By the way, he still wants the desk. Please give me a price and I'll need to meet Roger at the store on Monday so he can pick it up."

"Okay, but you're not going to be alone with him. I'll go with you."

"At least with you there he'll be less likely to try something." The kiss was promising, but Mark still had things to do. "I'm going to call Aunt Phyllis and let her know we'll stop by this afternoon." Tyler put his hand on his back, massaging the indentation above his butt and gently nibbling Mark's ear. He could feel the tension from the conversation with Roger start to leave Mark's body.

AUNT PHYLLIS lived in the same suburb where Mark had grown up. When Mark called her she invited them to lunch. As they walked up to her front door, Tyler gently placed his hand on Mark's back. "It's going to be fine; don't worry." Mark nodded and rang the bell. Aunt Phyllis answered the door. She looked to be about seventy, with hair that was almost white. She was quite striking, and Tyler could tell that in her youth she had been quite a beauty. Even though she walked with a cane, she still stood as straight and tall as she could. There was a certain dignity about her. "Please come in." As he entered, she gave Mark a hug, shook Tyler's hand, and directed them into her living room. The house was impeccably clean, tidy, and uncluttered. She had put snacks on the table and had a pot of tea ready as well.

After pouring tea, Phyllis said, "Mark, I want to apologize again for jumping to conclusions. I shouldn't have."

Mark smiled and took the offered cup of tea. "Thank you." He released the breath he had been holding. "It has been a hard few months and unfortunately Roger hasn't made them any easier."

"Amy told me some of the things he did when I spoke with her on the phone, and she also told me about the fire." Taking a sip from her tea and looking at Tyler, she asked, "Did you lose much?"

"Luckily, no. Most of the damaged pieces in the shop can be restored. There were a few pieces what were damaged beyond repair, but things are replaceable." He looked over at Mark and smiled.

"Mark, would you be a dear? In the cellar, there's some homemade raspberry jam. Would you please bring up two jars? I have trouble getting down those stairs." Mark smiled, got up, and went to the cellar. With Mark gone, she continued. "Tyler, I have a few questions for you. Please forgive me but I tend to be forward. Do you love him?"

Tyler smiled brightly. "More than I ever thought possible."

Phyllis smiled. "I thought so. I'm very pleased that Mark's happy. He hasn't been for quite some time." Mark rejoined them in the living room. "I was just about to tell Tyler that I admire your courage in telling your family the truth. I regret that I didn't say something to you earlier." Mark looked confused, but Phyllis just reached across the table and took his hand. "Mark, I've know for a long time that you weren't interested in girls and I didn't care then and I don't care now. What I do care about is that you're happy."

There were tears in Mark's eyes. "You knew?"

Nodding her head, she revealed, "I've known for a long time. Lately, with what happened, I've regretted not saying something to you earlier. It might have made things easier for you."

"It wouldn't have changed things with Mom." There was sadness in his voice. Tyler gently squeezed his hand.

"Mark, I spoke to your mother two days before she passed away. She regretted reacting the way she did. I'm just sorry she didn't act on those regrets before she died. She did love you." Using her cane to stand up, she said, "Now, I think it's time for lunch." The lunch was wonderful and they spent the rest of the afternoon with Aunt Phyllis. Mark felt free of a lot of his regrets and he was happy that his aunt really seemed to like Tyler.

Late in the afternoon, after being shown around the house and garden, they said goodbye at the front door. Phyllis hugged and kissed Mark, hugged Tyler as well, and asked them to please stop by again. Mark couldn't help smiling. On their way home, they stopped by the post office to mail the checks for Amy and Roger.

After dropping the checks in a mailbox, Tyler said, "Mark, let's go home. I have a surprise for you."

"Is this it…?" Mark asked, reaching across the seat to stroke the bulge in Tyler's pants.

"You'll see after dinner." He felt the leer from Tyler travel down his spine, and his body reacted forcefully. Tyler noticed Mark's reaction. "If you're good."

"What if I'm bad?" The leer was back again and Mark's butt was beginning to twitch. "Oooh, I win either way."

Tyler cooked a late dinner, and while Mark was cleaning up Tyler went to the bedroom, whispering, "Join me when you're done." Mark finished the dishes in record time. The sight that awaited him in the bedroom took his breath away. Tyler was lying on the bed wearing nothing but a black jockstrap, his skin glistening. "You like?" All Mark could do was nod and start shedding his own clothes. By the time he reached the bed, his shirt was off and his pants were around his ankles. Stepping out of his pants, Mark sat on the bed, his hands caressing Tyler's stomach and chest.

"Your skin feels so smooth, so hot." Mark's touch was like a branding iron, sending hot sparks through Tyler's body, moving from his chest, cupping the pouch of the jock, and gently stroking the contents. Mark whispered, "Is this my surprise?" as he pressed his lips to Tyler's, feeling a tongue press into his mouth in return. The kiss sent shockwaves through Mark as Tyler pulled him onto his body, caressing his back and wrapping his legs around his hips. The kisses were savored, the taste enjoyed, the desire building.

Standing over Tyler, Mark removed his underwear, freeing his cock. Bending forward, Tyler engulfed Mark's cock with his mouth, taking the entire length into him. Mark started to moan and gently buck into Tyler's mouth. Mark pulled out. "Too soon," was all he could manage between breaths. Lying back down, Mark nuzzled the contents of Tyler's jockstrap, teasing the balls. "Want me to fuck you with the jock on?" Mark's voice was deep with need as he inserted a finger into Tyler.

"Oh god…." The finger felt so good. "You could, but you'd miss your surprise." Tyler's voice was scratchy and deep with desire. Removing his finger, Mark removed the jock with a pull.

"Oh, that is so hot!" Mark's breath caught as he saw that Tyler was completely shaved and at the base of his erection was a large heavy silver ring. "That is so sexy," Mark breathed as he took the head into his mouth, feeling Tyler's heartbeat pulsing through his cock. Taking more of the cock, he worked his hands down Tyler's cleft to his opening, whimpering around his cock as he realized that was shaved smooth as well. "God, you shaved your ass as well. How did you know I've fantasized about this?"

Tyler could only groan. He was swallowed again and the finger reentered him. The finger was soon replaced with two, opening him, working into him, spreading him, sliding along his prostate over and over. "Mark, I need you. Need you bad." Mark added a third finger as he brought his mouth to Tyler's, fucking it with his tongue. Tyler was thrashing on the bed, gripping the sheets with his fists. Tyler cried out, "I want you now! Fast! Hard!" After lubing himself, Mark lifted Tyler's legs high, positioning his legs on his shoulders. Then Mark slowly entered Tyler, spreading him with his long, fat cock.

Tyler thought he was going to split in two as Mark entered him. The pressure of Mark's cock filling him, buried inside him, felt as though they were joined at the soul. Mark started to move almost immediately and ride Tyler's ass for all he was worth, the deep, thrusting strokes hitting the sweet spot over and over. "Oh… Mark… right… there… oh yeah!" Without warning, Mark pulled out, lying flat on the bed. Tyler immediately rolled over and straddled Mark's hips and plunged his ass onto Mark's cock, bouncing onto him, fucking himself. With each bounce, Mark thrust his hips up into Tyler, making Tyler's cock bounce against his stomach. "Mark, god, I love the way your cock fills me. Love the way you love me."

Tyler was stroking his cock as he pounded his ass onto Mark's hips. Mark replaced Tyler's hand with his as he pulled and stroked, pinching a nipple with the other hand. The sensation was too much and Tyler came, still pounding onto Mark's cock. With a huge thrust, lifting Tyler off the bed, Mark gushed his climax into Tyler's body.

It took a while before either of them could speak. "Shower, Ty," was all Mark could mutter.

After a long, hot shower, they crawled back into bed, Tyler wrapping himself around Mark. "Good night, Mark. I love you."

"Night, Ty. Love you more."

Chapter 16

TYLER spent most of Monday meeting with the architect and contractors to finalize plans for the store remodel. Mark was holed up in his studio working on a number of paintings. He had decided to include as many portraits in his show as possible and he currently had three in progress. The commissioned portraits of Tom and Bill had been completed and were being stored at Peter's until Tom was ready to take delivery. One of the portraits he was working on was of his Aunt Phyllis as she might have looked in her youth. When Mark told her about the portrait, she was thrilled and pronounced, "You'll make me immortal." The other two pieces in progress were portraits of Tyler. One was just a face, but the other was a full nude. They would be shown as a series with the portrait he had already completed, but he wasn't sure if he'd allow them to be sold.

Just before four, Tyler poked his head into Mark's studio. "The architect and contractor need to check in the basement. If you need me, yell, and I'll be right up. I shouldn't be long." Mark nodded. Tyler heard the back doorbell ring while they were heading down the stairs. He didn't like Mark being alone with Roger. After showing the architect and contractor where things were, he headed up the apartment. At the bottom of the stairs, he heard what sounded like a slap and then footsteps. Mark came down the stairs, followed by Roger.

"What hap…?" Tyler stopped in mid-word as he saw Mark tumble down the last six stairs, hitting his head on the railing and landing in a heap at the bottom of the stairs. Tyler wasn't sure if Mark had slipped or if Roger had pushed him. Racing to Mark, he knelt next to him, calling his name. He wasn't responding. Tyler checked for a pulse; there was one, thank god.

Looking at Roger, Tyler growled, "Did you slap him?" Roger just looked at Tyler without nodding or saying anything. Tyler stepped to Roger, slapping him with all his might across the face. "You ever hit him again and I'll rip your fucking balls off." Roger stepped over Mark and left. The contractor and architect came up from the basement. Tyler looked at them and shouted, "Call nine-one-one!" Tyler just held Mark's hand and waited. The architect found a furniture pad and used it as a blanket to keep Mark warm. The contractor directed the ambulance and EMTs to where Mark was lying.

The EMTs were very efficient. One worked on Mark, while the other asked all of the appropriate questions. They quickly had Mark on his way to the hospital. Tyler followed them. The architect and contractor said they'd make sure the building was secure. They both told Tyler to call them if there was anything they could do. Jumping in his car, Tyler sped to the hospital, arriving in the emergency room.

Tyler said to the nurse on duty, "I'm with Mark Burke. They just brought him in."

The nurse was very polite. "Yes, the head injury. The doctor is with him now. I'll have the doctor see you when he's finished."

Tyler sat in the waiting room and called Amy. He told her some of what happened, leaving out his suspicions about Roger. Amy said that she'd be right there. He called friends and let them know what had happened. He also called Aunt Phyllis. By the time he had finished, Amy had arrived.

"How is he? Have they told you anything?" she asked as she hugged Tyler.

"Not yet. They told me the doctor was examining him and would be out soon to let us know how he is." Tyler was sobbing into her shoulder. "He wasn't conscious when they put him in the ambulance." He was able to pull himself together and they sat in the waiting area.

About an hour later, a doctor came to speak to them. "Are you Mr. Burke's family?"

Before Tyler could say anything Amy spoke up, "Yes, we are. I'm his sister and this is his boyfriend." The doctor looked at Amy and started to explain. Amy held up her hand and corrected him, "Doctor, you speak with Tyler. He makes the decisions for Mark, not me." The doctor was a little surprised, but continued, "I've examined Mr. Burke and we believe he has a concussion. He has been taken down to radiology for a CAT scan. He hasn't yet regained consciousness, but we're hopeful he will soon. Once he comes back from radiology, he will be moved to the ICU, where you'll be able to see him."

"What's his prognosis?" Tyler could barely get the words out.

"We don't know. We will know more after the CAT scan. Once we have the results, I'll let you know. I hope it won't be too long." After telling them he'd keep them informed, he was gone.

Tyler just sank into a chair. All he could think was that he needed to keep it together for Mark. Amy went to get some coffee for them. When she returned, Tyler thanked her for the coffee, but didn't drink any; he just held the cup in his hands. "Tyler, he'll be all right. He's strong."

"Amy, I'm just scared. I looked for him for a very long time and…." He couldn't bring himself to finish the thought. "If anything happens to him, I don't know what I'll do."

The doctor eventually reappeared. "We got the results of the CAT scan and the injury doesn't appear to be too severe. Our biggest concern right now is that he hasn't regained consciousness. He's being moved to ICU now. Once he's settled, they'll let you see him."

"Thank you, doctor," was all Tyler could manage, and Amy led him to the intensive care unit. Once there, they were told it would be a few minutes. They sat down to wait again. "Amy, I have to tell you something. Today, Roger was at the store to meet Mark. While they were up in the apartment, he hit Mark, and as they were coming down the stairs Mark fell. I can't tell you if Roger pushed him or not, but he was right behind him." Amy's face registered horror. "I need you to speak with Roger, because when I found out he had hit Mark, I slapped him so hard I left a handprint on his face." Amy actually laughed.

"Good. He's deserved that for a long time. I'll talk to him, but I don't want to believe he'd push him." Amy was very concerned.

Tyler inhaled deeply. "To tell you the truth, I really don't want to believe it either." His voice trailed off as he saw a nurse approaching them.

"I'll take you back to see Mr. Burke," she said. They followed the nurse back to Mark's bed. He was attached to a lot of monitors. Except for a bump on his head, he looked fine. "Please be as quiet as possible." She then went back to her station.

Tyler gently took Mark's hand and started to speak to him. His words were soft, loving, and full of emotion. Amy stepped out for a few minutes because she felt as though she were intruding. Tyler held Mark's hand to his face, tears running down his cheeks. Amy rejoined him, putting her hand on his shoulder as the tears continued to flow. Mark's eyes were closed and he was connected to numerous instruments, which beeped softly. His breathing seemed regular and there was no IV or oxygen.

Tyler closed his eyes, willing Mark to wake up. Tears squeezed under his closed eyelids, running down his face. Tyler slowly leaned forward and kissed Mark very gently. "I love you."

"I love you too." The words were very soft, but he heard them. His heart leapt as he realized that Mark was regaining consciousness. Amy went to get the nurse. When the nurse joined them, Mark's eyes started to flutter. "Ty."

"Yes, Mark, I'm here." Tyler was still holding his hand and he could feel Mark squeezing it back.

"Where am I?"

"You're in the hospital. You fell on the stairs." Tyler was so relieved he could barely stand. The nurse had left and called the doctor, who joined them after a few minutes.

"Mark, can you hear me? I'm Dr. Phillips."

"Yes, I can hear you."

After a brief examination, the doctor turned to Tyler and Amy. "I think he'll be fine now. We'll keep him for a few days at least.

Tomorrow, we'll probably move him to a regular room. He'll be groggy for a while. I suggest you go home and get some rest."

"Tyler, don't leave." Mark moved his hand slightly and Tyler caressed it gently.

"I'm here." He held his hand to his cheek. "Amy, why don't you go home and I'll call you later." Amy kissed Mark goodbye and headed home. Tyler sat by Mark's bed for a while, holding his hand. Soon the nurse came in and said that she was giving Mark something that would make him sleep. "I'll see you first thing in the morning," Tyler said, kissing him gently on the lips.

As Mark drifted to sleep, Tyler left and headed to the store. Everything had been locked up properly, so he headed to East Side Terrace. He got a quick dinner, cleaned up, and collapsed into bed, sleeping poorly and waking often during the night.

In the morning, he cleaned up and headed to the hospital. When he got to ICU, they told him that Mark was being moved to a private room. The nurse took him back and he walked with Mark as they moved him. Once he was settled in his room, they brought him a small breakfast. Mark ate what he could and pushed the rest aside.

"Mark, what happened?"

Mark looked confused. "What do you mean? I tripped on the stairs. I was going too fast trying to get away from Roger after he slapped me."

"Mark, did Roger push you?"

Mark shook his head. "No." Tyler was relieved. "But he did slap me in the apartment when I told him he couldn't buy the table and to stop asking because we would never sell it to him."

"I heard the slap. After you fell, I asked Roger if he hit you, then I slapped him hard and told him if he ever hit you again I'd rip his fucking balls off!"

Mark laughed. "You didn't." Tyler nodded. Mark laughed again. "Don't do that; it hurts."

Tyler's eyes got wide and his tone serious. "I most certainly did and I meant it too. If I ever see him again in the store or around our home, I'll call the police." Tyler grinned mischievously. "After I rip his balls off, of course." Tyler got very serious. "You gave me a real scare. I thought I'd lost you."

"I know." The doctor and a nurse came in before they could say any more.

"Well, Mark, it looks like you'll be fine. All your vital signs have returned to normal. I'd like to see if you are able to walk." He helped Mark out of bed. Mark took a few steps and slowly walked around the room. "Excellent. There don't seem to be any lasting effects. We'll keep you here for a few days just to make sure."

"Thank you, doctor." Tyler was relieved that Mark soon would be home with him. He started to make calls, letting people know that Mark was all right. Everyone was relieved. Tyler even called Roger and let him know Mark was going to be okay.

Roger threatened, "I have a mind to report you to the police."

"You can do that, but Mark and I will press charges for you hitting him, sending threatening notes, and harassment, so I suggest you leave well enough alone. By the way, Roger, Mark and I will never sell you any of the items from your mother's. You may as well forget it." Tyler then hung up the phone. "Stupid bastard actually threatened to report me to the police for hitting him." They both laughed. "I am so relieved you're feeling better. Is there anything you need?" Mark asked for a few magazines and things to help pass the time. "I have to meet with the architect and contractor today, but I'll be back this afternoon." Tyler kissed Mark and left the hospital relieved and grateful.

The meeting with the contractor and architect had been tiring and exhausting, but productive. Tyler's mind had been at the hospital with Mark and he found it very difficult to concentrate. He stepped into the hospital lobby and headed for the elevator. As he passed the gift shop, he stepped inside to get some flowers to brighten Mark's room. The case had many arrangements, but Tyler's attention was drawn to a huge bouquet of deep red roses.

"May I help you?" the clerk behind the counter asked politely.

"I'd like the large…." Tyler's voice trailed off as a woman about sixty-five or so gazed into the window of the shop. Tyler watched her look around and then turn and head down the hall.

"Are you all right? You look like you've seen a ghost."

"I did." Tyler blinked a few times to get his mind back on track. "I'd like the large arrangement of red roses." The sales clerk smiled and helped Tyler with the purchase.

Mark was asleep when Tyler stepped through the door. Tyler set the vase of roses on Mark's bedside table and quietly sat in the chair next to the bed. His mind was whirling.

"Have you been here long?" Mark's green eyes were shining.

"No, I just got here." Tyler leaned to Mark, brushing his lips with a gentle kiss.

Mark's hand gently rested on the back of Tyler's head as he pulled him into a deeper kiss. "Thank you for the flowers. They're beautiful."

Tyler smiled and sat back in the chair. "You're welcome, love." A nurse came into the room and took Mark's temperature and pulse, and checked the monitors. "You're doing good, honey. The doctor should be in soon." Her gaze turned to the huge vase of roses. "Is this him?" Mark nodded and the nurse shook her head. "Damn, all the good ones are married or gay." She smiled as she left the room.

Mark turned to Tyler. "Ty, you're a million miles away. What's wrong? Is there a problem at the store?"

Tyler's fingers threaded through Mark's. "No. I saw my mother as I was buying the flowers." Tyler felt Mark's hand in his as a torrent of long-suppressed emotions flooded through him. "I thought I was over this."

"Ty, when was the last time you saw her?"

Tyler shook his head. "I don't know if I've seen her since I told my parents I was gay."

Dr. Phillips entered the room, pulling Tyler back to the present and giving him something else to occupy his mind. The doctor checked Mark's chart and looked into his eyes. "You're doing well but I'm going to keep you a few more days for observation. I want to make sure there are no residual effects." After saying goodbye, he headed down the hall to continue his rounds.

Tyler was able to bring Mark home a few days later. The doctor had said that Mark needed to take it easy for a few days, but he was going stir crazy after lying in the hospital and lying around the apartment. Mark was finally able to convince Tyler to let him go to the studio to work for a few hours; however, he had to keep the door closed because the remodel of the store had started and there was some noise. Sitting in his studio, he was enjoying being able to work again. Tyler was working to repair some of the pieces that had been damaged in the fire.

Mark was sitting at his easel when Tyler quietly entered the studio and pushed the door closed. He walked to Mark, cupped his head in his hands, and kissed him deeply. Mark moaned into Tyler's mouth, "It's been too long. I've missed you badly."

"The doctor said you have to take it easy, but I thought you could use a treat." Tyler opened the fly of Mark's pants and pulled out Mark's already hard cock. Slowly, Tyler bent down, licking the head and shaft. "Ty, I've missed this, missed you." Mark threw his head back, giving in to the sensations.

Taking the head in his mouth, he sucked and licked the underside until Mark was moaning loudly and begging for more. Tyler slowly took the shaft into his mouth and down his throat.

"Damn, you are so good at that," Mark whimpered between breaths as he tried to keep from slipping off the stool. Tyler kept working Mark's cock and he could tell that Mark wasn't going to last much longer; his need was too great. Mark started bucking into Tyler's mouth. With one final thrust, Mark buried his cock down Tyler's throat as he came. Tyler swallowed it all, cleaning Mark's cock before releasing it. Tyler brought his mouth to Mark's, kissing him deeply. Mark loved Tyler's kisses, especially when he could still taste himself on Tyler's tongue, and today was no exception.

While they kissed, Mark opened the front of Tyler's pants, pushing them to his ankles before lowering himself to his knees and swallowing Tyler to the hilt before using his hands and mouth to work the entire length. "Your mouth is magic." Tyler's legs were quivering and soon he was bucking into Mark's mouth before shooting directly down Mark's throat. Tyler helped Mark back to his stool before getting them both cleaned up and their clothes adjusted. Leaning to Mark, Tyler kissed him warmly. "I love you, Mark."

"I love you too." Mark looked at his easel and was relieved to see that he had been working on the portrait of Aunt Phyllis rather than either of the portraits of Tyler. He wanted those to be a surprise. "Tyler, I've worked long enough. Let's go home."

When they got home, Tyler settled Mark on the sofa, cuddling next to him. "While you're here, we should plan our vacation. There are two auctions that I'd like to attend, one in Rhode Island and one in Massachusetts, so I thought we could take the truck, attend the first auction, and then go on to Newport, Rhode Island, for a few days. Tour the mansions, go sailing, and enjoy the beach. Then we could head to Massachusetts for the second auction and then go camping for a few days near Plymouth. What do you think?"

Mark was a little surprised. "Camping?"

Tyler nuzzled Mark's neck. "Yeah, camping in a tent, cooking out, one large sleeping bag…." He whispered into Mark's ear, "Sex in the outdoors."

Mark was sold. "Okay. Camping it is."

"Great. I'll make the arrangements. You rest for a while." After kissing Mark, he went to make reservations for their vacation. When he was finished, Mark was awake and restless. "Mark, I have an idea for a painting. I'd like you to do a self-portrait."

Mark looked skeptical, but Tyler persisted. "Please come with me." He led Mark into the bedroom and had him stand in front of a full-length mirror. "Look at yourself in the mirror. Pay particular attention to your face." Mark complied, and then Tyler came up behind him and gently kissed his neck as he wrapped his arms around his waist. "Look in the mirror," he said quietly. Mark was surprised; the expression on his face was pure love. He glowed when he looked at Tyler. It was the same expression he'd captured in his portraits of Tyler. "I want you to paint that expression." Tyler gently nuzzled and kissed Mark in front of the mirror. Gently, Tyler guided Mark toward the bed.

Their lovemaking was slow, gentle, and sensual, their hands exploring, their tongues and mouths tasting, licking, nibbling. Tyler slipped into Mark, his movements slow, spreading, completing, and joining them together. Strokes long and slow, alternately emptying and filling, again and again; the kisses hot, wet, and longing, with hands caressing, touching, stroking. The need to touch, to be touched again, was overpowering, the joy of being in each other's arms enrapturing. Pressure built in both as they climaxed while whispering, moaning, and whimpering words of passion, joy, and love.

Chapter 17

THE closing on their house would be the week they returned from their vacation. Mark had quickly recovered from his injury, much to Tyler's relief. The remodeling of the store was progressing well. Tyler had finalized the details prior to their leaving, and any questions were to be directed to the architect. Mark had decided to equip two art studios: his main studio would be at the store, with a smaller studio on the third floor of the house.

Tyler was especially pleased that all their plans were coming together. They were currently in the truck, about an hour from their hotel in Providence. It had been a long drive. The truck had been packed the day before. Tyler had even managed to slip in a few surprises for Mark. They had packed relatively light: just their suitcases, some art supplies for Mark, and their camping gear. They both knew they'd need the extra space for items purchased at the auctions. They had left very early in the morning and had driven straight through, taking turns at the wheel. Mark was currently asleep, his hand on Tyler's leg.

It was nearly ten when they arrived at the hotel. As they were checking in, the desk clerk told them that the pool area was open until eleven. Quickly, they unloaded their luggage in the room, changed into their bathing suits, and headed to the pool area. Tyler was wearing a blue square-cut suit, while Mark wore a red patterned square-cut. The pool was a little cold, but the whirlpool was hot and soothing. They were the only people in the pool area, so they settled next to each other in the whirlpool, relaxing their bodies together.

"The auction starts at ten, with the preview starting at eight. If we get there by nine we should be fine." Tyler felt a hand on his leg, warm and comfortable.

"Good. That should give us time to rest and recover from our little cross-country marathon." Tyler kissed Mark gently. They were both very relaxed. "We'd better get out and head back to the room before we fall asleep." Getting out of the whirlpool, they padded back to their room, got ready for bed, and quickly fell asleep in each other's arms.

The following morning, after a quick breakfast at the hotel, they headed to the auction. Mark had never been to an auction and seemed fascinated. After looking at the items being sold, he gave Tyler a list of paintings and sculptures for possible purchase and the amount he should pay for each one.

"Tyler, the first item on the list I really want for the house." Mark pointed out the piece to Tyler.

"Okay, we'll see how the auction goes. Auctions can be very unpredictable." As the auction was about to start, they took their places and waited for each of their items to come up. Tyler had a number of items he was interested in, but he knew he wouldn't get them all. When the first item was about to come up, he handed Mark his paddle, gave him the limit on the item, and had him bid. Mark had a blast placing the bids and Tyler was thrilled because Mark got most of the items at really good prices. The last item they wanted was the sculpture Mark had pointed out for their house. "Mark, you bid on this one. I'm not going to give you a limit. Just ask yourself how much you'd pay for it if you saw it in Peter's gallery. Use that number as your limit." Mark smiled and nodded. As the item came up for bids, Mark started to get excited; he had a limit set in his mind. When the item was called, he decided to wait to bid. Mark kept his cool as the bidding started to climb: one thousand, fifteen hundred, two thousand dollars. The auctioneer was calling for last bids when Mark raised his paddle. There were no more bids and Mark had the sculpture. "Damn, Mark, that was good. You get to bid from now on. You have great luck."

Mark smiled. "I have good luck in other things as well." The smile was tinged with lust. Tyler paid for their purchases as Mark went to the truck to get packing material. "It looks like we did really well." They carefully packed each of their purchases, made sure all business was completed, and headed to Newport, about an hour away.

After checking into their hotel, Tyler and Mark drove into downtown Newport, a small beach and sailing community with expensive homes, beautiful boats, and cute shops. They wandered through town looking at the shops and the water, savoring the company, and just enjoying the wonderful September air. As the sun started to set, Tyler drove them to the start of the cliff walk. The cliff walk winds above the bay on the east side of the island, passing behind some of the grand houses. Walking together along the path, Mark was enthralled by the view. As they approached The Breakers, a huge summer mansion built by the Vanderbilts, they could hear the water breaking on the rocks. Taking in the view across the lawn to the mansion, Mark was awestruck by the beauty. "I brought my art supplies, but I wish I'd brought an easel."

Taking Mark's hand, Tyler smiled. "When we get back, look behind the seat in the truck."

"What did you do?" Mark was looking hopeful.

"As a surprise, Peter was able to find an antique portable easel. I packed it behind the seat. I don't know what they're called here, but the English call them an artist's donkey."

Mark was thrilled. "Would it be okay if I got my art supplies?"

"Well, the light will start to fade soon. We can come back tomorrow and plan it so you have more time." Mark was agreeable, throwing his arms around Tyler's neck. The other people on the cliff walk looked on a little sheepishly, but said nothing. They stayed for a few minutes, watching as the light played on the houses across the bay. After walking back to the truck, Tyler took a detour back into town, parking near the marina. "Let's walk a minute." Mark accompanied him as they walked, Tyler obviously preoccupied. Along the wharf was a booth offering sailing cruises. Tyler booked them on a two-hour sunset cruise the following evening.

"That sounds wonderful!" exclaimed Mark. They agreed to get some dinner and then head back to the hotel.

In the room, Tyler looked a little wolfish. "I have another surprise for you." Reaching into his suitcase, Tyler pulled out a set of long leather loops. Mark looked confused. "They're padded wrist restraints. Do you want to tie me to the bed?"

The look on Mark's face was almost pure delight. "That's so sexy. I'd love to do that, but only if you'll tie me up later." Tyler stripped to his underwear and Mark restrained his hands, making sure they weren't too tight. Standing at the foot of the bed, Mark slowly removed his clothes, performing a striptease for Tyler. "You like what you see?"

"Oh yeah!" Tyler whispered as Mark removed his shirt.

"You want to see more?" Mark slowly removed his pants.

"Oh yes! More everything!" The underwear went next. Mark stroked himself, making himself hard.

Tyler was entranced as Mark pinched his nipples and ran his hands through the hair on his chest. "You want some of this?" Mark knew he was driving Tyler wild.

"Yeah, I want that, want you." Mark continued teasing, rocking his hips slightly, making his weighty cock bob up and down, rock back and forth.

Mark bent over, giving Tyler a full view of his ass. "You like that?" Mark slipped a finger into his butt.

"Oh god, yes." Mark added a second finger, spreading his legs wide so Tyler had a good view.

"You want it?" Mark was fucking himself with his fingers, driving Tyler insane.

"Yes, I want you." Tyler tried to reach Mark, forgetting about the restraints.

Slowly he turned around and started stroking his cock again. With the sight of Mark, hard and ready, Tyler's legs seemed to open of their own free will. Tyler was painfully hard, begging for release. "Mark, hurry please. I need you." His voice was deep and raspy.

Mark picked up the bottle of lube and Tyler started to lift his legs, but instead Mark lubed Tyler's cock, working his hands along the entire length. Tyler's breathing became ragged, his voice needy, begging and pleading. Straddling his hips, Mark plunged himself onto Tyler. "You like that?"

"Uh-huh." Tyler could barely think he was so crazed with passion and lust.

Tyler bucked as Mark bounced; the sensation of being at Mark's mercy was incredible. "Mark, you feel so good!" Tyler's breathing was becoming heavier. "More, oh god!" Mark picked up the pace as he fucked himself on Tyler, stroking his cock. The bed started to move as Mark bounced harder and faster. Mark came in waves, shooting on Tyler's chest. Tyler bucked and sent streams of cum pouring deep into Mark.

Mark released Tyler from the restraints, cleaned him with a towel, and curled up next to him on the bed. "Ty, that was incredible." All Tyler could do was nod.

When they could move again, they changed into their bathing suits and headed to the whirlpool. The hot water was relaxing and soothing on their satiated bodies. Soon they were nodding off in the warm, swirling water. Heading back to their room, they climbed into bed early.

They spent the next morning touring the large summer mansions, The Breakers, Marble House, and the Elms. The homes were spectacular and Mark especially enjoyed all the artwork incorporated into the houses. After lunch, they took Mark's art supplies and easel to the cliff walk. Mark spent much of the afternoon quietly painting as Tyler sat in the shade reading. He must have fallen asleep, because Mark was gently rubbing his shoulder. "Tyler, I'm ready to head back." On his easel was a beautiful painting of the bay. All of the houses were gone, leaving only the pristine forests, beach, water, and sky. A large sailboat was the only indication of man's presence.

"It's beautiful." Tyler could never understand how Mark could do that: take a scene in front of him and remove what he didn't want to create beauty. Packing up Mark's supplies, they headed back to the truck so they could get dinner before their evening sail.

The boat was beautiful, seventy feet long, with two masts. The captain told them it was big enough for fifty people, but there were only about sixteen passengers that evening. The boat sliced smoothly through the water once the sails were raised and the crew had them set. In the middle of the bay, the view was beautiful. The sun was setting, casting warm tones on the water. Tyler took Mark's hand as they sat in the front of the boat.

He reached into his pocket and pulled out a gold band. "Mark, will you spend the rest of your life with me? Share my home? In short, Mark, will you be my husband?"

The question shocked Mark. He'd never thought he'd have this; not after his mother's rejection, not even after first meeting Tyler. This was beyond his wildest dreams, yet here it was. There were tears in his eyes when he choked out his answer. "Yes!" Tyler slipped the ring on Mark's finger. "But I don't have a ring for you." Tyler reached into his other pocket, produced a second ring, and handed it to Mark. "I love you, Ty. Will you be my husband?"

"Yes, Mark, I will, always!" Mark placed the ring on Tyler's finger. The crew then brought out the champagne that Tyler had arranged and glasses were passed to all the passengers. The captain and passengers toasted their happiness. Mark sat curled up next to Tyler, starting to feel a little chilled, but happy to be wrapped in Tyler's arms. When the sailboat docked, most of the passengers congratulated them as they disembarked.

Arriving back at the hotel, Tyler went directly to their room. Mark held back a minute, using his cell phone to call Amy.

"Hello."

"Amy, it's Mark."

"Hi, Mark. How's vacation?"

Mark was so excited he could barely stand it. "Amy, I just want you to be the first to know, we went for a sail this evening and Tyler asked me to marry him."

Amy was silent for a second and Mark was worried until he heard her sniffle. "Oh, Marky, that's just wonderful. I'm so happy for you."

"I'm pretty happy too. He had champagne ready on the sailboat and everything. It was magical. I better get back—he's waiting for me—but I wanted to tell you right away."

"See you when you get back, Marky. Enjoy the rest of your trip." Hanging up, he headed to the room.

Tyler was naked, lying on his stomach on the bed waiting for Mark. "How's Amy?"

Mark started getting undressed. "How'd you know?"

"Guessed. Now come here and keep me company. I'm lonely." Mark was naked as well when he joined Tyler on the bed, gently rubbing his back. The rubbing soon progressed to stroking and exploring, his hands gliding over the shoulders, back, legs, and butt. As he kneaded Tyler's butt, the legs parted, giving him access. The kneading turned to nuzzling and licking as Mark worked his tongue down Tyler's crack to his puckered entrance, tickling and teasing the rim before tonguing the opening. "Oh god, Mark, I love that. Don't stop. Fuck me with your tongue!"

Mark did just that, jabbing his tongue into Tyler's opening. "Oh god, Mark." Tyler purred, "I need you, I need more." Mark gently slipped a lubed finger into Tyler and the moans of pleasure increased. Soon the one finger became two as Mark prepared Tyler. "I want you, Mark. All of you."

"I know. I need to prepare you." The words were soft and comforting. A third finger was added and Tyler started thrusting himself onto Mark's fingers, clenching them tightly.

Slowly the fingers disappeared, replaced by the head of Mark's cock pressing into Tyler, filling and spreading him. Tyler bucked against Mark, taking all of him into himself, burying the cock to the hilt. The sudden movement caught Mark by surprise. "Ty, you feel so good, so hot, so tight!"

"Feel so hot... so full... so loved."

Lying on top of Tyler, Mark began thrusting, pushing into him with his cock, surrounding him with his body. Tyler's moans turned to gasps and sighs as Mark hit his sweet spot with each thrust. "Right there... oh, Mark, love you...."

"Ty, love you... so hot... so sexy... mine!"

"Yes, yours... all yours... only yours!"

Tyler came on the sheets as Mark continued to thrust into him. Tyler communicated his pleasure by contracting his muscles around Mark's cock, making his sphincter tighter.

"Ty, you're killing me." Mark continued thrusting until the pressure inside him was too great and he climaxed deep inside Tyler again and again.

Slowly, Mark withdrew, grabbing a towel from the bathroom and gently wiping Tyler and himself. After throwing the towel into the bathroom, Mark curled around Tyler, hugging, kissing, and cuddling. Gently stroking Tyler's smooth chest, he purred, "Ty, you're incredible."

"So are you. All I have to do is look at you, and I want you, all the time." Using his hands to cradle Mark's head, Tyler said soothingly, "I love you, always!" The kiss was warm, communicating deep love and affection.

IN the morning, Mark packed the truck while Tyler checked out of the hotel, and soon they were on their way to the second auction. They arrived at the auction in Massachusetts with just a half-hour to preview the items for sale. This auction went almost as well as the last one, with Tyler purchasing a number of lamps, a pedestal, a clock, and three art pieces. They did have some disappointments; there was a painting

Mark really wanted, but the price was too high. They packed their purchases and headed to Plymouth.

Tyler had reserved a space at a campground just outside Plymouth. Their space was larger than they expected and a little off by itself. After pitching the tent and getting everything set up, they headed into town to see the sights. Plymouth is a beautiful seaside community, and they spent the afternoon wandering through town, just getting their bearings and relaxing. They had dinner in a nice restaurant before heading back to camp.

Tyler bought some firewood from the camp store and built a small campfire. They roasted marshmallows and took turns feeding them to each other, laughing and telling ghost stories, sitting on a blanket near the fire. It was beautiful and quiet, the night sky a canopy of stars. As the fire started to die, Tyler lay on the blanket, his head cradled in Mark's lap. "Ty, this was a wonderful idea. Camping, being outside, and snuggling by the fire." Leaning down for a kiss, he quietly whispered, "It's so sexy. You're so sexy." More kisses followed and the talking ceased for quite a while. Mark's hands slipped beneath Tyler's shirt, caressing his chest and stomach, gently pinching each nipple, occasionally disappearing into his pants to gently cup his balls, a quiet moan coming from deep inside. The whisper was so soft and quiet. "Let's move inside."

Slowly, they went into the tent, watching each other as they undressed. A slight chill in the night air contrasted with the warmth of their sleeping bag. Mark snuggled close to his lover, feeling the warmth of his skin against his own. The evening breeze rustled the leaves outside as their kissing started, providing nature's musical accompaniment to their lovemaking.

"Mark… need you… always and forever." The wind picked up, echoing and punctuating the sentiment before again dying away.

"You've got me. Yours, only yours." Mark felt Tyler's fingers. Probing him, spreading him, as Mother Nature kept up her background music.

Gently adding a second finger, Tyler handed Mark the towel he had placed nearby. "Oh, Ty, that's nice… need you now, all of you."

Carefully, he slipped into Mark, slowly filling him, listening to the quiet whimpers and moans of pleasure. The strokes were careful, slow, and deep, with Mark meeting each thrust, Tyler gently kissing and nibbling Mark's neck and shoulders. Tyler wrapped his arms around Mark, holding him close, not moving, enjoying the feeling of the joining. "Us, together, we're one." A soft wind blew into the tent flap, wrapping itself around the happy lovers.

Tyler's movements were long, slow, and intimate. "Ty, love you, love being together."

"My love, my life." Tyler's slow movements continued. Mark moved with him in perfect harmony, taking their rhythm from the sounds of nature outside the tent.

"Ty, you're the love of my life." Those words sent waves of emotion coursing through Tyler and he came deep within Mark, filling him.

Tyler continued his slow intimate movements. Mark whimpered, "Oh, Ty," softly as he came on the towel. Rather than immediately withdrawing, Tyler pressed his back to Mark, keeping them joined together, pulling Mark tightly to his body. "You are the sexiest man I have ever met, and you're mine, all mine, and I'm yours, all yours, forever."

"Ty, I love you too." Slowly, Tyler withdrew from Mark, cleaning them both before settling back into the sleeping bag, spooning into Mark, pulling him to his body. The air had a slight chill, but the tent was filled with warmth and love.

In the morning, Tyler woke early, still cradling Mark to his body. Carefully, he rolled away, slowly slipping on his pants and shoes. He grabbed his shirt, and quietly left the tent. After cleaning up, Tyler built a fire and started a breakfast of sausage and eggs. Mark crawled out of the tent just before breakfast was ready. "Morning." Lazily, Mark slipped his arms around Tyler's waist, resting his head on his back.

"Good morning. Breakfast is almost ready. Would you get out the juice?"

"In a minute. This feels too nice." Tyler smiled, enjoying the arms around his waist and the weight against his back.

Breakfast was delicious. Maybe it was from being outdoors, maybe it was the loving, or maybe it was just the company.

After breakfast, they headed back into Plymouth, watched the boats, and toured the Mayflower replica. They were both surprised at how small it was and marveled that so many people could spend so much time living in such a small space. After a quick lunch, they headed to Plimoth Plantation to get a view of life in the early colonial period. Mark and Tyler both enjoyed the plantation, and marveled at the ingenuity of the early colonists as well as the nearly complete lack of privacy for some people based upon their social standing. They spent most of the afternoon at the plantation enjoying the demonstrations and talking to the people portraying both Native Americans and the early colonists.

After stopping in town for dinner, they headed back to camp, arriving as it started to rain. After making sure everything was secure, they headed to the camp game room, and spent the evening playing pool, cards, and watching a little television. Sitting together on the sofa in the TV area, they were joined by another couple and their two small children. The kids were playing games on the floor with a small dog as the parents watched. Introductions followed and they spent the rest of the evening talking and laughing. Mark kept reaching down to pet and stroke the small miniature dachshund. When the kids fell asleep, the parents excused themselves, and Mark and Tyler headed back to their tent. Climbing into the tent, they undressed, crawled into their sleeping bag, and held each other tightly, falling asleep to the gentle sound of the rain.

The trip home was uneventful and relatively leisurely. They stopped at a hotel in Ohio on the way, enjoying the hotel pool, whirlpool, and bed. The following day, they got up early, had a quick breakfast, and got back on the road, arriving at the temporary storage site by mid-afternoon. After emptying the truck of the auction purchases, they headed to the store. Tyler was anxious to check on construction progress.

Entering the store through the back entrance, Tyler was surprised to see that a lot of work had been done. The outside entrance to the apartment had been sealed. When he entered the store, he could see even more progress. The new staircase had been built and the basic configuration of the new store was in place. The construction foreman was checking out the work completed when they entered.

"Tyler, welcome back. Construction is going very well. There was less structural work than we thought and the drywall crew is available to start in the next week or so. We should be completed on time. By the way, an envelope was slipped under the back door yesterday. I put it on the easel in the studio."

"Thank you." Mark and Tyler went to look at the envelope.

Even before he opened the envelope, Tyler knew what he was going to find. He opened the envelope anyway.

Faggots

You burned once

You'll burn again

You'll burn in hell

TYLER dropped the envelope on the floor and turned white. "This has got to stop." He was starting to freak out. One fire he could deal with, but the thought of a second was too much.

Tyler's reaction concerned Mark. "Ty, I'm going to call the police." Mark placed the call and Officer Sam Davis showed up about fifteen minutes later. "Sam, we got yet another letter." Mark showed Sam the letter where Tyler had dropped it.

After picking up the letter, Sam tried to provide reassurance. "Ty, please don't let this get to you. The person sending these is a bullying coward. Sound like anyone you know?"

Mark and Tyler both nodded. "Roger," they said together.

"Keep your eyes open. He'll make a mistake eventually. Please call me if you hear anything or receive any other threats." Sam was just as frustrated as Mark and Tyler. "I'll ask in the neighborhood to see if anyone saw anything. I just wish there was more I could do." Sam took the letter and went back to the station.

"Ty, let's get to the apartment. We've had a long day." Tyler said good night to the construction foreman and Mark drove to the apartment. "Ty, please relax. This is just another of Roger's empty threats. Besides, we have other things to think about. Like… we get our house in a week."

Tyler actually smiled. "Yeah, we get to sleep in our own bed again, and in our own house." He looked very determined. "Besides, I refuse to let Roger intimidate us."

"Good. Let's get unpacked, make a quick dinner, and get to bed early. I think we need some quality time alone." Mark pulled the car off to the side of the road and leaned over to Tyler, kissing him hard. "Let's get to the apartment, fast!"

Chapter 18

THE closing on their new home had gone smoothly, and now the house was all theirs. Mark could barely contain his excitement as they walked up the path to their front door for the first time. Tyler turned the key in the lock and opened the door. Hand in hand, they wandered from room to room, marveling at their new home.

"I still can't believe it's ours. I have missed this house since I sold it years ago." Kissing Mark gently, Tyler mouthed, "Thank you."

Mark returned the kiss. "I don't know what you're thanking me for, but you're welcome."

Mark had used the time during the home inspection to decide on the colors for all of the rooms in the house. The trunk of the car was full of painting supplies, plaster repair supplies, ladders, and all the paint needed for every room in the house.

"Mark, let's bring in all the stuff and we can get started." They both headed out to the car to start bringing in supplies. As they were unloading, a familiar car pulled up behind them.

"Tom, Bill, what are you doing here?" Tyler was surprised to see them, especially since they were wearing clothes spattered with paint.

Bill opened the trunk, while Tom shook hands with Tyler and Mark. "I talked to Mark yesterday and he told us that you were spending the day painting. Bill and I thought you could use a hand."

Tyler was absolutely floored at the wonderful offer. "Thank you. We really could. There's a lot of work to be done." The four of them unloaded all of the supplies from both cars and hauled them into the house.

After giving Bill and Tom the grand tour, the two of them got to work on the living room, while Tyler and Mark started work on the master bedroom. The house was absolute quality construction throughout. The rich oak woodwork on the first floor continued through the hall and bedrooms on the second floor, and had never been painted. The floors on the second floor, like the first floor, were oak, and had been refinished by the previous owners. Mark started preparing the walls while Tyler set up the CD player, and soon the house was filled with music as well as companionship.

By noon, both the living room and master bedroom had their first coats of paint, and the dining room and upstairs family room had been prepped for painting. Tyler was about to order food when the doorbell rang. Tyler opened the door to find Amy and John with food and more painting supplies.

Amy smiled brightly. "We brought lunch and help." Tyler greeted them and ushered them into the house. Amy set up the food on the dining room floor, and everyone ate picnic style, talking, laughing, and joking throughout lunch.

Amy and John hadn't done much painting, while Tom and Bill were experts, so after lunch, Mark got Amy and Bill working together in the living room and dining room, while Tom and John worked in the library. Tyler and Mark worked upstairs and managed to get two coats of paint on the master bedroom and the family room. At six o'clock, only the dining room needed a second coat of paint. Everyone converged on that room, and by six-thirty the room was completed. Tyler had cleaned up the other rooms and washed out most of the brushes.

Tyler slipped his arm around Mark's waist, barely able to believe the generosity of their friends. "I have a reservation at Magellan's for all of us in an hour, to thank you for all your help. Please change clothes, and join Mark and me for a thank-you dinner." Everyone was all smiles as they packed up their things and headed home to change clothes. "I can't believe this. Their help was so wonderful and unexpected." Tyler had his arms wrapped around Mark.

"Ty, we need to get back to the apartment to shower and change."

Tyler winked at Mark. "Our clothes are in the car. I was planning to take you to dinner tonight, so I packed fresh clothes for us." Tyler headed out to the car to get their clothes as Mark headed upstairs to the bathroom.

Tyler brought the suitcase of clothes into the bathroom, laying out the towels and their kits. After putting their clothes in one of the yet unpainted bedrooms, he rejoined Mark in the bathroom. "Ty, you really planned this, didn't you?" Mark said over the sound of the shower.

"I just didn't know how long we'd be and wanted to be ready." Tyler undressed quickly, joining Mark in the shower. The bathroom had been remodeled recently, and the bathtub had been replaced with a large multi-head shower. Tyler opened the shower door, wrapping his arms around Mark's waist before closing the door again.

"Mmmm, that feels good," Mark purred as Tyler rubbed his hands over Mark's stomach and chest, gently kissing his shoulders and neck, as he pressed his body to Mark's. The rubbing and caressing continued. Mark slowly turned around, pressing his lips to Tyler's, using his tongue to explore his lips and probe his mouth. "Ty, what do you want?"

"I want you, inside me, now!" Opening the door slightly, Tyler picked up the lube he had placed outside the shower and handed it to Mark.

Mark placed the bottle on one of the corner shower shelves. "Ty, put your hands on the wall." Tyler complied. Soon his legs were spread and he felt Mark's hot tongue probing him, opening him, getting him ready. The sounds Tyler made delighted Mark as he continued probing his ass with his tongue and fingers. Mark soon had three lubed fingers inside Tyler, those sweet pleasure noises filling the bathroom.

"Mark, I need you. Please." Mark loved it when Tyler pleaded, begging for him. Removing his fingers, he replaced them with the head of his lubed cock, steadily pressing into Tyler. "More. I love the way you feel... need you... love you."

Soon Mark was buried to the root, filling Tyler completely. Mark started to move, gently at first, but steadily increasing the pace. With each thrust, Tyler made those wonderful pleasure sounds that Mark loved so much. Wrapping his arms around Tyler, he sucked on his shoulder, marking him, filling him, loving him.

"Ty, you're incredible. Love you... need you... always."

"Oh... right there... love... yeah...." Tyler could barely breathe.

"Forever!"

"Forever, Mark... mine!" Tyler was stroking himself to Mark's rhythm.

Mark pulled Tyler close. "Love you always."

With a shout Tyler came on the shower wall, clenching his muscles. The increased pressure was more than Mark could take and he climaxed deep within Tyler. Leaning against the wall, Tyler felt as though his knees would buckle, but Mark held him tight.

The water started to chill, so Mark shut off the shower and dried Tyler carefully, kissing him and stroking his skin. Mark then dried himself. They both got dressed, kissing through the process, left the house, and headed to the restaurant.

Arriving right on time, Tyler and Mark were shown to their table by the hostess. Their four guests had already arrived. Drinks and food were ordered. The dinner was a wonderful occasion and they spent the evening talking, laughing, and toasting their new house with champagne and friends.

TYLER was rushing to get everything ready before the guests arrived for Mark's surprise birthday party. This was their first party in their new home.

They had moved in a month ago. Not all of the rooms were fully furnished yet, but the living room and dining room looked beautiful. The painting Mark had found at the antique show hung over the fireplace, with the swinging mystery clock decorating the mantle. The paintings from Tyler's grandmother decorated the dining room walls, the candelabra illuminating the room, and her table stood imposingly in the center of the entrance hall. The portrait of Tyler was hung in their bedroom across from the large bed. The fabulous Herter Brothers table graced the library.

Mark was working in his studio at the store trying to finish a number of paintings for his show at Peter's gallery in late January and had no idea that Tyler was planning a surprise birthday party for him.

By five o'clock, Tyler had finished all of the preparations for the party and guests had started to arrive. Everyone had been asked to arrive by five-thirty. Amy arrived first, giving Tyler a big hug. "Is there anything I can do?"

"No, everything's all set. Mark usually calls when he leaves his studio. I just hope he does this time as well." Just in case, the only lights on in the house were in the hall and kitchen, making the house look like no one was home. The rest of the guests arrived within a few minutes and soon the house was full of people and yet very quiet and still, since no one knew when Mark would be home.

Even Aunt Phyllis was able to come, saying she wouldn't have missed it for the world.

At about six, the phone rang. "Hello."

"Ty, I'm heading home. Should I pick up something for dinner?"

"No, I've started dinner already." Tyler was trying to keep the excitement out of his voice.

"Okay, I'll be home soon." Tyler hung up the phone and let the guests know that Mark would be home soon. The house became very still once more. Only the kitchen light was on. The house looked, as Tyler had planned, as though no one was home.

About ten minutes before Mark was expected, the quiet in the house was disturbed by a loud popping sound from the back door. Sam recognized the sound, signaling to Tyler that he'd investigate. He heard Sam call from the kitchen, "Tyler, come here please." When Tyler walked into the kitchen, Sam had Mark's brother on the floor. "He was trying to break in. He popped the lock on the back door with a crowbar."

"Roger, what do you think you're doing?"

Sam didn't wait for an answer. "Tyler, look outside the back door." Tyler peeked outside the door and saw that propped up against the house were a crowbar and sledgehammer. Tyler realized Roger wasn't there to take anything, but to destroy, and he started to shake. That bastard was trying to take away their home, Mark's home. He'd done it once and he was trying to do it again. Tyler's hands clenched and unclenched as the anger washed over him.

Tyler marched back into the kitchen. His first impulse was to hit Roger and hit him hard, but he curbed the impulse. "We'll press charges. This man is an absolute nutcase and I want him put away." Thinking for a minute, he said, "I'll be right back." Tyler ran upstairs to the bedroom, returning a few minutes later. "Here's a pair of handcuffs; don't ask." Sam smiled at Tyler with a wicked look on his face as he cuffed Roger's hands behind his back. "Take him into the living room. I want our guests to see him." Sam hauled Roger to his feet and marched him into the living room. When he saw Amy and Aunt Phyllis, he started to cry.

Sam then took Roger back to the kitchen. "I'll call this in as soon as Mark arrives so we don't spoil the surprise."

Tyler bent to Roger's face. "You make any noise and I'll make good on my threat to rip your balls off, you understand?" There was fear in Roger's eyes as he nodded.

Mark arrived a few minutes later, everyone yelling "surprise" when he stepped into the hall. Mark raced to Tyler, throwing his arms around him. "I can't believe you did this. I love surprises." Tyler was trying to figure out how to tell Mark about the surprise waiting in the kitchen.

"Well, Mark, it seems that the rest of us got a surprise this evening as well." Tyler led Mark into the kitchen where Sam was still holding Roger on the floor. "He tried to break into the house while we were waiting for you."

Mark knelt near his brother. "Roger... why?" Roger said nothing. "Did you send the notes?" Roger just smiled a malicious smile. Mark turned to Sam. "Would you please call this in?"

Roger looked like he'd been shot. "But, Mark, I'm your brother." He was whining now.

"No, you're a burglar who tried to break into our house. You're a criminal. You're going to prison and the whole family will know." Mark looked at Sam. "Thank you for taking out the trash."

The police arrived a few minutes later and took Roger away. Mark and Tyler rejoined the party.

Tom cornered Tyler almost immediately. "Tyler, when's the grand re-opening?"

"I'm planning on mid-November. Construction should be done in two weeks. That'll give us two weeks to get set up and ready." Mark stepped behind Tyler, slipping his arms around his waist. "I'll be sending out invitations to the grand re-opening party next week."

Peter tapped Mark on the shoulder. "Getting ready for your show?"

"Oh, yes. I have twelve pieces completed and four more in progress. I think you're really going to like them." Mark had been working almost daily to get ready for the show. He still wanted to finish six to eight more pieces.

"Excellent. I can't wait to see them."

Tyler chimed in. "Me too. I've only seen the one piece he did while we were on vacation."

Mark smiled broadly. "I want everyone to be surprised." He would give no more information. The party was in full swing, with everyone eating, drinking, and talking.

Tyler gave Amy the prearranged signal. "Mark, I wanted to get you something special for your birthday, something that would add to the love in our lives." Amy appeared next to Mark carrying a beautiful long-haired miniature dachshund similar to the dog they'd seen on vacation. "Her name is Jolie. It's French for 'beautiful.' Happy birthday!" Mark gently took the small dog and she immediately licked his face.

"Where did you get her?"

"She's a year old and was rescued. Sam helped me get her. She's been staying with Amy for the past few days. I hope you like her; she sure likes you." Mark leaned forward, kissing Tyler gently. Jolie added her kisses to the mix as well and they both laughed.

The party lasted well into the evening and everyone enjoyed themselves. Tyler had placed Jolie's bed on the floor in their room. While he closed up the house, Mark took Jolie out and then brought her upstairs with him. Tyler got cleaned up and joined Mark in the bedroom. Jolie was already asleep in her bed. Tyler climbed into bed and waited for Mark to join him.

Mark was naked and ready when he walked into the bedroom, his hard cock swaying as he walked. Tyler felt his mouth go dry. Throwing back the covers, he pounced onto Mark, gently pushing him on the bed and taking his cock into his mouth, sucking it deeply down his throat. "Ty, I love that! Oh... man."

Straddling Mark, Tyler lowered his cock into Mark's mouth. Few things were better than sucking Mark while he worked his cock with his incredible mouth.

"Mark, that's... oh god." Mark used his tongue to work the head. "Oh... love that!"

Tyler quickly returned the pleasure, stroking the underside with his lips as he tickled the head with his tongue. Mark moaned around Tyler's cock, taking it deeply. "Mmmmm."

With Mark's cock deep in his throat, Tyler gently lifted his legs and slipped a slicked finger into his butt. Mark started bucking into his mouth as he added a second finger. Tyler continued sucking Mark as he fucked him with the two fingers. "Oooo... mmmmm." The sounds filled the bedroom like sweet music, swelling and building with their passion.

Mark started to buck more steadily and Tyler knew it wouldn't be long. Reaching under the bed, he found the butt plug he'd lubed earlier and slowly inserted it into Mark. "Oh, Ty, sucking and fucking me at the same time. Oh… yeah!"

He'd just seated the plug when Mark shot hard down his throat. Tyler swallowed every drop as he bucked into Mark's mouth, coming down his throat. Shifting positions, Tyler brought his lips to Mark's, kissing him deeply.

"God, I love it when you fuck and suck me at the same time!"

"Mmmm… so I noticed." Tyler gently removed the plug, cleaned it, and rejoined him in bed, pulling the covers over them. Tyler looked down at the dog, who was still sound asleep.

"Thank you for a wonderful birthday."

"You're welcome. Good night, sweetie." Tyler snuggled close to Mark.

"Good night, Ty."

Chapter 19

IT was a week before Christmas and Tyler was doing something he hadn't done in years: serious Christmas shopping. Before meeting Mark, he had exchanged a few gifts with people, but they were mostly business associates or people who worked for him in the store. This year was different. He needed to get gifts for Mark as well as gifts for Amy, John, and the kids. Tyler was so excited he thought was going to burst. For the first time since college, he was spending Christmas with people he considered family. Amy and John were adding a family room on to their house, but it wouldn't be finished in time for the holidays, so Christmas was being held at their house.

Tyler had gotten Mark a tuxedo to wear for his upcoming gallery opening and a leather jacket he knew Mark had been wanting. Those purchases were already in the car so Mark wouldn't see them. Tyler was currently on his way to meet Mark at the mall food court and then they were going to shop for the kids together. Heading into the food court, he saw Mark sitting at a table waiting for him and approached the table and sat down.

Mark smiled brightly. "Did you get what you needed?"

Tyler returned the smile and nodded. "Yes I…." Tyler stopped talking in the middle of his sentence and turned pale.

Mark turned his head to see what was going on, but he could see nothing. "Ty, what is it?"

His words were very measured, like he was trying to stay in control of himself. "Mark, that's my mother." Mark's head quickly turned and followed Tyler's gaze. "The woman in the green dress near McDonald's."

Mark could tell Tyler was very unsure of himself. It was obvious to him that Tyler was curious about her, but he was also scared of being rejected, which he knew was a distinct possibility. Then he got an idea. "Ty, do you want me to approach her?" The look on Tyler's face was incredibly conflicted.

Tyler made no move or sound for a long while. "Thank you, Mark, but no. We don't need to open all those old wounds. I have my own family now."

Mark watched as Tyler's mother got her food and sat down at a table on the far side of the food court, joining a man that Mark assumed was Tyler's father. They were laughing and joking together and looked very happy.

"Mark, that man? That's not my father." Tyler tore his eyes away from them and started to eat his lunch.

After finishing their lunch, they headed out into the mall to try to finish their shopping. They found some great gifts for the kids and Mark helped Tyler pick out presents for Amy and John. On their way out of the mall, they stopped by the pet store to get a few presents for Jolie as well. Tyler put all their purchases in the trunk, making sure Mark didn't see his gifts, before driving home.

Entering the house, they were greeted by Jolie, who wagged her tail and raced around the hall before running to the back door to be let out. Mark let her out while Tyler put Mark's presents away until he could wrap them.

Mark had done an incredible job of decorating the house for Christmas. There was pine garland running up the stairs with handmade gold bows. The living room was dominated by a huge tree that nearly reached the ceiling. The dining room was decorated with candy, sweets, and fresh poinsettias.

Tyler started dinner while Mark wrapped the gifts they'd purchased and put them under the tree. Amy and John had already started bringing over some of their gifts, so the tree was already bursting with presents. Jolie did not seem interested in the tree or the gifts, but they weren't taking any chances and no candy or treats had been put under the tree to entice her.

Mark headed into the kitchen. "Ty, have you worked out where everyone is sleeping Christmas Eve?"

"Yes, I thought Amy and John would stay in the guest room, and the two kids could stay in the family room. One on the couch, and I got a twin air mattress that we can put on the floor."

Mark kissed Tyler sweetly. "This is going to be a lot of fun, isn't it?"

"Yeah, I think so." Tyler had a faraway look and Mark figured he was thinking about seeing his mom.

After dinner, they finished wrapping their presents. Tyler got Mark's presents wrapped while he was out walking the dog. When Mark returned, he joined Tyler in the family room. They played with Jolie and watched television, curled up together on the sofa. As it started to get late, Jolie grabbed her favorite toy, walked into her bed, and went to sleep. Tyler locked up the house, got cleaned up, and joined Mark in bed.

Mark could tell that Tyler was out of sorts, so he spooned his chest to Tyler's back and held him tight, kissing him gently.

Mark was finding it difficult to sleep. He kept turning things over in his mind. In the small hours of the morning, his thoughts finally quieted and he drifted off to sleep.

TYLER opened his eyes. It was the morning of Christmas Eve and Mark was curled up next to him, still asleep, his butt pressed against Tyler's hip. Tyler rolled onto his side, spooning his body into Mark's. The warmth from Mark' body and the smell of his skin were making his body stir. Tyler let his hands gently wander over Mark's chest and stomach. Mark didn't move and Tyler knew he was just exhausted. Mark had been spending a great deal of time getting ready for his show at Peter's gallery and Tyler knew he needed the rest. Tyler luxuriated in the warmth of Mark's body as he drifted back to sleep.

Tyler woke again, and this time there was no doubt Mark was awake, because a pair of hot sweet lips were surrounding his cock, taking him in deep. "Oh, Mark... that's... oh...."

Mark looked up at him with a mischievous smile. "Didn't think you were ever going to wake up so I had to take things in my own hands—or mouth!" Mark grinned as Tyler pulled his face to his, kissing him deeply, communicating all his love through those lips. Mark tried to say something more, but he found his mouth otherwise occupied, and that was just fine.

Tyler's kisses always turned him on, but today they just drove him wild with desire. Mark could feel the heat from those kisses traveling through his body, his hips automatically grinding. He had to force himself to stop or he'd come; he was already incredibly close.

Those moans and whimpers coming from Mark sounded like heaven. Slowly, Tyler shifted them on the bed, his weight pressing Mark deep into the mattress. His hand found Mark's cock, stroking it, rubbing it, pulling those deep pleasure sounds out of Mark that always turned him on like nothing else. "Mark, need you. Need to love you bad!" Mark's response was a deep, long moan as Tyler cupped his butt, spreading his cheeks, using his fingers to tease.

Mark was trying hard not to shoot already. Tyler's hands were magic and he tried to think of something else to cool himself down, but it wasn't helping. "Need you so bad." Mark's words were raspy and deep. He felt a finger breach him, rubbing his pleasure spot over and over. Mark locked his legs around Tyler, exposing himself fully to Tyler's loving touches. The finger soon became two, stretching him, getting him ready for the loving to come. "Ty... need... more." Each word was an effort moaned between the jolts of pleasure traveling through his body.

"This what you want?" Tyler whispered, twisting his fingers gently as he reinserted them.

Mark bucked hard as the pleasure surged through his body. "Need... you.... Not... going... to... last!" Tyler stroked Mark steadily as he pushed a third finger into him, rubbing that wonderful spot deep in Mark that he knew so well. Those pleasure sounds came faster, becoming more insistent.

Tyler cooed into Mark's ear, "Your come makes the best lube," as he bit gently on one of Mark's sensitive nipples. Pleasure sounds built to a crescendo as Mark spilled himself onto Tyler's hand, clenching himself onto Tyler's fingers.

Without removing his fingers, Tyler shifted his body. "Mark, please get on your knees. I want you from behind." This was an unusual request, and Mark wriggled his butt in anticipation, clenching his muscles around the fingers. As he moved, Tyler shifted his fingers.

"Ty, that's, oh god. Each time I move, your fingers, oh... man." Mark's butt was wriggling and squirming like mad. Tyler reached under Mark, stroking his cock again, Mark starting to respond. Tyler just loved that he could do that to Mark. It was the sexiest thing he could think of.

Tyler slowly withdrew his fingers, replacing them with his come-lubed and dripping cock. Mark whimpered as Tyler buried himself deep inside Mark's hot, welcoming body, his hands on his hips, pulling him onto his cock. Mark turned his head and Tyler leaned forward. Mark's kisses were hot and needy, pulling his lips, tongue thrusting deep into his mouth as Tyler thrust deep into Mark, wanting to feel all of him at once. "Can't get enough, never enough of you."

"Yeah, always need you, Ty." Their bodies moved as one, loved as one.

Tyler could feel the blood rushing back into Mark's cock, filling it. "Love that I make you this hot."

"Only you... always you." Mark was bucking hard against him, fueling his passion, building his desire. The slight slapping sound as Tyler's hips met Mark's ass further drove his desire and soon he was pounding into him, with Mark meeting each thrust.

Mark's pleasure was almost transcendent. He was seeing stars as waves of pleasure coursed through his body, making him want more, need more, need Tyler like he'd never needed anyone in his life.

Tyler wrapped his arms around Mark and drove into him hard and fast, pulling on Mark's cock as he came in a flood, deep inside Mark.

When his breath returned, he withdrew slowly, kissing and caressing. Mark was rocking himself onto Tyler, still fucking himself on Tyler's cock. Tyler whispered, "I'm not through with you. Shower." Tyler lifted himself off the bed and headed for the bathroom. When the water warmed, he stepped into the shower and Mark slipped in behind him, his weighty cock pressing to his butt.

"Want you, Mark, deep inside me."

"Yeah?"

"Oh, yeah! Fuck me, Mark. Give me all your love." Mark's hands reached around Tyler's hot, wet body, pulling him into his body.

Wasting no time, Mark pressed himself deep into his lover's body, feeling Tyler's pulse as he filled him. "Ty, love you."

"Mark, so full… so completely full… love being full of you." Mark started to move, slowly at first. "Oh, yeah… right… there…." His breathing came in deep gasps as pleasure jolted through his body. Mark pressed his body to Tyler's back, his arms encircling him, covering him, filling him, and surrounding him with love. The bathroom was filled with a chorus of moans, whimpers, and deep, needy groans of pleasure and want.

Mark's hands traveled to Tyler's nipples, pressing against them. "Love that, love your hands on my nipples. Oh yeah, harder… yeah!" Tyler had completely abandoned himself to the feelings of pleasure and love.

Tyler felt as though he were riding huge waves of love as Mark came hard inside him, his cock pulsing wildly, deep inside his body. Mark started to withdraw, but Tyler shook his head. Mark reached to his cock, stroking him with hard, slow, sure movements, pressing his thumb against the head and slit. Tyler bucked hard against Mark's cock, thrusting himself onto Mark again and again. Rearing back against Mark, Tyler shot onto the tile, his knees nearly buckling.

Even before withdrawing, Mark started caressing and washing Tyler's body, and he was nearly finished when his cock finally withdrew from Tyler.

Turning around, Tyler threw his arms around Mark's neck, kissing him deeply and rubbing his chest and stomach against Mark's. They both loved washing each other, the act itself almost as intimate and special as their lovemaking.

After showering and getting dressed, Mark headed downstairs to make breakfast while Tyler made sure everything was ready for Mark's family.

He stopped and smiled as he made up the bed. Mark's family— my family. It had been a long time since he felt part of a family and the thought made him feel warm.

Tyler finished making up the beds and headed downstairs to the kitchen. Mark was putting breakfast on the table when he slipped up behind him, sliding his hands under Mark's shirt, letting them roam over Mark's skin. Mark just let his head fall back against Tyler's shoulder, moaning softly.

"You ready for more?" Mark's tone was skeptical.

Tyler smiled into Mark's cheek. "Maybe after breakfast."

"Yeah?" Mark's eyes were dancing at the thought.

"Can't get enough of you. Never will get enough of you."

Mark's response was a very contented sigh as he finished putting breakfast on the table. They sat close together during breakfast, lightly touching and smiling at each other.

After breakfast, Tyler was wandering through the house making sure everything was ready. The living room was stunning with the huge tree and so many gifts underneath that they spilled out into the room. As Tyler looked at the mantel, he noticed six decorative brass hooks that weren't there before. "Mark, what are these?"

Coming into the living room, Mark followed where Tyler was looking. "Ty, they're stocking hooks. I put them up yesterday." Mark reached under the tree and pulled out a flat gift box, handing it to Tyler. "Open it."

Tyler looked sheepish and opened the box. Inside, wrapped in tissue paper was a red Santa-boot-shaped stocking with white fur trim. On the trim, "Tyler" had been embroidered. The stocking was decorated with a Christmas tree, an antique clock, and books, pieced together and sewn on by hand. "Where did you get this?"

"Amy and I made it. We all have one, and I wanted you to have one as well." Tyler was floored. "Amy will be bringing theirs." Mark hung Tyler's stocking on one of the hooks, before hanging his next to Tyler's. Mark went back into the kitchen to clean up as Tyler looked at his stocking.

Amy, John, and the kids arrived after lunch. Mark got everyone settled in their rooms before hauling out lots of games. The six of them spent the afternoon playing games and watching A Christmas Carol on television.

For dinner, Mark put out a spread of finger food that everyone really seemed to enjoy. After dinner, Tyler put on some Christmas music, and John read, The Night Before Christmas to the kids.

During the story, Amy whispered to Mark, "Why do you keep looking out the window whenever a car goes by? What are you looking for?"

Mark nodded toward the office and Amy quietly followed. "I went to see Tyler's mother last week. I invited her to join us for Christmas Eve. I just kept hoping she'd come."

"Does he know?"

Mark shook his head. Amy gently kissed Mark on the cheek. "I never told Tyler because I didn't want to disappoint him if she didn't come. But I had to ask her. Even after Mom died, I still wished we could have made up somehow.... I guess I figured if there was a chance for Ty to have that, I'd try to give it to him." Mark smiled and headed back into the living room as John was finishing the story.

Amy and John put the kids to bed at nine. At about ten, they put out the gifts from Santa. Mark had finally stopped looking out the window, but seemed distracted. Tyler was starting to get a little concerned.

Everyone went up to bed about eleven o'clock. After cleaning up, Tyler climbed into bed, waiting for Mark to join him, which he did a few minutes later. Jolie was already asleep in her bed. "Good night, Mark. Merry Christmas."

Mark kissed Tyler gently. "Merry Christmas." Mark couldn't help regretting that Tyler's mother hadn't come, but Tyler was right: they'd built their own family.

In the morning, Mark was up early. After slipping on his robe, he let the dog out and got the paper. Mark thumbed through the paper while he drank his coffee. In the local section Mark noticed an obituary that caught his eye. The notice said that Martha O'Connor had passed away two days ago. It also said that her husband had passed away two years earlier. No mention of children was included in the notice.

Mark rested his head on his hands as tears ran down his face, looking at Tyler's mother's obituary. That small newspaper notice signaled the end. Both their sets of parents were now dead, they'd both been rejected, and all hope of reconciliation was gone. The last of the pain of losing his family, the pain he now felt for Tyler, knowing the man he loved still carried the pain and loss from losing his family, seeped away with his final tears. Enough was enough. They'd built their own family together and that was enough. No more grieving for what couldn't be.

Mark silently closed the paper, taking the local section outside the back door, and threw that section of the paper deep into the trash before quietly closing the door and heading back upstairs to their bedroom.

Chapter 20

IT was absolutely frigid, must have been the coldest day of the year, and he had to go out in it. "Ty, do we have to?"

"It wouldn't be good for you to miss your own gallery opening." Mark had just finished dressing and Tyler was in the bathroom getting cleaned up.

"I'm going to take the dog out one last time before we go." He headed downstairs, taking Jolie out and putting her on the cleared area of the lawn so she could do her business. Thankfully she was fast. Mark picked her up and took her back into the house. Tyler was coming down the stairs, looking incredible in his tuxedo. "You look good enough to eat." Mark actually licked his lips.

Tyler hugged Mark. "You look absolutely edible yourself." The leer he got from Mark made his cock jump. They put on their coats and headed to the gallery.

The grand reopening of Tyler's Antiques two months earlier had been a huge success. Business was better than before the fire. Gladys and Steve both now worked for Tyler on a regular basis. The larger store meant more buying trips, but Mark and Jolie went along on most of the trips anyway. Tyler had remodeled Mark's studio at the store to Mark's specifications. Mark had also set up a studio at the house, but rarely used it; he enjoyed working near Tyler.

Mark did tell Tyler about his mother a few days after Christmas, once everyone had left. They sat together quietly in their bedroom as Mark explained about seeing his mother's obituary in the paper. Tyler started to cry softly as Mark told him; not for his mother, but for the opportunities lost. Mark knew that while he never spoke about it, Tyler always held out some shred of hope that he'd be able to see his parents again. Taking his Ty in his arms, he rocked and comforted the man who'd been such a comfort to him.

As they headed to the car, Mark could feel himself getting nervous. "Ty, I think I'm going to be sick." Tyler reached across the seat and rubbed his back gently.

"You're going to be fine. Your work is stunning. You have nothing to be worried about." Leaning close to his ear, he reassured, "Besides when we get home, there'll be a little girl waiting for you, regardless, and there will be a large bed upstairs waiting for us, regardless." Mark calmed down and actually smiled.

They arrived at the gallery a few minutes before the opening. Tyler had not seen many of the items to be shown and he was very interested to see them. Peter had convinced him to allow the painting that normally hung in their bedroom to be shown even though it wouldn't be for sale. Mark led Tyler into the gallery and through the show. One room contained the portraits of Amy, Roger, Aunt Phyllis, and his mother, as well as a number of other portraits he had done of anonymous people and faces. The next room contained a collection of landscapes, including the landscape done in Newport and five others from around town. The final room took his breath away. This room contained four pictures of him: the one he had loaned Peter as well as three others. One was his face, one was a portrait from his waist up, and the other was a full nude from the side with him looking over his shoulder. Tyler was completely speechless. The pictures of him covered an entire wall. In front of those paintings was a bronze bust, also of him. There was a sign that said it wasn't for sale. That voice he loved so well whispered into his ear, "That's your final Christmas present."

Tyler started to cry right there in the gallery. On the wall opposite the portraits of him was a single self-portrait of Mark, staring across the gallery, looking lovingly at the portraits of Tyler. It was too much, and Tyler stood in the middle of the gallery, tears streaming down his face. Peter had joined them, whispering to Mark, "I told you he'd cry."

The gallery was about to open; Tyler pulled himself together, hugging Mark tightly before letting him go. After all, it was Mark's night. Tyler found Peter, reminding him that the one portrait of him wasn't for sale. Peter added a sign just before the gallery opened.

The gallery filled rapidly with people almost as soon as the show opened. Most of their friends were there, as well as many people they didn't know. Mark stayed by the door, greeting each person as they entered. The rooms were soon filled with people talking, laughing, and drinking wine, wandering through the gallery. Tyler noticed a very interesting phenomenon: people would laugh and talk in the hall and the first rooms, but the minute they entered the room with the portraits of him and Mark, they always went silent. Some gasped, and a few even cried. Tyler just smiled and tried to stay out of the way, until one of the ladies in the room saw him and recognized him. She walked up to him, patted him on the back, and nodded her head. "I had a love like yours years ago; hold on to it with both hands." She walked away with a tear in her eye.

Mark joined Tyler a few minutes after the lady left. "Love, how are you doing?"

"I'm doing just fine. I feel like a star."

Tyler looked into his eyes. "You are a star; you're my star, and you always will be." Tyler closed his eyes and gently kissed Mark on the lips. When he opened them again, half the people in the gallery were looking at them, most of them nodding their heads.

Aunt Phyllis gingerly approached them, using her cane. "In all my life I have never seen such a visual expression of love." Kissing both Mark and Tyler, she went back into the gallery to stare at her portrait. Mark walked back through the gallery and was surprised to see that most every item had a sold sign on it, except the three portraits of Tyler. As they were watching, a gallery employee put a reserve tag on each of the three portraits. Mark was a little confused, but figured he'd ask Peter later.

Peter looked thrilled as he approached. "Mark, I'd like you to meet Albert Fisk. He's the owner of a large gallery in New York."

"Mr. Fisk, it's my pleasure." Mark reached out and shook his hand.

"No, Mr. Burke, the pleasure is all mine." They made small talk for a few minutes. "Mark, I'd like to show your work in my gallery in New York in six to nine months. We'll need between twelve and eighteen new works. Is that feasible?"

"Yes, Mr. Fisk. I already have four additional works completed and ready, with four more already in progress. They were finished after we had laid out this show and I didn't want to upset the plans." Peter was surprised and pleased.

"Are any of them portraits of him?" He indicated the pictures of Tyler.

Mark grinned. "Yes, there are some of Tyler." He decided not to say any more.

"Good. They're incredible." Tyler and Mark were confused.

"Peter, why do the portraits have reserved signs on them?" Tyler inquired.

Mr. Fisk answered, "Because I wanted them for the show in New York and Peter graciously agreed." Mr. Fisk looked disappointed. "I'm just sorry the self-portrait was sold."

Tyler smiled. "I know who bought it and you might be able to talk them into letting you use it." The smile turned into a wide grin.

Mark looked at Tyler. "Who bought it?"

"Me…. Mr. Fisk, you may use the painting, but it isn't for sale and it never will be. The look on that face is for me and me alone." Tyler took both of Mark's hands into his and looked deeply into Mark's eyes. Mark stared back and for a few seconds the rest of the world disappeared.

Tyler heard Mr. Fisk mutter, "Oh my god." Tyler kissed Mark gently, releasing his hands. "But, how did you capture that look?"

Mark shook his head slightly. "We stood in front of a mirror together. I worked on the self-portrait for months, on and off."

"That's just amazing. That type of emotion is rare in real life, let alone captured so vividly on canvas. I think you'll be a sensation."

Mark was almost shy about accepting the praise. "Thank you, Mr. Fisk." He nodded. "Please coordinate the details with Peter and I'll have great work for your show." They said good night and Mark continued to mingle with the guests. Late in the evening, Mark entered the first room containing the portraits of his family and stopped short. Standing in the middle of the room was Roger, staring at his portrait.

He noticed Mark and whispered, "Is this how you see me?" Mark nodded. "I came here tonight to tell you that I'm in therapy and that I'm truly sorry for hurting you." The look on his face told Mark he was sincere. "I hated you for so many things, most of which were all in my mind, perceived slights that weren't real." There were tears in Roger's eyes.

"Your apology is accepted and you're forgiven." The only way to describe the look on Roger's face was complete confusion. "Hate, jealousy, and rage will eat you alive. I can't hate you, and I don't hate you. The hate I once had went into that painting; I've been able to let it go." Since they were talking, Mark asked, "Roger, did you send the notes?"

Roger said nothing. He just nodded slightly. Mark stepped forward and held out his hand. Roger took the hand. "Roger, get better and have a good, happy life. Everyone deserves happiness." Mark left the room to find Tyler as Roger took a last look at the portrait and left the gallery.

Mark found Tyler looking at Mark's self-portrait as he wrapped his arms around his waist. "I can't believe you bought the portrait."

"I couldn't bear you looking at someone else that way, even if it was only in a painting." Tyler turned in Mark's arms, kissing him deeply. "Let's find Peter and tell him good night."

"Before we find Peter, I saw Roger a few minutes ago. He was looking at his portrait. He admitted to sending the notes." The look on Tyler's face was pure relief.

They found Peter in his office humming a little tune to himself. "Mark, I have very good news. The art museum purchased one of your portraits. They want to add it to their permanent collection. In case you're interested, it's the portrait of your brother. The curator was enthralled by the emotional force captured in the work." Mark could only shake his head and smile.

Tyler started laughing and he couldn't stop. He kept laughing as Mark and Peter looked on, confused. Finally, holding his stomach, he spoke in his best teacher voice, "Now class, this painting is called 'Portrait of a Brother.'" Tyler breathed deeply, trying to keep control of himself. "There's a lesson here: be nice to your little brother or he'll grow up and paint you looking like this and hang it in a museum for the next hundred years." Tyler couldn't hold it any longer, laughing hard as Mark and Peter looked at each other before busting up themselves.

Mark croaked, "Ty, you're killing me." It took awhile, but they were finally able to get hold of themselves. "Peter, thanks for everything. We'll stop by in the morning to collect our things and settle accounts." Peter nodded and shook Mark's hand as they both chuckled. The evening was rapidly winding down and, after saying good night to people they met on their way out, Mark and Tyler headed home.

Jolie met them at the door, barking, running, wagging her entire backside, happy to see them. Mark gave her a small treat and they quickly headed up to bed. Jolie followed them into the bedroom, jumped into her bed, watching, making sure they were going to bed as well. Tyler got cleaned up and climbed into bed, waiting for Mark.

Mark walked out of the bathroom and climbed into bed next to Tyler. "I need you, Tyler. Make love to me." He didn't receive a verbal answer, just arms that wrapped around him and kisses that made him melt. The kisses continued as the hands caressed and kneaded, Tyler's weight pressing Mark into the bed. Mark's legs wrapped around Tyler's body. "I need you! Need you now!" The fingers tickled him, probed him, got him ready. A single finger breached him, carefully probing, then two fingers, spreading, stretching. Soon the fingers were replaced by Tyler, pressing, entering, completing him. Slowly, Tyler filled him, burying himself into his body, joining with him both physically and spiritually. "I love you, Ty," whispered Mark as Tyler gave what he needed, wanted, what they both needed and wanted.

"I love you, Mark" Tyler moaned between long, burning thrusts and passionate fire-hot kisses, the heat building… building… finally bursting from Mark and then Tyler.

"Ty, I'm incomplete without you."

Mark lay awake long after Tyler had fallen asleep in his arms. He couldn't help marvel at all he'd found—a home, a family, love—and all those things were wrapped up in one person: Tyler, his love, his home, and his family.

Epilogue

"GOOD night. Thank you for coming," Tyler said to his last customers of the day as he locked the door to Tyler's Antiques at the end of a long Saturday. He couldn't help smiling to himself as he headed through the store to Mark's studio. When he'd remodeled the store five years ago, he'd included an artist's studio in the plans with a separate outside entrance as well as an entrance off the store. As he reached the door, it was opened by a stunningly handsome man.

"Oh, you've already closed. Should I go out the other door?"

Tyler smiled. "That's not necessary. I'll walk you out." Tyler led the man through the store to the front door.

"Are you Tyler?"

Nodding his head, Tyler replied, "Yes."

"I'm Brad." He extended his hand. Tyler shook the offered hand firmly. "Mark was talking about you during our sitting. If half of what he says is true, Mark is one lucky man."

Tyler smiled a happy, contented smile. "I feel like I'm the lucky one." Tyler opened the door for Brad, wished him a good night, and locked the door behind him. Quietly, Tyler headed through the store to Mark's studio. He knew that Mark would still be working to get his vision and ideas onto canvas. As Tyler expected, Mark was hard at work. Tyler stood in the doorway, watching as his brush moved over the canvas.

Tyler knocked softly on the doorframe before stepping forward, slipping his arms around Mark's waist. "Hey, Mark," Tyler whispered seductively into Mark's ear.

Setting his brush down, Mark leaned back on his stool, bringing his lips close to Tyler's. "Hey yourself. Is the store closed?"

"Uh-huh." Tyler's hand slipped beneath Mark's shirt, carding his fingers through the hair on Mark's chest. Tyler felt Mark lean against him as Tyler circled a hard fleshy nipple with his fingers.

"Ty…." Tyler's hands stroked the skin of Mark's stomach, slowly edging lower. "Oh… that's nice." Tyler's lips found Mark's as a hand slipped beneath the waist of his pants before slowly retreating again. Tyler kissed Mark deeply as his hands continued to stroke and pet the hot skin of Mark's chest.

"Lift your arms." Tyler's voice was deep and a little unsteady. Mark complied, and Tyler slowly pulled Mark's shirt over his head. Tyler could feel the warmth radiating off Mark's skin as the nibbled and sucked the base of Mark's neck. "Do you remember when we christened this studio?"

Mark moaned deeply, recalling something he would never forget. "I take it you want a repeat performance?" Tyler lightly pinched Mark's nipple as he sucked gently on Mark's shoulder blade. Tyler slowly lifted Mark off the stool, lips sucking on Mark's shoulder as Tyler's nimble fingers unfastened his belt. Tyler pulled off the belt and dropped it on the floor. He gently turned Mark around to face him, their lips coming together as if magnetically drawn. Without breaking the kiss, Tyler unfastened Mark's pants and slowly lowered the zipper. Running his hands down Mark's back, he slipped the now-open pants past Mark's hips and they fell around his ankles.

Mark stepped out of his pants as Tyler's tongue thrust deeply into Mark's mouth. Mark sucked and pulled on Tyler's tongue as skilled fingers gently traced the outline of his cock through the fabric of his briefs. Mark moaned into Tyler's mouth as fingers ran softly along the ridge of his cock. Tyler slipped his hands along Mark's hips. As he lowered his hands he caught the waistband of the briefs and pulled them down past Mark's hips until they fell around his ankles.

Mark leapt into Tyler's arms, curling his legs around his body as Tyler's hands cupped his butt. Lips pressed together tightly as Mark lost all control and completely gave himself over to his heart's desire. Tyler sat Mark on his stool, their kisses increasing in intensity, Mark's body vibrating with excitement. "Mark, what do you want?"

Mark just moaned between kisses. "Trust… you." Mark's hands wrapped around Tyler's neck as Tyler shifted Mark's body on the stool so his lower back was supported, his legs now in the air. Tyler knelt as he spread Mark's legs wide. Mark shivered as Tyler blew on Mark's tight, pulsing entrance. Tyler's tongue circled the opening as Mark writhed in pleasure.

"Is that what you want?" Tyler's tongue darted inside.

"Oh god! Yes!" Mark's head fell back as Tyler darted his tongue into Mark again and again. Each thrust was accompanied by a small whimper or moan. A smile crossed Tyler's face as he licked a path to Mark's balls, and then up the length of his cock before swirling his tongue around the head and then retreating back down the shaft. Tyler swirled Mark's balls in his mouth and then licked his way back to Mark's now throbbing entrance. Over and over, he licked and sucked his way from Mark's opening to the head of his cock.

"Tyler, I need you… need you now!"

Tyler smiled. "What do you need, Mark?" Tyler stood up and lowered the zipper of his pants and fished out his now leaking cock. "Is this what you want?"

"Oh god, yes! I want you now! Please!"

Tyler slipped two fingers into Mark to make sure he was ready for him. Mark writhed and clenched his butt on the fingers. "Don't tease me, Ty. I need you!"

Positioning himself between Mark's legs, Tyler placed the head of his cock at Mark's entrance and pushed. Mark's body opened for him, almost drawing him in. Tyler steadily pressed his cock into Mark while Mark begged for more. "Need all of you, Ty." Tyler let Mark have what he wanted, thrusting deeply into Mark, burying his cock to the hilt. "Yeah, Ty, that's it, that's what I want." Tyler pulled back and then thrust deeply and firmly into Mark. "Yeah, give it to me, Ty." Those words broke all of Tyler's self-control. He drove his cock into Mark again and again.

The stool started to rock, so Tyler drove deep into Mark, wrapped his legs around his waist, lifted Mark off the stool, and lowered his body to the drop-cloth-covered floor. Tyler was still buried in Mark, and with Mark now safe on the floor, Tyler drove into him. Mark's head rocked back and forth, his eyes rolled into his head, his hands clutching at the drop cloth in absolute ecstasy. Tyler pulled off his shirt as he continued pounding his cock into Mark, sweat pouring off his body. "Ty, I love you, so much." With those words, Mark came in torrents onto his stomach and chest, clenching the muscles of his butt around Tyler's cock.

The added pressure sent Tyler flying and he climaxed deep in Mark's body. The words "I love you too, Mark," ripped from his lips. Tyler withdrew from Mark and collapsed next to him on the drop cloths, both of them panting heavily. Tyler wrapped his arms around Mark, pulling him close. "I'm the luckiest man alive to have you." Tyler's kiss conveyed all his love and Mark's kiss returned that love to him.

"I love you, Ty." Their kisses were now sweet, warm, and languid as they lay on the drop cloths, their bodies curled up together.

Eventually Mark got up and started to get dressed. "Tyler, it's almost six and we need to get to the gallery by seven." Tyler reluctantly got up from the floor; his cock was still hanging out of his pants. Both men laughed as they gathered their clothes, dressed, locked the store, and headed home.

Jolie met them at the door, wagging her entire body. Tyler fed her and let her out while Mark headed upstairs. Mark was in the shower when Tyler entered their bedroom. The walls of their bedroom were covered with their memories. The portrait of Tyler and Mark's self-portrait graced the walls, along with numerous framed photographs of them on vacation as well as pictures of Amy's family, Aunt Phyllis, and Tyler's grandmother.

Tyler quickly shed his clothes and headed into the bathroom. "Can I join you?" Tyler didn't wait for an answer; he didn't need one. He just slid open the door and stepped into the shower as a pair of arms wrapped around his waist, while lips sucked gently on his shoulder. Showering together was something they still did on an almost daily basis.

After washing each other, they stepped out of the shower, dried themselves, and went into the bedroom to dress for the gallery.

As they finished getting dressed, Tyler could tell that Mark was nervous. Well, maybe more excited than nervous. He always seemed to get nerved up at these things. "Will I ever get used to this?" Mark had a smile on his face, so Tyler knew he wasn't too worked up.

Tyler just smiled as he helped Mark straighten the bowtie of his tuxedo. "What do you have to be nervous about? I'll tell you the same thing I told you before your first opening. When we get home, there'll be a little girl waiting for you, regardless, and there will be a large bed waiting for us, regardless." Mark smiled as he remembered those words, and they had the same calming effect they'd had almost five years ago.

Tyler was right. What did he have to be nervous about? Mark had opened shows in New York, Los Angeles, and even Paris. All of his shows had been huge successes and he'd had portraits commissioned by movie stars, politicians, socialites, and businessmen. But tonight's show was special. Very special.

A year ago, Mark had come up with a concept for a series of works. Peter had been enthusiastic when Mark had explained the concept to him, and he was overjoyed when Mark told him he wanted to hold the opening in his gallery. Peter had been very good to Mark, giving him his first break and acting as his agent for the past five years with honesty and absolute integrity. "Besides," Mark had told him, "I want to show these paintings in Milwaukee. It's very important that they be shown here."

When Tyler was finished with Mark's tie, he looked him over and pronounced him "the most handsome man I know."

Mark kissed him gently. "You look handsome yourself." Mark opened his mouth and sucked gently on Tyler's tongue.

Tyler's arms were around his waist, pulling their bodies together as his lips met Mark's in a scalding, deep, loving kiss. Tyler felt Mark melt into the embrace and he could feel Mark's erection against his hip, his own erection rubbing gently against Mark. Slowly, Tyler released his embrace. "We do need to go, because if we keep this up we'll never make it to the opening." Taking Mark's hand, he led him out of the bedroom and down the stairs with Jolie on their heels, her tail wagging expectantly.

Mark went to the kitchen to get her a chew while Tyler got their coats from the hall closet. Tyler glanced around the rooms as he got the coats. They had indeed filled the house with antiques and art. Over the past five years they had built an impressive collection of antique furniture, decorative arts, and painting and sculpture. Every piece had been chosen because they'd loved it. Their home was a reflection of themselves. They both still treasured the Herter Brothers table and they had refused to sell it, even when contacted by staffers from the White House after their home had been featured in the lifestyle section of the newspaper. When Mark was ready, Tyler handed him his coat, and they locked the door and walked to the car.

In the car, Mark was fidgeting while Tyler drove to the gallery. As usual, Mark arrived an hour before the opening so he could make sure everything was prepared and so he could talk to Peter. Over the years, the two men had become very good friends as well as business associates.

When they pulled up to the gallery, Peter met them at the door. Peter hugged both Tyler and Mark before ushering them inside and giving them a tour of the exhibit. Mark had entitled this exhibit "Family." The paintings featured were pictures of families, both conventional and unconventional. Among the paintings in the exhibit was a painting of Tyler, Mark, and Jolie. Mark and Tyler were shirtless, with Tyler holding Jolie while she kissed Mark's cheek. There was a painting of Tom and Bill; both men were dressed in leather. Included in the exhibit was a painting of Steve and his dad; both father and son were in their work clothes with the deli counter in the background. The exhibit included paintings of a lesbian couple and their two children, a gay couple and their adult daughter. One of the most powerful paintings was of two women, Barb and Dottie, who had been together for almost fifty years. The look on their faces showed everyone that these two women loved each other as much today as they did when they met. There were portraits of some famous unconventional families, including a movie star and the three children she'd adopted from Africa. There was a portrait of a local minister with his son and his partner. The minister had insisted that he be depicted with his collar because, in his words, "God made my son this way and God doesn't make mistakes."

Hanging next to the picture of Mark, Tyler, and Jolie was a painting of Amy, John, and their now three children. Peter had already put a yellow "sold" dot on the painting. When he saw the painting, Tyler leaned to Mark. "Does Amy know about the painting?"

Mark smiled. "No, but John does. He and the kids sat for me. I added Amy from memory." Hanging on the opposite wall was the signature piece of the exhibit. The single canvas was the largest Mark had ever done; it covered the entire wall. On this canvas were faces, dozens of faces, each rendered in exquisite detail. Each face was unique and represented a wide variety of races and ethnic origins. It was a very powerful painting. Mark had just titled this painting "Family."

"Mark, this is an incredibly moving work of art. Every time I look, I see something new." Tyler had an arm around Mark's waist as he stared at the painting. "I'm going to miss it." The painting had hung on the large wall in their family room for months until it was moved to the gallery last week.

"I know, Ty, but I need to let it go." Tyler knew Mark was right.

Tyler and Mark headed back to Peter's office to relax before the gallery opened. Tonight's opening was an invitation-only reception with the gallery opening the exhibit to the public starting tomorrow. Mark had provided Peter with a list of his invitees and Peter had handled the rest of the invitations.

Peter stuck his head into the office. "I'm opening the doors. Just relax and come out when you're ready."

Tyler leaned to Mark, kissing him on the lips. "Don't be nervous. Your work is incredible. Just enjoy the evening."

Mark placed his forehead to Tyler's. "Thank you."

"For what?"

"Thank you for the support, the love, and most of all, for being my family." With another kiss, Mark and Tyler stood, clasped hands, and headed into the gallery.

Fall into a world of fantasy in Andrew Grey's series about the Children of Bacchus.

Coming Soon – Thursday's Child

Check out this and other short stories from this series at

www.dreamspinnerpress.com.

ANDREW GREY grew up in western Michigan with a father who loved to tell stories and a mother who loved to read them. Since then he has lived throughout the country and traveled throughout the world. He has a master's degree from the University of Wisconsin-Milwaukee and works in information systems for a large corporation. Andrew's hobbies include collecting antiques, gardening, and leaving his dirty dishes anywhere but in the sink (particularly when writing). He considers himself blessed with an accepting family, fantastic friends, and the world's most supportive and loving partner. Andrew currently lives in beautiful, historic Carlisle, Pennsylvania.